I0788716

L.C. Scandiuzzi
The Death Of A Mystic

SDK Publishing
www.sdkpublishing.com

IV

THE DEATH OF A MYSTIC

L.C. SCANDIUZZI

VI

Contents

Prologue

At first he thought he was looking at a huge mirror lying flat on the ground in front of him. In it, he could see the reflections of trees and clouds.

Suddenly, a gust of wind ripples across the glossy surface, breaking the illusion, and he realizes he is looking at a lake. A breathtaking lake on top of a mountain. He approaches the shore, kneels on the ground, and leans forward to quench his thirst. Satiated, he withdraws a few paces from the shoreline and sits on the grass. In the faint sun of the morning, the breeze is actually quite cold.

Then there is a man. A man walking toward him across the surface of the lake, his abundant copper-colored hair tousled by the wind. Calmly and silently, the stranger comes to shore.

He thinks he should rise in greeting, but the stranger gestures for him to stay seated.

Crouching down, he asks, *"Why kneel before the lake to drink?"*

Then, *"Know this: the lake is there to serve you. You need not kneel before it. Simply crouch down and drink bountifully with your hands."*

He can't find the words to reply.

The stranger continues, *"And now, if you'd like, you may ask the question that is on your mind."*

He knows the question. He wants to know what is stopping him from working miracles such as walking on water.

"So then, as a follower there down below, you don't know?"

He is astounded that the stranger knows of his life. He responds to say that no, he doesn't know, and he asks him to explain it in a language he can understand.

"*The trouble is in the legends themselves. You will only come to see the truth when you cast aside the lies.*"

The lesson continues and he listens and marvels. He wants to retain everything. Excitedly, he interjects that he has an infallible method of remembering anything he has learned: he mentally devises symbols that only he can understand, and they work as a sort of index. Later, whenever he thinks back to a particular symbol, he can remember everything connected to it.

"*And what good is that?*"

The question seems beautiful to him. He simply wants all the incredible knowledge to remain in his memory and available for recall—for when he comes down from the mountains.

"*Remembering means nothing without doing. Memory kills the word.*"

"What do you mean?"

"*Memory stores nothing but useless letters. The word must enter your heart. From this springs the fountain of life.*"

While speaking, the stranger rises to his feet and offers his hand. He accepts the help, and he too stands up. Then he wants to know if the stranger is an angel.

"*Will it make any difference if I say yes?*"

Taking three steps back, the angel returns to the surface of the lake and begins walking away. He stops suddenly. Turning around, he says, "*You've learned how to do it. So why don't you?*"

He begins walking again. He crosses the lake, reaches the opposite shore, and disappears into the woods. He vanishes without looking back.

Frustrated, he is left thinking that the angel had hoped he would follow. And perhaps he should have done so. He looks at the water before his feet. What was he waiting for? He need only take the first step.

"You won't be able to do it," he hears.

Turning quickly, he sees an old man sitting on a rock in front of a hut. How had he not seen him before? He approaches the new stranger. The man is incredibly old and nearly bald with a wild, whitish beard. His tiny eyes are opaque and seemed of little use.

He asks the old man's name.

"My name is unimportant, young man. What matters is that I too once climbed this mountain in search of the power to perform miracles. I was your age. I never left."

He asks why.

The elderly man points an accusatory finger at the lake. "It's the lake's fault. It won't let me go."

He bursts out laughing. He looks at the lake. Looking left and right, he can see countless trails, all well-worn. The old man must be insane. No doubt the mountain sun has fried his brains.

Indifferent to the scorn, the old man fixes him with an unseeing glare and says, in a defeated tone, "When... when I arrived here, there was another old man sitting right where I am now... and he also told me I would never be able to leave. I laughed in his face—just as you have done to me. Then he said that I would bury him, and then... then I would take his place on this rock. The same had happened to him. And this is what will happen to you too, young man."

"Impossible," he says to the old man. The angel had taught him the secret of walking on the lake. He could leave whenever he had wrapped his head around it.

"The angel taught me as well... a long, long time ago. To this day I keep it in my memory—what I learned. But I can't seem to remember what he taught me. Do you understand? The same will happen to you."

No, it wouldn't. Not to him. He never forgot anything. He had developed an infallible method of memorization.

"Everything repeats itself, young man. I buried that old man... and you will bury me. Then you will wait for the day someone comes to dig your grave. And so on, and so on."

He lets loose another volley of laughter. How absurd! Even if the old man doesn't want to walk on the surface of the lake, he could easily leave using one of the many well-worn paths.

"The paths? They are only dead ends. Most lead off cliffs... and the others simply stop. Look, young man, I've spent my whole life trying each and every one of them. Then I gave up. The only way out is over the lake."

All right. Let it be over the lake. But he would show him how easy it was.

The old man stands aside to allow him to return to the water's edge. He watches as he impetuously sticks his foot in. He is unperturbed by the young man's scream and his desperation, as he just barely manages to grab hold of a lakeside branch to prevent himself from drowning.

The old man laughs from his rock.

"You look like a bedraggled little dog climbing out of a bath."

Then, saddened, the old man lowers his voice, "The only thing I remember is that... remembering means nothing without doing. Here you will stay, young man."

"No!" he screams, throwing himself onto the shore. He rages and flails against the earth, beating his head against it.

◆ ◆ ◆

GIANCARLO AWOKE. He was on the verge of tears. He was tired. He opened his eyes. The day would soon be dawning, and the cold had begun to seep in through the fabric of his sleeping bag. The cutting north wind whistled through the cracks in the half-cap of rock he took shelter under on this part of the mountain. He readjusted his blanket and looked up. The first glimmer of dawn revealed the spiky silhouette of the Apennines. But he no longer had the desire to continue his ascent. The dream had left an impression.

He then realized that he could remember nothing of what he learned in the dream. He only knew that he was the prisoner of a lake. And that remembering means nothing without doing.

Desperately seeking understanding, trying to articulate why he felt the need to cry, he sensed that it was not because of the dream. There was more. A lot more. This certainty arrived in a wave of anguish that caused him to begin sobbing. Uncontrollably.

Half suffocating and midway to panic, he quickly pulled himself partway out of his sleeping bag. He pulled his blanket over his shoulders but shivered despite its warmth—spasms that came from deep within and had nothing to do with the mountain cold. He sat with his head resting on the stone behind him, immobile, breathing deeply. And crying.

"But why? Why?" he almost screamed.

Twenty-five minutes later, it had dawned a clear day and he began his descent down the mountain. There was no longer any room in his mind for a lake. His decision to return home now had a name: Father.

A name that carried with it the bitter aftertaste of tragedy.

One

The day had gotten off to a bad start.

The old truck rounded the last bend before the small town of Vigneto, in southern Italy. Tullio Bertinezzi, a rugged man of twenty-nine, was then able to speed up. He was tense. He wiped his face with his arm, temporarily ridding it of the sweat that was permeated with red dust from the road. Sitting beside him, with his right leg held tight in a splint, his father groaned in pain.

Tullio turned to look at the blood oozing from his father's thigh. He thought he was going to vomit. He stuck his head out the window and retched noisily. That was enough: the urge was gone. A quick word of encouragement to his father, and he renewed his focus on the road.

Just twenty-five minutes later, Tullio was lifting his father in his arms and carrying him into a shabby little hospital. Luckily, it was ten in the morning—a good time to be at the hospital/pharmacy. Paolo Rossi, the local doctor, who also happened to be the village drunk, was in his brief sober interlude between the morning's hangover and the afternoon's imminent bender.

He saw Tullio Bertinezzi enter with his father in his strong arms, and he immediately directed him to the last room, where they did emergency surgeries. He shouted the nurse's name. A middle-aged woman emerged. She and the doctor went into the room and closed the door.

An hour and a half later, the doctor emerged from the room, stopped in front of Tullio Bertinezzi and removed his blood-stained gloves.

"What fell on your father, Tullio? A whole forest? He lost his leg, and he also lost a lot of blood."

Tullio recounted his father's absent-mindedness that morning and the first oak they felled together. As for the second tree, he didn't really know what happened. His father had turned and walked away to rest a bit and drink some water.

"I kept on working, *Dottore*. All of a sudden, the tree started to fall. I thought my father was somewhere behind me, so I wasn't concerned. I even expected him to let out a celebratory shout like he always does when a tree is falling. But I didn't hear anything. And I couldn't see my father. Only after, when he…"

Excitable as ever, Tullio suddenly had something stuck in his throat. The doctor patted him on the shoulder a couple of times.

"It's okay, Tullio. With only one leg, Giuseppe might not be up for felling trees anymore, but he will get on with his life. Now, you go find your mother. It would be nice if she could stay with your father tonight. I have to go to Cosenza, and I might be gone a day or two."

♦ ♦ ♦

Albertina had always been a calm woman. Those who do not know her well might mistake her serenity for a lack of courage. She had had her first child at the age of nineteen, and now, at the age of forty-eight, each new dawn seemed to bring her the portent of some new misfortune. And sharpened the lines on her face.

The more Tullio told her his father was doing fine, that he had been lucky—although he was left with just the left leg—the more his mother felt that the day's misfortune had not yet truly come knocking. She sensed a much greater misfortune was still in store.

She stood at the kitchen window, her arms crossed, and stared in silence at the mist obscuring the mountaintops. There, at the foot of the Apennine mountains, used to be where their fertile land ended. *Ah, Albertina! Albertina…!*

Whatever happened to the Bertinezzi farm—how nice it used to be! What remained of the grapevines? And the stream, who was draining its waters?

Looking again at those blue mountains, she also thought of her youngest child. Giancarlo. *Where could he be, oddio? When would he come home?*

But her chestnut eyes could see, like a spotlight shining into the future, that the restless feeling in her soul was not because of the exhausted lands before her. Nor the continually falling numbers of calves each year—nor even Giancarlo's absence. The real problem was at the hospital—with her husband, Giuseppe.

"Let's go, *Mamma*," Tullio called.

Later that night, Tullio returned to the farm alone, having left his mother at the hospital.

11:10 PM. Giuseppe Bertinezzi stirred and began to mutter in the dim room. "Gian..."

Albertina turned on the light. After squinting and blinking his eyes got used to the brightness, Giuseppe looked up at his wife. With fear in his voice, he said, "Where is Giancarlo, Tina *mia*?"

With quick hands, she smoothed out the creases her husband had made in the sheet while trying to move his right leg—the leg that was no longer there. The bedclothes had been tucked in tightly to ensure that Giuseppe would not discover the missing limb on his own.

Albertina replied, "Try to stay calm, Peppe. And don't move. Before he left, *Dottor* Rossi told me not to let you move—and that means you also need to keep your mouth shut. You lost a lot of blood."

Then she added, "And you know where Giancarlo went. He's up in the mountains."

"Ah, the mountains... Giancarlo always liked the mountains, ever since he was a boy. He takes after his *nonno*." Giuseppe let out a small sigh, "Tina... I'm very happy that... Giancarlo is back. What a fine *ragazzo*! And doesn't the graduation ring look nice on his finger! *Nevvero*?"

It was true. But she didn't respond. She kept straightening and tucking the sheet.

"*Oddio!*" her husband resumed. "How the years have flown by! And just like that, Giancarlo is back—and with a degree. And he came at just the right time. Our area can't keep going without an expert who can understand the land.

Gian... he will rehabilitate our grapevines... he will build a dam... and he will..."

"Enough talking, Peppe. *Dottor* Rossi said..."

"Ah! *Dottor* Rossi. He never had a son, Tina."

But Giuseppe fell silent.

Moments later, his face fell, and his countenance looked different. Heavy. He said, "Giancarlo really takes after his *nonno* Enrico. My father also used to like going up into the mountains and spending a few days alone up there. Oh, how he liked it!"

With that, out of the blue, Giuseppe began to cry. His sobbing was bitter, tormented, unhinged. And he started talking about his father again. He lamented that they had never had a good relationship.

"Tina... I... I have a confession to make."

"I am not a priest," his wife responded from above him. "And no one here is dying."

Giuseppe explained that his confession was a family matter. Not something for a priest. It was about his father, Enrico.

"Why go digging up the past?"

"This isn't in the past. You have to listen to me."

She sat and waited.

"Tina... I... I lied to all of you."

"What are you talking about?"

"About my father."

Albertina remained silent while he told her everything. Until he calmed down.

Rising from her chair, she crossed her arms and walked slowly around the room, finally returning to her husband's bedside. His eyes were anxious, and he looked at her as if expecting some words of comfort.

She said, "*Dopo*... we'll have plenty of time to talk about this later, Peppe. Now see if you can sleep and get some rest."

Giuseppe grumbled a bit. But he quieted down.

♦ ♦ ♦

An hour passed. Albertina was snoring on the next bed over when she heard her husband wake. He sounded like he had been having a nightmare. She went to look. Giuseppe's eyes seemed to be bulging out of their sockets, his mouth dry. A round lump had formed around where the tube went into his arm. Albertina went to alert the nurse.

"The IV's come out of the vein," said the nurse ten minutes later. She looked tired. She dug around in two or three places and finally found a vein on the back of his fist.

When the woman had left, Albertina asked her husband, "Why are you looking at me like that, Peppe?"

He puffed.

"Tina... if something were to happen to me, you... you... I want you to tell Giancarlo everything. Not Tullio. Telling Tullio won't help anything. He's like me. A brute. But not Giancarlo... Giancarlo is different... he's educated. I want you to tell him everything, Tina. Do you promise?"

Just to placate him, she promised. But she did not intend to honor that promise. What her husband had told her caused her to feel great shame—a shame she did not want to share with anyone else.

Albertina Bertinezzi stood up. She went to the window, pushed a few bad thoughts out through the pane of glass and returned. Placing a hand to her husband's forehead, she thought he might have a little fever.

"Time to take your medicine, Peppe. Then try to get some sleep. And see that you don't have another nightmare."

In fact, Albertina wanted to believe that her husband's whole revelation was all part of a bad dream. Giuseppe drank some water. But he didn't fall asleep. His fever was getting worse. Delirium had set in.

"Aquila...! Aquila...!"

Albertina thought he must still be thirsty[§]. But just after he had wet his throat, he started again.

"Aquila...! *Papà*...! I must go! Aquila... Colorada. Oh, *stella... stella mattutina*, will you take me there?"

Three o'clock in the morning and Giuseppe Bertinezzi was burning up. Frowning, the nurse came to administer another dose of antipyretic through his IV. However, the fever would not abate by more than two degrees.

At nine-thirty the next morning, with the nurse unable to get hold of the doctor in Cosenza, septic shock caused Giuseppe's kidneys to fail. Eight hours later, the raging infection and accompanying circulatory collapse closed

---

§   Aquila sounds like the Italian "acqua" meaning "water."

his eyes for good.

◆ ◆ ◆

THE FOLLOWING AFTERNOON, dressed all in black, Albertina stood on the ground-floor veranda looking out at the blue mountains. Tullio came out of the kitchen, his hot Calabrian blood seething in his veins. He inserted himself between his mother's eyes and the mountains.

"Thinking about our *vagabondo* Giancarlo again, *Mamma*? Don't you think he's big enough to take care of himself?"

"Tullio, my child!" his mother's response was tempered. "Giancarlo is your brother. Don't call your blood a *vagabondo*. You worked in the fields, and he worked in books. He has a degree now... he's an expert who understands the land. Now the two of you will have to work together. He can help us. You know how much we need this."

Tullio spoke through partially gritted teeth. "You can't understand the land, *Mamma*, unless you've had your hands in the dirt—not by having your nose in books. He's the type who prays for rain, and then cries when too much of it falls. Giancarlo's books will never bring our grapevines back to life."

His mother stayed silent. She went back to staring at the mountains. She finished by saying, "Something might have happened to your brother, Tullio."

"There's always something happening to my little brother," he responded harshly. "Get this straight, *Mamma*: this land can't feed more than two mouths anymore. Books...! I'd rather see Gian to go to hell!"

"Tullio!" his mother cried, bestowing a sharp slap on his face. It had been many, many years since her children had caused her maternal Calabrian blood to boil in her veins. But the slap was not just for Tullio's harsh words: it was a spilling over of feelings of trauma, of loss. Of fear.

In stony silence, Tullio left to do his work. Albertina let herself fall, defeated, to rest on a stool.

A few minutes later, she raised her head. Even though her chestnut eyes couldn't yet see him, she could sense that her younger son was coming down from one of those blue mountains. Coming back home.

◆ ◆ ◆

THE FIRST ONE TO SEE GIANCARLO arriving was actually Tullio. He wasn't expecting his brother to approach the veranda. Setting his task aside, Tullio ran over to intercept him.

"It's your fault *Papà* is buried, you...!" Tullio shouted, raising his hand to strike Giancarlo.

"What?!" Giancarlo shrank back, straying from his path. He grabbed his brother's fist firmly. "What did you say, Tullio?"

"Exactly what you heard, you *barbone*! The day it happened, father had been worried about you all morning. He couldn't get his head in his work. He got hit by a tree."

"*Oddio!*"

Giancarlo let himself fall into a crouch. It was also a way of escaping Tullio's wrath. Their mother came out of the kitchen door.

"What did you do to your brother, Tullio?"

Face knotted, Tullio turned around.

"*Niente*! I didn't do anything to your precious little boy!" he spat, turning his back to his mother, and storming off.

Staring down at his feet, Giancarlo lowered his head between his knees. And wept. Albertina approached. Grabbing him by the arm, she pulled him up off the ground.

"Crying won't help, *figliolo*. It isn't going to bring your father back."

Giancarlo wiped his eyes with his arm. Then looked at his mother.

"I... I was warned about *Papà*'s death, *Mamma*," he said.

"Warned? By who?"

"By the pain, *Mamma*. I could feel it. It was preparing me up on the mountain. I was next to a lake and... it was a dream, I know. But it was also a warning. As I was coming down, I got the feeling that something terrible had happened."

Albertina didn't understand but she was too exhausted to press him further.

"We waited as long as we could, *figliolo*. But at noon we had to bury your father."

"Where, *Mamma*?"

"On the way up... at the bend, next to..." his mother's voice faltered. She looked away and lowered her head. "Next to *Nonno* Enrico's grave. That was where your father wanted to be buried."

Albertina sat and watched her son approach the grave half a mile from their home. There he remained, between the two crosses—one worn, one new—for nearly two hours.

Never in his life had he felt so guilty, so useless, and so unforgiveable. Yet in the midst of his acute suffering, he had flashes of the pain he had experienced at the edge of the lake that kept him prisoner high in the mountains. From one pain to the other, back and forth, and then mixed. He wished—yearned—to have spoken to his father before he had died. His soul was wounded by the shards of the lie embedded in it.

Dusk was falling as he returned home. Tullio was on the veranda. The rage had gone from his face but he still received Giancarlo coldly.

"Tullio," Giancarlo wanted to talk. "Now that *Papà* is gone... we have to think about *Mamma*. I know I think one way, Tullio, and you think another, but you're gonna have to deal with her."

Tullio thought he understood. Giancarlo had decided to go away again. Thank goodness.

"Do you understand me, Tullio?"

Still looking away, Tullio responded, "*Sì, sì, capisco.*"

Giancarlo gave his brother a pat on the shoulder and entered the house. Albertina was watching it all from the kitchen door. She said nothing. And Giancarlo knew she was happy to see her two sons make peace.

Their mother turned to the stove and was about to start tackling dinner. Giancarlo came over to her.

"*Mamma*... I... I have something I have to tell you."

She didn't say a word. Just kept moving the wood around in the oven. Giancarlo walked over to the door. He looked outside, as if searching for the right words. He returned to where his mother stood. Hesitating before the difficult confession he knew he needed to make to relieve his conscience, he ran his left fingers from his mouth down to his jawline.

"*Mamma*... I... I didn't want *Papà* to die before I... before I..."

"Where is your graduation ring, Carletto?" his mother asked when she saw his naked fingers.

"That's what I wanted to talk about, *Mamma*. I..." Giancarlo retrieved the ring from his pocket, "I decided that I won't be using this ring."

"What?"

"I won't be working in the fields, *Mamma*."

Albertina's eyes froze. Her hands, too. Her whole body went rigid for a few seconds. Maybe she hadn't heard right.

Sensing the confusion in his mother's mind, Giancarlo said, "I should have told you as soon as I got here, *Mamma*... that I... I... that I'm interested in other things. Things that are more important to me."

"More important than eating?" his mother blurted out. "And what might that be? So, you spent all that time studying for... for nothing?"

"*Bravo, caro!*" Tullio called ironically from the doorway. "*Bravissimo!*"

"You shut your mouth, Tullio," said their mother without taking her eyes off Giancarlo.

After a moment or two longer standing there like a gaping statue, Albertina realized she was holding a stick that was already halfway into the oven. She quickly tossed it in. Then she allowed the stove to take her weight so she wouldn't sway and fall. But she wasn't in pain from the burning stick: it was her strong desire to scream, to spew forth her discontent, to curse—to blame her husband and the oak tree that fell on his leg.

"It's a good thing your father is six feet underground!" she abruptly threw in the face of her younger son. Her voice came out cutting, cold, defeated. Giancarlo kept his mouth shut.

But not Tullio.

"Didn't I tell you he's a *vagabondo*? I always said you were wrong about Gian. All he wanted was to get himself out of doing the hard work. He's been that way ever since he was a child. All he wanted to do was draw trees and bulls. He wanted to be idle, spend *Papà's* money. Only a blind man couldn't see that."

"I told you to shut your mouth!" his mother shouted at him without taking her eyes off Giancarlo. "Stay out of this, Tullio. This matter is between me and your brother."

Tullio fell silent. Giancarlo hung his head low. He hadn't intended to upset his mother or make her suffer this much.

His voice saddened, he said, "I already told Tullio that I want no part of it, *Mamma*. And he understood me."

Then, stepping forward, Albertina took the graduation ring from Giancarlo's right hand and placed it on his right ring finger.

"There's no rush to start working, *figliolo*" she said as if she trusted him. "I understand that it must have been hard for you to leave your training in art that you so loved and to start a new path in agriculture. I know you did this to please your father. But you are still young. You have your whole life ahead of you. And lots of time to show us everything you learned at the university."

Giancarlo took a breath and was about to say something, but he couldn't find the courage. Instead, he looked at his mother's face. Then turned his head to look at his brother before again facing his mother.

"I don't want anything to do with this place, *Mamma*. I... I'm going away."

"Away? Away where?"

Giancarlo lowered his gaze and began to retreat to his room in silence. Tullio's ridicule exploded from the kitchen door,

"*Bravo*! That's better! Now that's what I like to hear. This land doesn't need you, *caro mio*. It never did and it never will."

The Calabrian blood had by now cooled in Albertina's veins. This time she did not react to Tullio. But from somewhere deep in her heart, she felt the tug of a premonition of pain. Along with it came a question for her son, who was walking away, "But... then where will you go, Gian?"

Even from ten feet away, Giancarlo could feel his mother's gaze, an apprehensive gaze. He didn't respond. He had nothing to say. He merely wished that things were different. He went to his room and partially closed the door, leaving it slightly ajar.

His mother soon followed him. Seated on the bed, Giancarlo tried to think of a response to her question. He had to be careful. Though his mother was a simple country woman, that didn't mean she wasn't shrewd.

Before she could open her mouth, he said, "*Mamma*... I have a different path to follow. Rest assured, I know what I'm doing."

Albertina sat down next to her son.

"A path? But what path?"

"You see, *Mamma*. My head is not in the land. It is not in the fields and it is not... not in this ring. My head is not in the books that taught me how to do a graft... or how to increase the production of grapevines. Can you understand that?"

"*Sì, sì*. But then where is your head—can you tell me?"

As if defeated by some fierce strain of remorse, Giancarlo slowly removed the ring from his finger.

"*Mamma*, I cannot use this ring."

"*E perché?* It's yours, your father set money aside for a long time so you could earn and use it. You are an expert with a degree, *figliolo*. Whether you like it or not."

Giancarlo's eyes seemed to plead for forgiveness.

"*Mamma*... while I was away I... I wasn't attending the agricultural school... recently, that is... I only went to classes for the first two years."

After hearing this, his mother fell silent. Regaining her composure, she said, "Tell me again what you just said. I didn't understand."

Giancarlo had to struggle to meet his mother's gaze.

"I... I didn't graduate, mother. That is the truth. I didn't finish my degree. I was lying. For these past few months, I spent my time learning about painting... reading... meditating... traveling... that's all. That's why I said I'm leaving."

Albertina lowered her head and let her hands fall dead in her lap. Her gaze was lost in a knot in the floorboards. Her thoughts were divided between the lie her son had confessed to and another lie—the one she had heard from her late husband at the hospital.

She exploded again—more outrage this time but less noise, "*Oddio!* How long will lies run in the Bertinezzi blood? What madness! This must be a curse your grandfather Enrico brought upon all of us. It all started with him."

Giancarlo swallowed his rebuke. As if trying to dodge the subject, he asked, "With *Nonno* Enrico? *Perché?!*"

Going against her initial intention not to air that dirty laundry—and driven on by the rage instilled in her by her son —Albertina began telling the story.

The first thing Giancarlo learned was that there was nobody buried under the old cross next to his father's grave.

"What are you saying, *Mamma?* That *Nonno* is not buried next to *Papà?*"

"There are only stones in the casket."

"Stones? In *Nonno* Enrico's grave, only stones? But... then where is *Nonno*'s body?"

Albertina Bertinezzi kept her head half bowed. She was still struggling to overcome the distress Giancarlo's confession had caused her.

"Who's to say?" she finally answered. "Some cemetery or other out there

—if he's even dead yet."

Stunned, Giancarlo didn't ask any questions. He just let his mother continue talking.

"One day, I remember it like it was yesterday... after being widowed by your *nonna*, your *nonno* went up into the mountains saying he was going to find God. That was when it all started. When he came back down days later, he had the crazy notion that he should go traveling. He was influenced by some books he had read... just like you were. Did you think I hadn't noticed them among your things?"

Giancarlo absorbed his mother's gaze.

"Then your father, being the only male child, convinced his three sisters to go along with it. We all thought losing *Nonna* Rosa was weighing heavily on him. And your *nonno* left. That was twenty-five years ago now. You were two and Tullio was about to turn five."

"Nine months later, your *nonno* came back. But what a struggle, *oddio!* When he came back... your *nonno* seemed to have lost his mind. All he wanted... and who knows where your *nonno* had been, but... he wanted to sell the Bertinezzi property, put an end to everything and start a new life somewhere else. He said this land was cursed."

"But why?"

"Nobody understood your *nonno's* mind. Then your father pulled him into the barn and they had a serious conversation. When your *nonno* came out of the barn, he said he was going to leave for good. That was all we heard.

"But who believed your *nonno* would actually go through with it? We thought the madness would pass and he would be back soon. But no, that wasn't what happened. Your *nonno* never came back."

Albertina looked into her son's green-brown eyes. They were the same as the eyes of *Nonno* Enrico. Giancarlo was looking more like his grandfather all the time. She stressed, "Then... on his deathbed, the remorse was eating away at your father."

"Remorse at having let *Nonno* leave, *Mamma?*"

"Worse: remorse at having put your *nonno* out on the street."

"What?"

"I only just learned what your father said to your *nonno* that day in the barn: that he was going to have him thrown in an insane asylum and divvy up his lands. Your father lied and told him it was what we all wanted. Your *nonno* had no choice, Gian. He was forced to leave for good."

Getting up from the bed, Giancarlo put his hands in his pockets and paced back and forth to the window a few times. He stared out at the Apennine mountains, way out there where he had just spent seven days and seven nights—and where he too had gone looking for God. But... would having an experience with God imply he was crazy too—like *Nonno* Enrico?

He returned to his mother's side.

She said, "Your father wanted his leg to heal so he could go after your *nonno* one day, *figliolo*. I told him he was twenty-five years too late. Yet even as his tongue slurred its words, he kept repeating, until the last minute of his life, that he was going to go after your *nonno*. Poor thing. He died thinking that he still had two legs. He was living a lie. And he died in a lie. Such is the fortune of this family."

Soon a deep silence fell between mother and son.

"*Mamma*... I don't understand. I remember a scene. I think I was about to turn six, and my father was burying my *nonno*'s body, which he had gone far away to find. That is what I believed for all these years. But in the end, what is the truth?"

Albertina gave a deep sigh.

"Three years after your *nonno* disappeared, your father wanted to get the legal paperwork to divide up the land and city houses with his sisters. But he ran into problems with the red tape. So, your father went traveling. A few days later, he came back with a death certificate—and a casket containing your *nonno*'s body. A closed casket."

She looked for her son's eyes.

"Lies are so ugly, *figliolo*. When we tell them, we then want to hide from ourselves. But they always take root like seeds planted in the ground. Fear of death made your father confess everything. The death certificate was fake, Gian. Your father paid a document forger for it. I don't know where. Then he put some rocks in a casket and came home. And then the inheritance could be portioned out."

"Tullio said a tree took your father because he was thinking of you. But that isn't true. Your father told me. He had been thinking about your *nonno* for some time. If the accident hadn't happened, I think he would have ended up going after your *nonno*."

"But where would he look?"

"I don't know, maybe a place called Aquila Colorada. In his fevered delusions, your father kept repeating that name."

"Aquila Colorada sounds kind of Spanish, *Mamma*."

"Indeed, it is. On your *nonno's* first trip, he went to the north of Spain. That much I do know. Perhaps your father knew your *nonno* was there all along. Your father, poor thing, kept saying the *stella mattutina* would take him there."

"The morning star?"

"It was just the fever, *figliolo*. But you know what I think? I think your *nonno* must have met another woman somewhere. He married, had children and those other children buried him."

"But what makes you so sure he's dead?"

"The living always turn up again, *nevvero?*" Albertina continued her lament, "The only thing I know for sure is that now and then the hand of God has come down heavy on the Bertinezzi family. It seems there may even be a curse on our family. And the land? What happened to our land, Giancarlo? It's all Tullio can think about, the land. It's eating him alive. It already consumed your father. He sold the city house to buy a truck, but it's already in very rough shape. Your uncles and aunts... where are they now? And me, for my part, I don't think I can take this much longer. Ah, my child...! I want... I want this curse to come to an end!"

Giancarlo could see that his mother was a wreck. He pulled her into a hug, to rest on his shoulder, where she stayed comfortably for a moment. And he said, "Perhaps *Nonno* wasn't the crazy one, *Mamma*. Maybe he really did find what he was after. Maybe we are the crazy ones... me... you, Tullio... and not the people like *Nonno* Enrico."

Suddenly, Giancarlo associated his grandfather—a grandfather he couldn't really remember—with the sad old man sitting on the rock in front of a hut he inhabited alone. It was like a call, a cry for help. He said, "I will go find *Nonno* Enrico, *Mamma*."

Albertina sat looking at her son in silence. Then she left, walked to her room, and returned holding a crucifix on a gold chain.

"This belonged to your father, Gian. And before that to your *nonno*. Now it belongs to you."

"It's mine? But... what about Tullio?"

"Your brother got first pick, and he chose your father's watch."

Albertina placed the chain around Giancarlo's neck and stood up from the bed.

"Do you have money, *figliolo*?"

"*Sì*, I have enough."

"Then go, Gian. Do what your father should have done many years ago. Bring your *nonno* back home." Albertina finished, "Him or his bones."

Two

"*Eccomi!*" *Barone* Vittorino Tedesco Piomondo celebrated his granddaughter's surprise with the face of a mischievous boy. He shook his old cane in the air, its copper head adorned with a shallow relief of the coat of arms of the Tedesco Piomondo family. He was seventy-four years old but sometimes he still acted like a naughty child. Mostly when he got wound up.

"*Nonno!*" scolded Jill. "You scared me! I almost dropped the paint can."

"Poor *Signorina* Jill, *Nonno*! You shouldn't frighten her like that."

Nonno Vittorino looked at Genoveffa and said something in reply. Nonetheless, he wasn't mad about the casual tone coming from an employee. Because Genoveffa was more than an employee: she had been born in that mansion and knew nothing of the world outside despite her forty-three years. Furthermore—the old man pondered—the times when he was called "*Barone* Vittorino Tedesco Piomondo" at the villa were long gone. These days, even the horses had no respect—or memory of it.

But he adored being close to his granddaughter, Jill. She was youthful, active and, above all, a beautiful *ragazza.* She clearly took after the lineage of the Tedesco Piomondo family— although her father's name and American ways had won out in her upbringing.

"*Signorina* Jill Lane Piomondo Heston," her grandfather said cunningly, "are you painting the rafters or... dying your hair?"

"Good eyesight, eh, *Nonno*?" Genoveffa said. "For someone who complains day and night about his cataracts, it's astonishing you can make out the brown paint in *Signorina* Jill's hair!"

Dark chestnut and curly, Jill's hair was flecked with the brown paint she had been applying to the woodwork of the veranda. *Nonno* Vittorino pretended not to hear his aide Genoveffa's observation. He was admiring his granddaughter's handiwork.

"Hmm! This is turning out beautifully! I might just have to hire you as a painter for the main house here at Villa Piomondo. How about that? Can you give me a quote?"

Jill laughed freely but stayed where she was at the top of the ladder. Then, bothered by the observing shadows down below, she stopped painting and looked down at her grandfather. Her *nonno*'s intelligence never aged—she reflected. Nor his pride. A beleaguered pride driven to the bitter end by a man who had no other options. And indeed, her *nonno* had no options: he had to pretend to keep dancing that old and happy waltz. He had to keep going, following the missteps of a deceptive old age. And he always did his best to do it with style. He dreamed he was still rich. Poor old *Nonno*.

Jill felt sad for her grandfather. In Atlanta, during her many years studying, she often caught herself thinking about the preordained life her maternal grandfather led at the villa. A life that carried with it a certain degree of infamy and shame—the shame of an ancient family in which each generation was taught to add new conquests to their ancestral patrimony. Poor old *Nonno*! Poor *Barone Vittorino Tedesco Piomondo*!

He seemed to have suddenly forgotten all his many successive mortgages, the need for extreme penny-pinching... how he'd fired his old staff. He had forgotten all that in the vain hope, disguised in a frustrated joke, of getting a quote for the complete renovation of Villa Piomondo. Poor and dear old *Nonno*! He didn't have a single cent to his name.

With almost childish eyes, *Nonno* Vittorino continued to examine his granddaughter's work. Climbing down the ladder, Jill set aside the can of paint and the brush. Then she allowed herself to be embraced and pulled close to the chest of her tall and rather thin grandfather. But she dodged the gaze of his glistening blue eyes.

Still engulfed in his affectionate arms, she held back a smile as she watched her grandfather raise his fingers to his eyes. Referring to his own sentimental tears, he said, "*Oddio! Questa mia cataratta* gets worse every day!"

Jill had no time to laugh at his joke because her grandfather suddenly began to cough and complain of dizziness. His nose started to bleed.

"*Signor* Dante!" she shouted the name of another aide. Inside the mansion, Dante quickly dropped what he was doing and rushed over to help.

Minutes later, Dante, Genoveffa and Jill were carrying *Nonno* Vittorino into the villa's main house.

♦ ♦ ♦

By the end of the afternoon, Jill was plagued by worry as she drove the long road home to the villa from Salerno, where she had taken her grandfather to the hospital.

Later, alone in a room with her mother, Jill repeated what the doctor had said when examining her grandfather's X-ray: advanced cancer in the right lung.

"They don't know how *Nonno* is still alive, *Mamma*."

Maddalena Piomondo Heston lowered her head in silence. She had been born here at Villa Piomondo, and educated abroad at a school in Marseille, France. After that, she married Wesley Heston and lived in the United States for ten years, in Boston. She had learned from a very young age how to deal with great joy or great pain without showing it on the outside.

But now she felt the urge to scream. She needed to sit down and gratefully took a seat on the straw seat of the colonial two-seater sofa nearby. Her daughter sat down next to her.

"*Oddio!*" Maddalena Heston cried out. Jill took her hands and held them.

Maddalena Heston had lost most of her zest for life when the Villa Piomondo telephone rang two months back to announce that her husband was dead. The Consul had not survived a devastating heart attack that had occurred right in his office. He would have been fifty-six years old the following month.

And now she was receiving the news that her father was terminally ill.

"Does your *nonno* know, Jill?" They were speaking Italian, as her mother preferred.

"No, *Mamma*. I asked the doctor not to tell him. He thinks he has a nasty case of pneumonia. That's all."

Jill walked out onto the terrace and stared at the Mediterranean. A cold breeze was blowing in from the sea, so she crossed her arms to keep warm. Then she turned and went back to her mother's side, still looking quite preoccupied.

Returning to her seat, Jill placed her hands on top of her mother's hands, which lay limp in her lap.

"Your hands are cold, *Mamma*. You'll have to overcome this too. And so will I."

Maddalena Heston looked up at her daughter.

"Jill… you have to know what is happening. You still don't know everything."

"What don't I know, *Mamma*? Is it about the villa? I know it's super mortgaged… I know about the bank debt. But with time we'll figure something out."

"Time is running out, *figliola*."

"What is that supposed to mean, *Mamma*?"

"We're living here as… as a courtesy, a kindness."

"As a courtesy? What do you mean? The villa has a mortgage with the bank and *Nonno* has lifetime enjoyment. That's not a kindness."

"That's what I thought, too. But your father explained it to me. In a legal sense, one can only 'enjoy use' of property that belongs to someone else. In the villa's case, a fiduciary agreement was drawn up to take over from an old mortgage. It has a clause affording lifetime enjoyment rights to your grandfather."

"But…? Then who owns Villa Piomondo, mother?"

"The bank."

"The bank?"

"And it must be said that this special lifetime enjoyment clause was a courtesy of theirs, of the bank's…. out of respect for the ancient home of the Tedesco Piomondo family. The bank did this to avoid putting the villa up for auction, sweetie. Your *nonno* would have died of shame."

Jill was bewildered.

Her mother resumed, "But still I had hope. There is also a clause giving your *nonno* the right to pay back the debt. And if he does, he will be immediately reinstated as the owner of this property. But now I've lost hope. Without your *nonno* around, Jill, nothing can be done. And you know what that means, don't you?"

Jill had no response. She was still stunned.

Her mother continued, "I know that you, Genoveffa and *Signor* Dante... you did a lot of work in renovating the mansion. But your father's plan has come to an end."

Looking at her daughter, she concluded, "You can no longer bring the children. You must accept it, Jill. Accept it and get in touch with Missionary Marshall. He has to know that the dream is over."

"No, *Mamma!*" Jill exclaimed, falling to her knees on the floor. Her face raised and eyes apprehensive, she was looking for safety in her mother's arms. "We cannot fail! We cannot allow the children to be taken back! Father's honor is at stake!"

◆ ◆ ◆

They met at the agreed-upon time.

When the waiter had departed with his now-empty tray, William Benjamin Benson said, "Anyway, *Pingue*, what is the mystery you couldn't tell me about over the phone?"

Tonelli felt like his face was on fire. Normally, calling him *Pingue*—Chubby— would be a reckless move. But he couldn't just walk away from William Benson. That would be highly foolish. Bill Benson was the right person to help him.

So, ignoring the jibe, he responded, "It's that million dollars again, Bill. I wanted to know if any new information had surfaced."

"Wait a minnute, Tonelli. I can't believe you took me away from a nice calm weekend so I could hear this old story again. Don't you have anything better to do?"

At almost thirty-eight years of age, the journalist Massimo Tonelli had achieved the great honor of being named *persona non grata* in three member states of the European Union. And it wasn't actually much different in his former hometown near Rome. Certain socialites had decided he was best kept in fine restaurants where they could stuff his face with so much rich food that he never had time to ask any questions. But there was one tiny detail that few knew about: Tonelli's shrewd brain was powered by his stomach. William

Benson, however, was aware of this.

For his part, Benson was not oblivious to the fact that Massimo Tonelli was hungry for an international dish that would bring him glory—and leave some money in the bank. But he also had to admit that Tonelli's blind hunger sometimes broke down walls that almost always led to something that others might have overlooked. In a nutshell: they had both benefited from each other's work in the past.

Taking a sip of whiskey, Bill Benson asked, "What are you fishing for today then, *Pingue?*"

"*Io?!*" Tonelli nearly chortled, hand reverently on his chest, just slightly off where his heart was. "*Niente, caro mio!* Nothing at all."

"Then I've got the same old fish to sell you: stop by the zoo and try to do a report about the zebras... or the alligators."

This time Tonelli did chortle.

But Bill had another suggestion, "Or, for that matter, how about going out for a sports review? Roma has an amazing team this year."

Pulling back his hand in a surfeit of laughter, Tonelli said, "I got myself transferred temporarily to nearby Naples, Bill. So, I'm rooting for Napoli now."

Tonelli poured the rest of the wine down his gullet. Then he stared into the American's face. To his surprise, Bill Benson mentioned calling the waiter over to pay the bill so they could leave.

Dropping his best peacemaking smile, Tonelli clung to Bill's arm and said, "All right. I'll find a way to watch a couple of your team's games. Okay? But now I must go back to the issue at hand. It's a serious matter. Bill... does that mean you still believe those children actually exist?"

"They do exist, Tonelli."

"*Sì*, of course. I know they exist. Millions of them, starving. And not only in Africa and Asia, *nevvero?* But this is a different matter, Bill. In Consul Heston's case, it was all nothing but a... a sordid farce. A con. Wounded girls and boys... malnourished... Wasn't it the keystone of Frank Borsato's election campaign to drain his campaign fund of a million dollars in, let's face it, a completely demagogic gesture, to save the little war victims the kindhearted Consul Heston would have then sponsored? An old trick, but it still works at the ballot box, no?"

The use of the conditional *would* had a sharp, ironic resonance. But Bill Benson held back and just stared into the face of his Italian colleague. Then he said, "This isn't all coming from you, *Pingue*. Who is paying you to uncover what happened to the money Senator Frank Borsato donated and how much have they paid you?"

"Ah!" Tonelli rejoiced, "so you admit that the dollars are out there somewhere!"

"Don't play stupid, *Pingue*. I just want to know what your interest in this whole story is."

"To stop a bomb from going off, *caro mio*. But I will respond to your question: I'm working for myself. I am simply after the facts. Now, Bill, you know better than I do: the late Consul's father-in-law is an old ruined *barone* from Campania. And did you know that selling Villa Piomondo won't pay off his debt to the bank?"

Tonelli laid out the hypothetical scene for his colleague. "Frank Borsato stuck his hand into his own pocket to donate the money. The dollars came and—poof! They disappeared. And did anyone see or hear of the Consul's orphaned children again? Huh? As for the money... okay, the story isn't over yet. Maybe we will all be surprised. The late Consul's father-in-law's debt might suddenly be paid off."

Bill Benson shook his head.

"You really are nuts, *Pingue*."

"Bill... did you know that Consul Heston died minutes after receiving a phone call from Frank Borsato? And did you know that this phone call was accidentally recorded?"

"You're bluffing."

Tonelli leaned forward with his upper body, for emphasis, and said, "Bill, Consul Heston died of distress... died of panic when he learned that his scheme had been uncovered. That was what made his heart explode, blowing away his triple bypass. *Capisci*"

In response, Bill Benson stood up and signaled to the waiter for the bill. Tonelli remained seated. The *conto* came and Bill put some money on the little tray. Then, in his bad Italian, he told the waiter to keep the change.

"*Grazie, Signore.*"

After the waiter had left, Bill Benson shot Tonelli a severe look. Then he too got to his feet.

"*Pingue...* I thought you invited me out for a nice weekend conversation. You know, I've always enjoyed watching you suck back a bottle of wine or two... and the conversation always led to something. I think I even owe you a couple favors. But now forget about me. I'm not in this game. Now you root for Napoli, and I root for Roma."

"*Sì, sì*" Tonelli responded, forcing out an uncomfortable attempt at laughter. "But we are still playing for the same cup, *nevvero?*"

Ignoring Tonelli's irony, William Benjamin Benson walked over to the iron railing of the restaurant's upper terrace. He took a cigarette from his bag. He lit it, took a drag, and blew the smoke upward. From up here, he could see a long portion of an old road that was almost always taken over by a tourist market. The stalls extended in both directions, and there was a constant stream of people.

Tonelli approached. He gave a deep sigh. Then said, "I envy those people down there, Bill. Today they're here... tomorrow in India... in Madrid... Lourdes... Rome. They're like beings from another world, *no?* They live for trivial things like silks... handicrafts... traditional food... miracles. I'd like to be one of them. Even if I had to be a crazy mystic like that one there, the yogi with his entourage. Look at how he walks. Maybe he thinks he's levitating. He looks like an ancient god surrounded by his faithful subjects. For them, there's no such thing as good or bad news."

William Benson continued smoking in silence.

Tonelli turned to him to say, "You know, Bill, one day someone told me there are only two types of people: those who eat, drink, laugh and cry—and those who dream. We two are definitely not like that group of spiritualists. *Noi due...* we write stories in the papers and they read them. Then they throw the paper away and get back to dreaming. But we still have the dirt of the news on our hands."

Turning to look at the market again, with an intentional touch of drama, Tonelli steered the conversation back to the matter at hand, "*Noi italiani*, Bill, we like to be well informed about the world. Think about it, Bill."

Bill Benson let the rest of his cigarette fall. Stomping it out, he stuck one of his hands into his pocket, made a discrete gesture with his other hand and took a step aside.

"*Arrivederci, Pingue,*" he said and headed for the stairs that would take him down to the ground floor and outside.

"*Arrivederci, bello.* And *grazie* for the wine."

Massimo Tonelli turned toward the market down below and stretched his arms out along the railing.

Moments later, he caught a glimpse of Bill Benson as he appeared amongst the market stalls. He watched him until he disappeared behind one of the rows. At the same time, Tonelli has his eye on the unusual group in tow behind the yogi. He looked like a magnate on a luxe vacation. But nevertheless, you could see he was a leader. A leader who knew how to attract and keep hold of a small yet still flabbergasting number of people.

Filling his lungs with cool air, Tonelli left the dreamers to their fantasies and went back to the table to work on the real and concrete task of giving himself a belly ache.

Throughout the meal, he chewed and drank through his muddled ideas. One of which made him think he should abandon everything and go back to the gossip columns. At least that generally yielded good *vino* and delicious *lasagne.*

Then Isabella's image came crashing into his thoughts. His fiancée was his last hope. He promised himself that if Bella couldn't get any leads, he would drop it all and return once and for all to the comforts of Rome.

◆ ◆ ◆

HALF AN HOUR after the succulent pasta had been washed down with more red wine, Tonelli was back home. It was a little apartment he rented near the Bay of Naples. He took off his shoes and laid back on the sofa. Within ten minutes, he was fast asleep.

Suddenly, his deep snoring was silenced by the ringing of a bell. He opened his eyes, thinking of Isabella. But it wasn't the doorbell that woke him—it was the telephone. He extended his arm and grabbed it before it could stop ringing.

"Tonelli?"

"*Sì.*"

"It's Bologna. So, how's it going?"

"Nothing yet, *caro mio.* I just had a talk with Bill Benson, but it looks like he's out."

"Be careful. Don't even come close to mentioning Francesco Ricotta."

"Don't worry. Bill thinks I believe the Consul ran the scam to pay the mortgage on his father-in-law's villa. I went as far as to say I have a recording, but he thought I was bluffing."

"Oh, so you got the tape! How wonderful. That's a good start. We have to hurry: the head honchos are asking questions."

Tonelli was about to say no, that he didn't have the tape—that he really was bluffing to Bill Benson. But he kept his mouth shut. It was a way of keeping hold of Nezzo Bologna by the reins. Bologna and all the bosses.

"One of these days, you'll all be in for a big surprise, Bologna."

"That's gonna be great for you. Call me when you have news."

Hanging up the telephone, Tonelli was soon asleep again.

Minutes later, his renewed snoring was again interrupted by another wake-up call. He opened his eyes, thinking about Nezzo Bologna. But this time it isn't the telephone—now it's the doorbell. Getting up, he crossed the room and opened the door.

"*Ciao, amore* mio!" Isabella's voice burst into the room, accompanied by her dazzling smile. Setting down her bag, she embraced her fiancé and kissed him two or three times on each cheek. Maybe four.

At thirty-five years of age, Isabella was pretty. Her blonde and curly hair, blue eyes and eternal smile endowed her with extreme likeability. She loved her fiancé, Massimo Tonelli, who she affectionately referred to as *Amore*.

Normally so quick to smile, Isabella was becoming deeply concerned by their interminable engagement. After all, when she first met her *amore*, she was full of hope and aspirations. But it had now been fourteen years since they first met and twelve years since he had popped the question.

Bella—which is what only Tonelli was allowed to call her—was a talented software engineer but, during this vacation, she had again proven herself to be an excellent chef in her fiancé's kitchen. This talent was perhaps Tonelli's favorite thing about her. Nevertheless, for dessert he always had the arduous task of defending his suggestion to delay their wedding yet again.

Tonelli's arguments were strong: he wanted to give his beloved—as the journalist of international renown he would surely soon be—an unforgettable honeymoon on a luxurious cruise around the world. He claimed to be struggling day and night to get them on that boat. And he had been at it ten years now.

"Twelve, *Amore*," his fiancée corrected.

Like an obliging bloodhound, Isabella had spent the past week working as an efficient spy for her beloved—using skills she inherited from her father, a retired police commissioner. All Tonelli had to do was give her the likely address of a proverbial bone, and Isabella would sniff around until she found it.

And today—at long last—his fiancée-turned-spy had brought her *amore* a fine trophy. She grabbed her bag off the sofa and drew out a cassette tape in a case.

"Here. I got you a birthday present."

"Bella...! Bella *mia*! You got the recording?! *Fatti dare un bacio!*"

Isabella had earned one kiss but stole another on top of it. Tonelli laughed out loud with joy. It was true—he would be turning thirty-eight next week—but who was thinking about birthdays? What he wanted was that much desired present. He smothered the cassette case in kisses and sat down lightly on the sofa with a tape recorder.

Moments later, he heard, "Heston? Is it you?"

"Yes. Who is it?"

The same voice continued in cold and metallic-sounding English, "Frank Borsato, Heston."

"Oh, Senator, pardon me. I didn't recognize your voice. Go ahead."

"Where in the world have you been this morning, Heston? I tried to get a hold of you three times. It's about Missionary Marshall. Anyway, just what is going on over there? Do you still not know about the funds I sent for your project?"

"Yes, of course, I just got off the phone with Missionary Marshall. Everything is fine, I just have to thank you yet again. But what's the matter, Senator?"

"I'll be asking the questions, Heston. What's the matter? You needed money, asked me for it, and I was able to convince some of my colleagues to send over this humanitarian aid. So, what is that idi... what is Missionary Benny Marshall complaining about? I even made it easy for him and had the money delivered in person and in cash. What a circus! I don't like people messing me around, Heston."

"I... I don't understand."

"You already got the funds you needed. End of subject. Now find some way to keep the mouths of the people connected to shut and, most of all, keep Missionary Marshall's mouth shut. And get it done fast, Heston. Do we understand each other?"

"Y-yes, of course."

"Okay then. That was all I wanted to hear."

Dial tone.

Tonelli's eyes bulged. Jumping up off the sofa, he lifted Isabella and started spinning her around in the air. She laughed, thrilled, and clung to her fiancé's neck. She felt compensated for having sacrificed a week searching and negotiating for that trophy.

Exhausted, they both collapsed onto the sofa.

"It wasn't easy to convince Anita, *Amore*. She didn't want to bring me the recording. She was afraid of compromising herself."

Anita Manfrini had been Consul Wesley Heston's secretary. When he died, she decided to quit her job and become a freelance literary translator.

Isabella had more information, "Anita says the Consul died the same day this phone call was placed. He also made a call to his wife at Villa Piomondo and received another call. But Anita doesn't know who that was from. Those ones were not recorded because he used his *cellulare*. Anita had some papers for the Consul to sign and she was waiting for him to finish that last phone call. Five minutes later, upon entering the office, she found Consul Heston on the floor. He was already dead."

Isabella stressed, "But that was not the same day she discovered the existence of this recording."

"And when was that?"

"The Consul's office stood empty for a few days after his death, *Amore*. So, when she decided to quit, she went to organize a few papers in the archives. That was when she discovered the received call log. It seems it was recorded by accident, Anita said. Maybe the Consul had meant to turn the recorder on for an earlier call but hadn't started it properly, so when that call ended and he pressed the button to turn the recorder off, he actually turned it on and recorded this call instead. Anita doesn't know why she decided to take the tape. She came to regret it. She was very reluctant about bringing it to me. And of course, it came with a price: I had to dip into our honeymoon savings, *Amore*."

"Oh!" escaped from Tonelli, opening his hands. "Well, what can you do?"

He savored a long sigh. Reflecting on his luck, he started to smile. Things were looking up.

He said to his fiancée, "I was already sure of one thing, Bella: that the money from America made it to Italy. And do you know whose hands it ended up in?"

"No, no I don't."

"Francesco Ricotta—who just so happens to be married to the late Consul's sister. It's a family con, *cara mia*."

Tonelli had a sharp glint in his eyes. And Isabella's brow was already furrowed.

"I can't believe it, *Amore*. I can't believe that cocky politician is gonna try to get himself reelected again. Who in their right mind would vote for Ricotta?"

"Bella...!" Tonelli pitied his fiancée's naivety. "With a million dollars, even *io*, Massimo Tonelli, could get elected to office. But this is a different story. What matters is that Bologna is right."

"What?" Isabella said shrilly, placing her hands on her waist. Her antenna had intercepted an additional plot in the air. "Nezzo Bologna? I can't believe you're working for that guy!"

"*I-iio*, Bella?" Tonelli said, laying an innocent hand on his chest. "I'm just looking for a journalistic scoop... a piece of heavyweight international reporting—how many times have I told you? And our honeymoon, Bella... our round-the-world cruise."

Isabella was not convinced. But she decided to drop the subject for the time being. She didn't want to start an argument with her fiancé.

Getting up off the sofa, Tonelli turned and walked partway down the hall. On the way back, he said, "We have two names, Bella: Missionary Benny Marshall and someone called Pellegrino. What does Anita know about them?"

Isabella opened her bag and took out an electronic organizer. It had a few recent entries.

"The Consul was a very private man, *Amore*. She had never heard of Missionary Benny Marshall before, just on the tape recording. But Anita says she has heard the Consul say the other name a few times—Pellegrino. Then, on the afternoon this all happened, she saw a pad of paper on the Consul's desk with a note reading: Domenico Sbroggio Pellegrino. And the name Pellegrino was underlined."

"Hmmm! Domenico Sbroggio Pellegrino—or simply Pellegrino. Now we have two names, Bella. That's a good start."

"We also have Jill."

"Who's she?"

"She's the late Consul's daughter. His only daughter. She is twenty-eight or twenty-nine years old and spent most of her life in America. She completed her PhD in Clinical Psychology in Atlanta. According to Anita, she is now living at Villa Piomondo. Anita is of the opinion that this Jill came over here from Atlanta to take care of her late father's affairs."

"Hmmm!" Tonelli replied again.

"The villa is to the south of Salerno, on the Mediterranean coast. And her grandfather, *Barone* Vittorino Tedesco Piomondo, he is..."

"Ruined," Tonelli finished. "I know. I know all about that old man."

Isabella closed the electronic organizer. Meanwhile, Tonelli went over to the shelf, retrieved a small package, and took a handful of nuts from inside. He chewed a few and swallowed them. Then, seated on the sofa, he took out his cell phone. He dialed the number of the newsroom of *Il Faro* in Rome.

"It's Tonelli, Mila. Put me through to Vaccaro."

Vaccaro was the crime reporter. Before Tonelli could even begin speaking, Vaccaro blurted out, "What's the matter, Tonelli?"

Tonelli gave him the names Domenico Sbroggio Pellegrino and Missionary Benny Marshall. He asked Vaccaro to find out anything he could about these names.

"I'm about to leave for Sicily, Tonelli. There's been another grisly murder in Palermo. I'm gonna cover my story first, then I'll look into this for you. It'll cost you a bottle of whiskey."

"*D'accordo*, Vaccaro. You have my number. Call me when you have news."

♦ ♦ ♦

Jill slowly sat back down.

Every manner of aggravation washed over her like an unbridled swarm of bees. Her mother's words were echoing in her head—*You can no longer bring the children.*

She got to her feet, visibly irritated, she dropped her arms to her thighs.

"I even spent money on renovating this house! What are we going to do, *Mamma?*"

Maddalena Heston looked at her daughter, who was pacing both indecisively and furiously. Jill had always been tough, a warrior woman—but also overly vulnerable. Any mildly strong wind that fluttered against her face she saw as a tempest.

"Jill! Please," her mother nearly shouted. "Stop pacing like that! It's annoying me! And it's not making anything better. Sit down and let's think of a way out of this."

Jill returned to her mother's side. She breathed a deep sigh.

Maddalena said, "What we have to do now is stay calm and think. But one thing is for sure: if you want to move forward with your father's plans, the villa's debt has to be paid off. And before your *nonno*..."

"But where will we get help, mother?" Jill asked, getting to her feet again. "What if... what if we asked the consulate?"

"No, don't even think about that. You know what things were like there for your father before he... No, *figliola*. We have to respect his wishes."

"What about Uncle Francesco?"

"Definitely not your Uncle Francesco. You know what your father thought of him."

Jill sat down next to her mother again.

"What a tragedy!"

"Calm down, Jill. We have to keep thinking."

They heard two light knocks at the door. Maddalena Heston could tell it was Genoveffa. She shouted for her to come in. Genoveffa was carrying a letter that had just arrived for Jill.

Maddalena waited for her daughter to read it. Jill went over to the balcony. Once she had finished reading, she came back over to her mother.

"Why the happy face, sweetie? Was it a letter from America?"

The look on Jill's face was not actually one of joy—her smile was almost cynical. Instead of responding, she just handed the letter to her mother.

"Hmm!" Maddalena said when she finished reading. "Like it fell from heaven! Mike was always so considerate—and he always adored you."

"It really could have fallen from heaven," she said, looking vaguely at a point on the wall opposite, "but it fell three months too late, mother. Mike... he doesn't know how badly he hurt me in Atlanta, during those terrible days when I needed his support the most. Out of the blue, he left me all alone and made up some big business trip to Australia."

"Jill! He loves you! And he must have had his reasons. He explained himself to you, didn't he?"

Jill looked at her mother.

"Maybe one day I'll understand. But today is not that day, *Mamma*."

"Jill," Maddalena, swayed by the letter's words, grabbed her daughter's hands, "he wants to marry you! He wants to start over! All you have to do is call and he'll be on the very first flight. What more do you want from Mike?"

Jill fixed her mother with a penetrating gaze.

"Are you thinking of me, or of the stocks Mike's dad has on the New York Stock Exchange, *Mamma*?"

"Jill!" came Maddalena's rebuke.

"I didn't mean anything by it, but I know you understand me. I can see the grief... the uncertainty in your eyes over everything that's been happening. I feel the same way, *Mamma*."

Maddalena Heston sat in silence.

"Ah, how I wish everything had ended well between me and Mike...! These problems would all be solved now. I know that."

And, looking deep into her mother's eyes, "But I can't do something like that, not even for the villa, *Mamma*. Not now. And I don't know if I can do it in the future either."

"What about for the children?"

Jill breathed a deep sigh. She felt like she was up against a wall. "There has to be another solution," she finally said.

"You're right. It was just a silly idea that crossed my mind. But let's keep going, we can't lose hope. We will find a way out of this."

Now she ran her hands through her daughter's hair. Jill felt her hair fall back onto her shoulders.

Maddalena started again, "The solution has to come from here, from Italy. Maybe... Maybe the time has come to go looking for your grandfather's old friends. After all, they all owe him favors. I remember he used to have four friends—all quite rich men."

Jill quickly raised her head.

"What did you just say, *Mamma*?"

"Your grandfather would have never accepted the idea of asking any of them for help, but now..."

"Explain this to me properly. Four? All friends of my grandfather—and all rich? Richer than *Nonno* Vittorino used to be? I've never heard about this."

"Of course," her mother said, pushing a lock of Jill's hair back into place. "Your head was always in Atlanta. But go get *Signor* Dante. He knows the most about your grandfather's past—and how much money they threw away." Maddalena Heston exclaimed, "We could really use some of that cash now!"

Jill got up decisively.

"I'll look into it, *Mamma*. I'll go talk to *Signor* Dante straight away."

◆ ◆ ◆

"**What are you thinking about**, *Amore*?"

Tonelli chewed and swallowed a few more nuts.

"Let's start with *Barone* Vittorino Piomondo's granddaughter. What was her name again?"

"Jill Heston."

"Jill. Pretty name. If she is taking care of her father's affairs as Anita said, she probably knows everything. *Nevvero*, Bella?"

"*Amore*..." Isabella hesitated because she was already imagining her fiancé's displeasure with the news she was about to tell him. "Anita is of the opinion that those refugee children really do exist. And that they are most likely somewhere in Italy."

"What?"

Isabella looked at Tonelli's astonished face.

"Anita thinks it's this girl, Jill, who has the refugees from Kurmania."

Tonelli quickly shook himself out of the shock.

"How ridiculous. That's a lie. Anita didn't know the Consul very well—she was just his secretary. She knows as much about the children as I know about Bologna—maybe even less."

Isabella's frown returned.

"Ah! Nezzo Bologna again...!"

Realizing his blunder, Tonelli changed the subject.

"That was a con, Bella. A shameful con the Consul was running to drum up some cash for himself and his brother-in-law, Francesco Ricotta. There were never any refugee children from Kurmania—not those involved in the Consul's story, anyway."

Isabella forgot about Nezzo Bologna.

"Then why don't you make a phone call to Villa Piomondo?"

"Call the villa? And what for?"

"To ask about the Kurmanian children," Isabella said, opening her electronic organizer again. "It almost always works. If you ask the right question, then the person who answers ends up saying something they shouldn't have."

Tonelli thought it wasn't a bad idea. However, he suggested she make the call herself. Isabella consulted her electronic organizer, took the phone, and dialed the number.

"*Pronto!*" said a woman's voice on the other end of the line. "Villa Piomondo."

"Ah, yes, *grazie.* I'm calling from the newspaper *Il Faro* in Rome. To whom am I speaking?"

"Genoveffa. I work here."

"Hi, Genoveffa! How's it going? We wanted to make an appointment to speak to someone there about the Kurmanian children staying at the villa."

"What? I don't understand. There... there are no children here."

"Oh, is that so, Genoveffa? Okay... and *Signorina* Jill Heston... may I speak to her?"

"Just a moment, I'll see."

Isabella put her hand over the phone's mouthpiece to listen to Tonelli's excitement.

"What was she saying, Bella?"

"That there are no children at the villa. But she wasn't telling the truth. She hesitated a bit."

Seconds later, Isabella heard, "*Pronto!* Jill here."

"Ah, *Signorina* Jill, it's nice to hear your voice. I'm calling from *Il Faro* in Rome and we wanted to know about the children..."

Isabella fell silent for five seconds. After that she lowered the telephone. Tonelli was left puzzled.

"What happened, Bella?"

"That Jill must be crazy. She hung up."

"*Ma come?* Just hung up, that's it? She didn't say anything?"

"Yes, she did. She said she is not married. Nor is she a single mother."

Isabella batted her lashes. Tonelli celebrated, rubbing his hands together. It was good news.

"Mmmm! Great! Didn't I say that the refugee orphan children were a machination of her father's?"

"Don't be a fool. No woman would respond that way—not unless she was somehow covering up the truth. I only see one option."

"What?"

"We pay a visit to Villa Piomondo. Do a little snooping and figure things out. Maybe the children do exist, and they are, in fact, there—and in that case you won't have a story to write. And then we can go back to Rome."

"*Brava!*" Tonelli quipped, not accepting the setback. "What else does that foolish little head of yours have to say, Bella?"

"What else? Well... then we can finally start planning our wedding."

"Wedding?! And continue living this life of... of poverty? Never!"

"N-never, *Amore?* Are you saying that us two... that *noi due* will never be married?"

Tonelli already regretted having started this war. His fingers tried to find peace with his fiancée's cheeks.

"Bella, Bella *mia...!*"

Nothing else came out.

Then she said through the threat of tears, "I don't want a round-the-world cruise for our honeymoon, *Amore...* I never asked for that. I just want to get married... I want to have children..."

"*Bambini?!*" Tonelli jumped aside. "How absurd!"

"Absurd? What's so absurd? Now me wanting to have children is absurd? My *nonna* had seventeen of them and they're all still alive. What's so absurd about that?"

The high number spooked Tonelli even further. But he knew how to get around it.

"No, Bella! I wasn't saying it's absurd to have children. I was talking about those imaginary children. That girl... What was her name again?"

"Jill Heston."

"That's it. I was talking about those children. It's absurd. I don't believe they exist. They never existed, Bella. And I know I have a big international corruption story on my hands."

His torment finally overcome, Tonelli paced around the little room clutching the cassette tape. He needed to reconsider everything. Maybe it was a good idea to take a trip to Villa Piomondo. Yes, that was what he was going to do. The story of orphan children sponsored by the late Consul Heston was nothing more than a dirty con to raise money for the Francesco Ricotta campaign—and other family interests. And that was that. It had to be made public and he was the man to do it.

He finished the remainder of the nuts in the bag but kept throwing out ideas.

"Bella..." he said, stopping his circuit of the room to stand in front of his fiancée, "there's really no harm in getting to know this Jill Heston. If she has taken over for her father as Anita Manfrini said, she should know what the money was for. And that's all I'm interested in."

Isabella was still dabbing at her eyes with a handkerchief to dry them of the tears her passing rage had provoked. But her antenna still picked up the signal of intrigue.

She said, "Yes, it's possible that Jill Heston could have been involved in Ricotta's reelection campaign. After all, he is her uncle."

Encouraged by Isabella's agreement, Tonelli spent the next four minutes hashing out the next steps in his plan. Then, gently, mewling and cajoling, he played an old trick. While yammering on nonstop, he conducted his fiancée and her bag over to the front door.

"*Ma cosa...?*" Isabella screeched. "Are you trying to get me to leave again, *Amore*? I only just got here!"

"No, Bella, of course I'm not making you leave. The thing is I... I have a lot of work to do, you know how my life is... the boat never stops... and now I need to pack my suitcase. *Ciao! Un bacio.*"

"Suitcase? So, are we going traveling?"

"*Noi?*"

Tonelli blocked his fiancée from coming back in the door.

"I am going traveling, Bella. Me! I am going to work. And you can go back to work too. You can busy yourself with our hope chest."

"Our hope chest?! It's been ready for ten years now! You know that very well."

"Then make it even better, Bella. Embroider things... put another flower on every towel, add some branches and leaves—you can figure out something to do while I take care of our future. *Ciao*, Bella."

Isabella was a happy woman because she was always practical. She smiled, closed her eyes, and offered up her lips for her beloved to deposit a kiss or two on them. Tonelli gave her half a kiss. She opened her eyes and took the other half too.

Then, heading toward the stairs, she said, "Goodbye, *Amore*."

Locking the door behind him, Tonelli took in all the freedom the air had to offer. He was euphoric about everything that just happened. He could already sense financial independence just an arm's reach away. He went over to the sofa, picked up the cassette tape and gave it another audible kiss.

Then he fell from his dream back into the bitter reality: money. For now, he was alone on this job. Nezzo Bologna wasn't offering anything up front, just two hundred thousand dollars after the fact—and even so he was talking about passing the hat to the brass. But what now? What about funding? His only chance at funding was currently walking down the stairs and out the door.

He quickly opened the door, ran over to the stairs to the ground floor, and shouted down them.

"Bella, Bella *mia*! Wait!"

Isabella was an extremely practical woman. Smiling from down below, she said, "I already know, *Amore*—money. Don't worry, I'm going to withdraw some from an ATM. I'll be back within two hours with my suitcase, and I'll help you pack yours. *D'accordo*? And tomorrow, bright and early, the two of us are going to Villa Piomondo! Goodbye! *Un bacio!*"

Isabella blew him a kiss and left.

"*Va bene. Noi due,*" Tonelli resigned himself on his way back into the apartment.

◆ ◆ ◆

MADDALENA HESTON saw the bewilderment on her daughter's face when she hung up the phone.

"Why did you respond that way, Jill? Who was it?"

"Some newspaper from Rome. They know about the children, *Mamma*. I'm going to find *Signor* Dante."

Dante Migliano was of Celtic ancestry, balding, seventy-three-years old but still quite strong. He had also been born here at Villa Piomondo, one of three brothers. Another was Genoveffa's father, who had been a sort of nanny to *Nonno* Vittorino when he was a boy. Dante often said that he couldn't breathe properly when he wasn't on the property. He was dismayed by hearing of the *Barone*'s grave state of health.

But Jill had another subject to discuss with Dante Migliano that afternoon: the four wealthy men. According to her mother, no one knew better than he did about the indulgent life her *nonno* had led twenty to thirty years ago—he and his four inseparable rich friends.

Always loyal to his employer—even if he was broke—Dante asked, "*Ma perché, Signorina?* Why should I discuss this without *Barone* Vittorino?"

"Because a doctor has just given my *nonno* thirty days to live, *Signor* Dante. And that means that soon we'll all be looking for another place to live. Got it? And that would also mean all the hard work and money we put into renovating the mansion will have been for nothing. Where will we house the children?"

Dante was baffled. The *signorina*'s eyes were aflame and her words inflammatory. But it was all too much for the mind of a simple man like him. And it was all really painful. So, he agreed to tell the story of the four rich men.

◆ ◆ ◆

"THEY WERE FOUR MEN—enviable, fiery and highly successful businessmen. At the time, *Barone* Vittorino had three other estates too, all over the Sorrentine Peninsula. But he was considered poor compared to his four friends. People used to say that half of southern Italy belonged to those four men, along with a couple nice tracts of the Po valley in the prosperous North. However, the only one with a noble title was Vittorino—*Barone* Vittorino Tedesco Piomondo. And that made him an obligatory companion on all their nights out in Sorrento, Naples, Venice, and Paris."

Back then, Dante Migliano was the Baron's shadow. He didn't know much about the others, but at least once he had washed a shirt stained with the acidic vomit of one of their nights in the cabarets.

"I don't know about the others, *Signorina* Jill. But last year one of them came here to visit the *Barone*. It was *Signor* Luigi Decchi. He is one of your *nonno*'s four old friends. *Signor* Decchi spent one afternoon here at the villa and left."

"Do you know what he came for, *Signor* Dante?"

"No, *Signorina.* I don't."

"And do you know where he lives?"

Dante was hesitant to respond. It was difficult to talk about this. It felt like he was betraying the *Barone*— and admitting to eavesdropping.

"*Signor* Dante... I know that you know. It's okay. You can tell me."

The best way out he could find was to ask a question, "Isn't *Signor* Decchi the owner of Decchi Industries in Turin, *Signorina?*"

Jill cracked a smile.

"How nice, *Signor* Dante. That straightens everything out. We'll leave for Turin early tomorrow morning."

"Me too, *Signorina?* But... what about *suo nonno, il barone?*"

Jill understood. It was his ingrained loyalty. Her *nonno* would have to be informed that Dante would be absent from Villa Piomondo.

"Don't worry. I'll talk to my *nonno.* Is it okay if he is there to say goodbye to us early tomorrow morning when we leave?"

"*Sì, sì, Signorina*" said Dante, smiling.

When he opened the door so Jill could go outside, he found Peppino sitting in the doorway. He was crying softly with his head buried between his knees. Dante sighed. It was a sigh of pity. And of impatience for the young man.

The son of a Villa Piomondo staff member, Peppino had the body of an eighteen-year-old, but the mental faculties of a five-year-old. He was docile, sentimental, and dependent like a child of that age. And of course, highly impressionable. The work he absolutely enjoyed doing was looking after a small flock of sheep. Of late, however, Villa Piomondo's many hungry mouths had been eating away at that flock, day by day, and at his joy.

"What's wrong, Peppino?" Dante asked. "Why all the tears? And why are you sitting there?"

Looking up, Peppino said, "*Signor* Dante... is it true that... that everyone is going to have to leave the villa?"

Peppino didn't have to say anything else. Dante understood. He went back to Jill.

"*Signorina,* Peppino, he... he heard everything about the *Barone*'s troubles. He tends the sheep... the few we still have. Caring for the flock is the one thing he likes to do."

Walking forward, Jill came over and crouched down next to Peppino. He was still sitting with his head hanging low.

"Peppino, listen to me," she said. "None of that is going to happen, got it?"

The boy raised his head.

And she repeated, "None of that is going to happen, no one is going to have to leave the villa. No one. And you can keep your flock. We're even going to buy a few more sheep on our way home. Do you understand me?"

His spirits already lifting, Peppino vigorously hammered his head up and down.

"I'm going to look for help, Peppino. I'll get a lot of money, and everything at the villa will go back to the way it was before."

When Jill got up, Dante ordered Peppino to get back to work. Like a child with a head full of plans, he ran off.

"What time do you plan on leaving tomorrow, *Signorina*?"

"Before eight, *Signor* Dante."

"I will be ready."

◆ ◆ ◆

DAWN WAS BREAKING.

Camouflaged behind the bushes that lined the old cobblestone road, the old lead-gray four-door sedan couldn't easily be spotted by anyone at Villa Piomondo. But Tonelli—and mainly Isabella—were able to keep tabs on one whole side of the property.

"How long are we gonna wait around here, Bella?" Tonelli wanted to know.

"Calm down, *Amore*. We just got here."

"It's been half an hour already. And I haven't seen any sign of the children. If it were up to me, I'd go ring the front doorbell and get straight to the point."

"*Amore*! You are a fool," Bella mocked. "And I suppose she'll just come right out and tell you everything, *nevvero*?"

"And why not?"

"You silly! If she has nothing to hide, you won't have a story for the newspaper. And then say goodbye to our trip around the world."

"*Va bene*," Tonelli resigned himself. "But then what did we come here to do?"

"To observe. And wait for someone to show up, obviously. Then we can ask questions."

◆ ◆ ◆

NOT FAR AWAY, when the last sheep had left the fold, Peppino picked up his crook and set off after his flock. Soon after, the sheep filed past the old straw-yellow mansion and headed for the north of the property. Over there, from the bluffs of the Mediterranean to the boundary fence east of the villa, was a separate grazing area for the young shepherd and his small herd.

But today was different. Peppino stopped when he saw *Signorina* Jill taking *Barone* Vittorino Piomondo's old Alfa Romeo out of the garage. She saw him watching and waved at him.

"Goodbye, Peppino!"

Peppino's face broke into the joyous smile of a child who has been promised a gift. He smiled and waved in return.

From the balcony of his room on the upper floor of the main house, *Nonno* Vittorino also waved at the car as it drove out of the front gate. Recollections—or regrets—made his blue eyes tear up. Next to him, his daughter noticed.

Raising his hand to wipe away the tears, the old man said, "*Oddio! Questa mia cataratta!*"

Maddalena Heston flashed a smile. Her father didn't have to suffer like this. Nor blame his cloudy eyes for the tears. She had already forgiven him. Already forgiven him for the extravagances of the past.

◆ ◆ ◆

PEPPINO CLOSED THE FRONT GATE when the car had gone. Then he went back to his flock and they kept walking.

North of the villa, Isabella saw the sheep come out from behind the old mansion.

"Let's go, *Amore*," she said, opening the car door.

Nearing the fence, she waved and shouted, "Hey, *ragazzo!*"

Peppino obediently came over to her. He looked like a curious and gullible boy. Isabella asked him about the children.

"*Bambini?* There are no children here anymore. *Signora* Gioconda took her children with her when she moved away."

Isabella realized the boy had a learning disability.

"What is your name?"

"Peppino."

"My name is Isabella, Peppino. I'm not talking about Mrs. Gioconda's children. I wanted to know if *Signorina* Jill brought some children here to the villa... lots of children."

Peppino stood with his mouth agape. He didn't seem to know what she was talking about.

"*Signora*... I don't know anything about that, I'm a shepherd. I have my flock... even though it's little because *Signor* Dante had to sell a few sheep. But *Signorina* Jill said she will buy me more sheep."

Ever-impatient, Tonelli butted in.

"That's nice, Peppino, that's nice. Forget about the children. I want to know about *Signorina* Jill. Is she at the villa?"

"*Signorina* Jill?" Peppino cracked a smile. "She went to get money... *molto denaro*."

Tonelli raised his eyebrows.

"What? Money? You said *molto denaro*, Peppino?"

"*Sì*. And *Signorina* Jill is going to buy me some sheep on her way back. She went to Turin to get money. She just left."

"What?" Tonelli asked again. Isabella was more practical,

"Turin. Okay then. What car did she take, Peppino?"

"*Signor Barone*'s Alfa Romeo."

"What color?"

"Black."

"*Grazie*, Peppino. Let's go, *Amore*. Quick."

Isabella grabbed her fiancé by the arm and started dragging him off toward the car.

Three

Quasi-desperate barking pours out of the two unleashed dogs running past him. He wrinkles his forehead and sits—watching. Their run extends to a wall. Stretching out vertically, Caesar uses his front paws to stabilize himself on the high wall. He is still barking ferociously. Nero, a bit behind, is now entertaining himself with something on the ground.

From his position beneath the flowery garden pergola, he sees the caretaker head over to where the dogs are. Caesar is still barking while pursuing his vain attempt to climb the wall. Meanwhile, Nero picks something up from the ground. Coming over, the caretaker takes it out of the dog's mouth. Next, the man turns and approaches him.

"I saw this get thrown over the wall, *Signore*," the caretaker says, moving to hand him the object.

He rebukes his employee for bringing it over instead of throwing it in the trash. It looks like some kid's artwork.

"It has a piece of paper inside, *Signore*."

He picks up the object. It's a piece of inch-wide black tubing, the kind used in construction, no more than eight inches long. He examines it confirming that indeed a piece of paper is inside. He asks Donato to get him something narrow to pull it out with.

The caretaker takes out a gray pocketknife, opens it, and hands it to him. He slides the paper out of the tube, unrolls it and reads:

YOuR DAYS ARE NuMBEreD

His face turns pale. The message has been pasted together with letters that have probably been cut out of a newspaper. He hands the pocketknife back to the caretaker. The man walks away.

With the note in his left hand and the tubing in his right, he stays planted in the grass for a whole minute. He looks at the walls of the property. They are high—but easily climbable. Then a growing fear starts to take hold of him and he is gripped by an icy sweat.

◆ ◆ ◆

Amaro Maggio was woken by the barking of his dogs. He fought his eyelids open and stared at the wall clock: seven forty-five in the morning. The dogs were still barking. Mouth dry, eyes wide in fright at the nightmare, he jumped up out of bed and briskly walked over to the window. He slid back the curtain. His eyes scanned the walls next to the metal-plated front gate. The dogs. Still. Caesar was now almost fully vertical and barking ferociously. Nero was entertaining himself with something on the ground.

"How strange... exactly the same as my dream," he said to himself. Then he saw the caretaker heading over to where the dogs were.

Maggio followed him with his eyes and saw Donato taking a black object from Nero's mouth. Straightening up, the caretaker began walking toward his little house.

Opening the window, Maggio stuck his head out of it and shouted, "Hey, Donato!"

As usual whenever his employer called him, the caretaker hurried over.

"What do you have in your hand, Donato?"

The man held up the object. It was a simple piece of black plastic tubing, the kind used in construction. Maggio swallowed a dry lump in his throat. The nightmare was still present.

"It's nothing, *Signore*," replied the caretaker. "I saw it get thrown over the wall. It must be some kid's artwork."

But Maggio's nervous fingers called for the object. Donato brought it over to him. He checked that there was no piece of paper inside. Finding it empty, he felt relieved and handed the piece of plastic back to the caretaker.

"I'll throw it in the trash, *Signore*," said Donato and left.

There was no paper at all—but the atmosphere was still permeated with apprehension. The dogs continued to bark and bark and bark. Maggio remained at the window.

"Donato!" he shouted again. The caretaker stopped and looked up at him. "What's going on with these dogs? Take a look out front."

Donato obediently went, opened the gate, looked outside, and closed it again.

"There's nothing, *Signore*... nobody," the caretaker shouted back.

Maggio continued to watch the dogs for some time. They continued to bark, walk, stop, look up the wall, and bark. Bothered, he swallowed another dry lump. The walls were high—but not unclimbable.

Then he gave a strong whistle. The Dobermans came quickly, entering the house through the back door, and were in front of him only moments later. Maggio stroked the black fur on their backs and spoke to them. Then he ordered them to lie on the rug outside the studio door. The Dobermans obeyed. He closed the door with his guard dogs outside. He immediately felt safer.

Ten minutes later, Maggio was sitting on the carpet in the middle of his studio. He crossed his legs and put his hands on his knees. The big window curtain was closed, and all the lights in the studio were off. The room was immersed in shadows. He closed his eyes and started the relaxation.

In a punctuated cadence, Maggio repeated a sequence of ritual words one after the next. In less than two minutes, his brain waves fell to the seven cycles of a hypnagogic state. The channeling was complete. Maggio could already distinguish the characteristic fog-filtered light in his closed eyes. And he sensed *him*. He hoped that *he* would appear before him to open a dialogue.

"I..." Maggio hesitated, "I need help... I got really spooked by a terrible dream."

"I do not fight against my equals," *he* said, "but remember this name: Vallencantado."

"Vallencantado?"

◆ ◆ ◆

THE NEXT DAY, the precise moment of Giancarlo's arrival at Amaro Maggio's country house near Genoa coincided with his master's sacred hour. Giancarlo could tell because the main gate's doorbell was disconnected. For those two hours, nothing and no one could get Maggio away from his ritual.

But the barking of Caesar and Nero—elegant black-furred Dobermans—called Donato, the caretaker, to the gate. He was a man of fifty-two years, a bit thin and of humble bearing.

Opening the door for Giancarlo, he said, "Come in, *per favore. Signor* Maggio told me you would be coming, and he wanted me to make you comfortable. Let me take your suitcase, *Signor* Bertinezzi."

"Thank you, *Signor* Donato. But you needn't trouble yourself."

"As you wish. Follow me, *per favore.*"

Restless, snarling and baring their teeth, the dogs kept their distance at about thirty feet away. Giancarlo was two steps behind the caretaker at all times. The closer they got to the arbor in front of the house, the more the dogs' restlessness gave Giancarlo pause. He turned around. On the spot, as if frightened, the Dobermans let out a high-pitched snarl—almost a whimper—and backed away. One of them had his gray eyes fixed on Giancarlo. His snarl was a languishing whimper.

"What's the matter, Caesar? Why are you giving me trouble?" Giancarlo asked, extending a hand to touch the dog. As if to avoid contact, Caesar dropped to the ground, almost commando crawling. Then, tail between his legs, he shot off and disappeared behind the house. Nero did the same.

Waiting a few steps ahead, Donato had been observing the scene. He kept shaking his head as if to beg forgiveness on the dogs' behalf.

"Sorry, *Signor* Bertinezzi. You can never trust a *cane.*"

"It's all right. Let's keep going."

Sixty feet to the right, behind his studio window, Amaro Maggio was lurking in silence. He had been roused by Caesar and Nero's strange whining. The scene he had just witnessed intrigued him.

◆ ◆ ◆

FORTY MINUTES LATER, after tapping twice on the door with his fingers, Amaro Maggio entered Giancarlo's room with a broad smile.

"How's it going, Gian? Have a good trip?"

"Great. Except the bus was late."

"It happens."

Without ceremony, Amaro took a seat on the edge of the bed. Giancarlo did the same.

"You know, Gian... your phone call caught me off guard. I'm sorry you lost your father."

"Thank you, Master."

"But don't let it get you down, *caro*. Our lives here on planet Earth are like that: transient."

"But it did come as a shock. My father was only fifty-one."

"How did it happen?"

"He... *Papà* was harvesting wood with Tullio and a tree crushed his leg. Then there were complications from the amputation. He lost a lot of blood. When it happened, I was in the mountains... meditating about my life. I needed to make some decisions, Master. And I came down with the firm intention of having a frank conversation with my father. But I was too late, and that hurt."

Still traumatized, Giancarlo was speaking in a strained manner, in fragments. Amaro Maggio patted him on the shoulder in support.

"Take courage, *caro mio*."

"And I..." Giancarlo hesitated, "I came here because I owed you an explanation."

"Owed me an explanation? What do you mean?"

Giancarlo briefly held the silence, then said, "I... I have decided that I won't travel with you anymore."

"What? Say that again, Gian."

He repeated himself.

Now more serious, Amaro Maggio thought for a moment, then said, "But what made you change your mind? Why won't you tell me what's happened to you over the last twenty days, Gian? Maybe I could understand you better. Because... frankly, leaving everything behind because of your father's death...! It doesn't make sense. I hope you have some stronger reasons."

"I think I do: a dream."

"A dream?!" Maggio let slip a short snicker. "It must have been a pretty special dream then. Tell me about it."

Giancarlo told him the dream. When he finished, Amaro Maggio got to his feet and cracked some of the knuckles on his left hand. He walked over to the window and looked out. Unbidden, his eyes scanned the walls of the property. Then he looked at the dogs. They were still restless.

Maggio returned to where Giancarlo was.

"Very well. Then... then you mean to say you don't remember anything you learned in the dream," Maggio said as if asserting.

"Nothing except that remembering means nothing without doing. And that I was a prisoner. But the idea that stuck with me was that I belong to the world of failures. I was taking the place of an elderly man, who took the place of another before him. Generation after generation—all failing."

"Generations provide us with tradition, my boy," Maggio retorted with a certain harshness. "Have you forgotten that?"

Giancarlo gave no response. Then, distinctly enunciating his syllables, he said, "When I came down from the mountain, I found my father dead and buried."

"Yes, you already told me your father died—so what?"

Ignoring Maggio's new somewhat rough tone of voice, Giancarlo continued, "Next I discovered that the grave next to his, where I always thought my grandfather was buried, contains nothing but a casket full of stones."

"Stones?"

Maggio sat back down on the bed.

Little by little, in the same stilted manner, Giancarlo laid out everything that had happened in the last few days on his family farm. The he reached the part about the graduation ring.

Maggio could see a look of profound repentance on Giancarlo's face. But he just couldn't let it go.

"'Never regret anything' Have you forgotten that rule of ours, Gian? Any kind of regret is harmful to a person. It limits your spiritual progress."

Yet again, Giancarlo gave no response. Maggio was beginning to get irritated.

"That's why I came here, Master. I didn't want to say it on the phone, but my mind is made up: I am going to find my grandfather. And I also came because... because I know that... that dealing with this last-minute change will end up falling on your shoulders. I wanted you to understand, and..."

"Of course I don't understand," Maggio cut him off and got to his feet again. "All I understand is that your answer is no—you will not finish what you started. You're running away again, like you did last year. You always run away. Unbelievable! It's all happening again."

Maggio briskly walked a couple of angry circles and stopped in front of Giancarlo again.

"It's a shame that all this happened right now, Gian. It *really* is a shame. I'm afraid that you'll have to start all over again from the very beginning in the future—and that's if they give you another chance."

Pacing in another circle, Maggio changed his rhetoric. His voice took on a chill and came out many degrees colder.

"You, Gian… you're one of those people who see life like a box of surprises. Am I wrong? Every morning you want to open it up to find out what the rest of the day has in store for you. Fool!" Maggio emphatically said. "Yes, we have to seek. Of course! But no one ever succeeds when they're seeking two different things at the same time."

Fighting to control his voice so it wouldn't come out sour, Giancarlo replied, "I am not seeking two things. I am only seeking one."

"A pile of bones. Such a wonderful thing to look for!"

They both fell silent for a moment. Maggio managed to regain his composure. He returned to where Giancarlo was on the bed for the third time, but this time his eyes were lost in the floorboards. The next thing he said came out in the form of an accusation,

"Yesterday I contacted McDowell, the emissary of the Order. He has already confirmed the day, time, and location. What do you have to say about that? Aren't you ashamed to break your word?"

Silence. Leaning forward, Giancarlo supported himself with his arms on his thighs.

"I… I'm very sorry, Master. But I have to follow what my heart desires."

"Heart?" Maggio wanted to laugh. "Ah, Gian, Gian…! What madness."

"It's something that's trapped inside me. I don't know how to get it out."

Amaro Maggio was about to say something—perhaps even curse and swear—but he managed to control himself. He remained standing. He didn't take his eyes off Giancarlo.

"You know what I think? I think you lost your good sense up in those mountains."

As he spoke, Maggio walked over to the door and opened it. Then he stopped. He turned back. The rage finally seemed to have subsided. Half smiling, he said, "In any case, Gian, you will always be welcome here. I cannot hide that I am happy to see you, even with this sappy sentimentality of yours. I don't want things to change between us. Why would I want that? I am not just going to this huge celebration in honor of my disciples. In fact, I... let's say I've been feeling like getting away too. I need this, believe me. I have to get myself out of Genoa for a while... away from my business. It's a shame you won't be on this trip. You're the one losing out here, Gian."

After a brief pause, Maggio added, "Menendez should be arriving at any moment, and I agreed to pick up Michel in Avignon tomorrow at midday so we can stay on schedule. But if I can do anything for you... take you somewhere, just say the word. Do you have any idea where to start looking for your grandfather?"

"Yes," said Giancarlo, getting up off the bed. "In Aquila Colorada. It's north of Zaragoza."

Maggio's face lit up. Leaving the door ajar, he came back to stand next to Giancarlo.

"Zaragoza, you say? Really? But that's fantastic news, Gian! The universe is conspiring in our favor!"

"I don't understand."

"We're going to the northwest of Spain and our route will take us through Zaragoza! Do you understand now?"

Maggio's face was different. But Giancarlo did not share his enthusiasm.

Still festive, Maggio said, "I won't hide that I still hope you might change your mind, *caro mio*. But now let's raise a toast to this splendid occasion."

As he said that, Amaro Maggio walked over to a side table and returned with a bottle of wine and two crystal glasses. He handed the glasses to Giancarlo and opened the bottle. He filled both glasses and took his from Giancarlo. After returning the bottle to its place on the side table, he raised his arm to make a toast.

"To your search, Giancarlo."

Suddenly, a jagged crack split through the glass in Maggio's hand. Shards of crystal fell to the floor. The wine spilled out onto the floorboards. Maggio went pale, his gaze on the mess on the floor. He couldn't believe what he was seeing. He sought Giancarlo's eyes.

"What the...?" he muttered, white and tense. "What just happened?"

He looked back at the floor. He again saw the shards of glass, the wine pooling on the floorboards. And he raised his head again to look Giancarlo in the face.

"I... I don't know what happened, Master."

Walking over to the side table, Giancarlo left his intact glass there, still full of wine, and returned to stand next to Maggio.

Amaro Maggio ran his right hand through his hair, which was graying at the temples. His eyes were still bulging, his cheeks pale. It wasn't from fear simply of the glass shattering in his hand. That could have had a simple scientific explanation. But that wasn't the whole story. Maggio could sense that it wasn't.

Then the images he had seen shortly before Giancarlo arrived paraded through his mind again. He saw the strange way the dogs greeted a man they knew so well—someone who had spent entire months in his home with him. And now the shattered glass. Something eerie was afoot.

Maggio ran a hand through his hair. He strode over to the window and looked out. Caesar was walking in circles, stopping, sniffing the lawn, walking again, barking. Nero was doing the same. They looked lost. Maggio felt the need to look at the front wall once again. It was high—but not unclimbable. *Vallencantado—escape to that place and wait for me. That is where I will instruct you and free you from this threat of death.* The memory was still alive inside him. Vallencantado was not a mere promise—it was something he needed… to survive.

Still at the window, he sighed and tried to pull himself together. Leaving his post, he walked back to Giancarlo again.

"This..." he tried to analyze what happened, "this is not rough crystal, Gian... do you understand me? But nevertheless, it absorbed the negative energy in this room. Do you see what I'm saying? You brought very strong negativity with you."

He ran a hand through his disheveled hair again.

"It's partly normal considering everything that has happened to you in the past few days. But I... I can sense something else. Perhaps something even more unpleasant is going to happen."

They looked at one another for a few seconds.

"Okay, I'll send someone to clean the floor. Please, Gian, let's forget this, okay? Dinner will be served downstairs in about an hour. Then we'll gather everything we need for the journey. I intend to leave at seven in the morning."

"That's fine, Master. I'll be down shortly."

It was a formal, dry dialogue without their usual casualness. They could both feel it. Amaro Maggio left the room without saying anything else, closing the door after him.

Giancarlo looked for the bed to sit down. He continued to stare at the pieces of crystal and the wine stain on the floor. He felt it was an omen. He could feel that something was breaking in his relationship with the man he considered his master. Some kind of invisible wall was going up between their separate lives.

But how? Why? And who was orchestrating this?

Then, like a reverse avalanche of snow blasting out of the abyss up onto a luminous mountaintop, for a fraction of a second he felt like the explanation was simple, genuine, and crystal clear. But he only felt it very briefly and soon that threat of greater understanding left him. Like rolling snow, the light tumbled away and was lost again in the depths of oblivion.

◆ ◆ ◆

HALF AN HOUR LATER, just as he had finished showering himself clean of his journey, Giancarlo heard the sound of a vehicle arriving outside. This time, the dogs were barking excitedly, throwing a party. Giancarlo could tell it was Menendez. Going over to the window, he watched the commotion down below.

It was indeed Menendez. The dogs were celebrating his arrival.

With that, Giancarlo left his room and went downstairs to eat dinner.

Four

They had spent the whole day traveling.

It was eight-thirty in the evening when Jill and Dante Migliano arrived at the hotel in Turin. The next morning, they headed for Decchi Industries. A series of letters running from one end to the other at the top of the office building read: DECCHI INDUSTRIES. They went inside.

"I'd like to speak with *Signor* Decchi, please," Jill said to the receptionist.

"Who?" the other woman was surprised.

"*Signor* Luigi Decchi?"

The receptionist was about to say something but she seemed to change her mind. She picked up the phone.

"*Signor* Federico, there's a woman here asking for *Signor* Decchi."

"Who is it?" The reply from the other end of the line was audible.

The receptionist covered the mouthpiece and looked at Jill again.

"Could you tell me your name, *per favore?*"

"Jill Heston. Please tell him I'm the granddaughter of *Barone* Vittorino Piomondo, a great friend of *Signor* Luigi Decchi."

The employee conveyed the information and was told to have Jill come up to the third floor, which was reserved for company management. Dante waited in the reception area.

Federico was thirty years old at most. The first idea that occurred to Jill was that he might be one of Luigi Decchi's sons, possibly his youngest.

"I'd like to speak with *Signor* Luigi Decchi. Are you his son?"

"No. My father is Salvatore Pinatti. Our family acquired Decchi Industries last year."

"Oh, but...?"

"Everything is still the same as before, *Signorina*... the Decchi brand is still going strong. Just with new owners. Why? What brought you here today?"

"Okay... the surprises just keep coming. Are you able to give me *Signor* Luigi Decchi's address?"

Standing up from his chair, he said, "I'm very sorry, but I have some appointments to get to. I don't know about *Signor* Decchi. Perhaps... perhaps you'll be able to find him at The Village."

"What is that?"

"The Village? You've never been to Monaco? The Village is a casino in Monte Carlo. Now, if you'll forgive me, *Signorina*, I have an important meeting to get to."

Shortly after, outside of the building again with Dante, Jill tried to make sense of it all.

"What do you think a man like Luigi Decchi would be doing in Monte Carlo, *Signor* Dante?"

"*Signor* Vittorino's companions were so extravagant, *Signorina*...! I wouldn't be too surprised to find out that *Signor* Luigi Decchi branched out."

"But buying a... a casino?!"

They walked back to the parking lot and got into their car.

"What now, *Signorina* Jill?"

"What now? We've gone too far to come back emptyhanded, *Signor* Dante. We're going to Monaco."

◆ ◆ ◆

IT WAS A BEAUTIFUL DAY IN MONACO. The radiant light of the Mediterranean carried with it a fresh breeze. After three and a half hours of driving, Jill stopped the car in front of The Village Casino in Monte Carlo.

A uniformed guard wearing the red and white colors of the casino was standing next to the door. Jill walked up to him.

"Does the name Luigi Decchi mean anything to you?" she asked in improvised French.

"Luigi Decchi? Certainly, *Signorina*" the guard responded in perfect Italian. "I speak Italian. I'm from Arezzo. I saw that your car's license plate is from Salerno. One moment."

He opened the casino door and called for a woman, Françoise. She hurried over. She appeared to be in her late 50s. The guard spoke to her in French, explaining that the woman here was asking after *Monsieur* Luigi Decchi. Françoise said something in response and the guard turned back to Jill.

"She wants to know what you want with Luigi Decchi."

"I understood what she said," Jill said in French. She stuck her face into the half-open door. "It's a private matter, Madame Françoise. My grandfather is a great friend of *Signor* Luigi Decchi."

"Who is your grandfather?"

"Baron Vittorino Piomondo, from Campania."

The woman pondered that for a moment. Then she said, "See that little bar on the other side of the street, near the corner? Luigi is there."

"*Merci, Madame.*"

Leaving the car, Dante closed the door behind him and followed Jill over to the bar. It was midday and the staff were starting to get things ready for the evening ahead. The presence of a woman at that hour in what was clearly a nocturnal bar made the two men stop digging though crates of bottles.

"I'm looking for *Monsieur* Luigi Decchi," said Jill in French.

One of them motioned with his head. Jill turned in the direction he indicated. Down at the end of the small lounge, sitting with his back to the door, she saw a man sitting at a small rectangular table. She went over.

Standing across the table, she waited for Luigi Decchi to finish the drink in his glass and raise his head.

He had a thin face and a troubled expression. Luigi Decchi's squinting and anxious eyes tried hard to recognize the pretty lady in front of him. They gave up and went back to staring at the glass. Then, in one swallow, Decchi drank it down.

The smell of the strong alcohol made Jill feel sick. Pulling out a chair, she took a seat and said, "*Signor* Decchi, my name is Jill. I am Vittorino Piomondo's granddaughter."

The man stopped fiddling with the pieces of a matchstick on the table. He looked at her but said nothing.

Ever since she spoke with the French woman a few minutes earlier, Jill had had some idea of what she would find in the bar and now she was sure: this man had come to the villa one year ago, probably to ask for the money he had loaned to *Nonno* Vittorino. Money to add to the whole fortune he had gambled away at the roulette tables. She felt a mixture of disappointment and pity for the man. He didn't just seem like a failed businessman—before her was the total wreckage of a man. She looked at his shabby suit: it was a nice garment but pretty threadbare at the elbows and around the collar.

Suddenly, the man's thin dry lips forced themselves into some semblance of a smile. With a touch of irony—and as if talking to the bits of matchstick or perhaps the finger playing with them—he said, "So, your *nonno* sent his granddaughter out to see if it was really true!"

"If what was true, *Signor* Decchi?"

"This," he said, blowing forcefully at the pieces of matchstick, sending them all to the floor. "What's become of me."

Next, turning toward the balcony, Decchi shouted a man's name. He turned his head. Decchi asked him to bring another bottle. He consulted another member of staff, who consented in silence, and another bottle of liquor was brought over to the old man's table.

Jill waited as Decchi poured himself a huge drink. Then she said, "I came to do the exact opposite, *Signor* Decchi. I came to ask you for help. Help for my grandfather."

"Help for... your *nonno!*" the man mocked. "*Signorina...* the *Barone* turned his back on me, did you not know that? He turned his back on me when I needed him last year."

"You must be mistaken, sir. He simply didn't have the courage to confess that he was ruined."

Luigi Decchi showed the beginnings of a smile. Then he said scornfully,

"*Barone* Vittorino Piomondo... is ruined?"

He said more. He made a mockery of Jill's words.

Keeping her cool, she replied, "What I said is true, *Signor* Decchi. The only difference between you and *mio nonno* is that he quit drinking some time ago."

The man wilted. That last double shot seemed to have knocked him out. His voice now thick with drink, he asked,

"And how could I... how could I be of help to you?"

"I won't deny it: I have come seeking financial assistance. I need to pay off my *nonno*'s mortgages on the villa before he... Well, *Signor* Decchi, we can't lose the villa. I can't let the bank take everything. That's why I came. But I didn't know about Decchi Industries... or that you..."

"Say it!" he shouted brutishly, pounding his hand on the table. "Why did you stop? Are you afraid to say I'm poor... that I can only come to this place to drink because of Françoise? Why are you afraid to tell the truth?"

Jill stood up. The man, half reeling, drooled a bit out of the corner of his mouth. His little eyes were glassy.

"I'm very sorry, *Signor* Decchi," she said.

She really was sorry, and she couldn't bear to be in that place any more than a minute longer.

His head fell solidly onto his arms atop the table, knocking his glass to the ground, but Jill had already walked away. She stopped. Retraced her steps. Luigi Decchi was still half leaning on the tabletop.

"*Signor* Decchi... *per favore*, can you tell me where I can find my grandfather's other old companions. There were four of you, weren't there? You know what I'm talking about, don't you, *Signor* Decchi? Please answer me."

But there was no answer. The man only turned his head away and was lost in trying to forget his own existence. Jill left.

Out on the street again with Dante, the two of them suddenly heard a loud bang.

◆ ◆ ◆

Tonelli looked at Isabella.

"Was that a gunshot, Bella?"

"*Sì*. And Jill went running back into the bar, *Amore*."

"Let's see what's happening. *Sbrighiamoci!*"

They left the car quickly, crossed the street and entered the bar. Other people did the same.

"Please," asked one of the barmen, "we need to ask you to leave. The police have already been notified."

Nobody moved. Other onlookers arrived. Meanwhile, Isabella's stomach began to churn.

Somehow having gained an extra moment of life, Luigi Decchi slightly opened his eyes.

"*Signorina...*" he muttered, "find... find Gio... Giovanni... Giovanni di Stefano... Stefano..."

"Giovanni di Stefano," Jill repeated. "But who is he? Where do I look?"

"Villa... Villavieja... del Campo... Spain. Gio- Giovanni... he... he knows..."

His eyes stopped moving, stuck at half-mast. Jill stood up slowly, noting that he was barely breathing. She looked at Dante's apprehensive face.

"Please, please," the barman came back, "we'd like you to leave. The police are already on their way and you'll all end up getting involved. We have experience with this kind of thing. We'd like you to leave, please."

Isabella had already walked away in search of a chair. The scene made her feel nauseated.

Coming over, Tonelli asked, "Did you hear everything, Bella?"

"I think... I think I'm gonna throw up," she responded, her face white.

"Throw up? Could it be yesterday's dinner, Bella? I said that chicken was no..."

"Enough, *Amore*. I'm going back to the car."

"Please, we'd like you all to leave."

Tonelli extricated himself from the barman's anxious attention.

"Wait, Bella," he said, going after his fiancée.

◆ ◆ ◆

BACK IN THE CAR, Isabella returned to a normal color.

"Better?"

"*Sì,*" she said, retrieving the lipstick from her bag.

"Did you hear everything the old man was saying, Bella?"

"*Sì.* The poor man was so drunk he shot himself in the leg."

"Whoever this Giovanni di Stefano is... he must be taking care of everything. *Sei d'accordo?* He might be the link between Domenico Sbroggio Pellegrino and the consul's brother-in-law, Francesco Ricotta. Sending the money out of Italy until everything cools down really was a stroke of genius... *nevvero*, Bella?"

"*Sì, Amore.* That's true," Isabella responded after applying the lipstick. "Do I look better now?"

"Much better. But what is Giovanni di Stefano's address again? Do you remember?"

"*Sì.* Now stop talking and start the car, *Amore*," Isabella said turning to look at the other side of the street. "They're already leaving."

Five

They arrived in Avignon at dusk. They were tired. Maggio intended to get back underway the next morning, but Michel said he had a few last-minute issues to sort out at the school he taught at. Amaro Maggio was irritated.

At lunch he announced that they were going to the northwest of Spain. They had to be there in two days. He had promised to give a talk at the closing of the Pasonuevo New Age Festival.

"Pasonuevo?" Michel asked. "Where is that, Master?"

"Sancho knows better than me."

They all looked at Menendez. "It's west of Leon."

"But the initiation ritual for you two is going to be farther away. I'm keeping its location a secret for now. You all need to be up at six o'clock tomorrow. I'd like to stick to a schedule, and we're already a day behind. I want to spend the night in Zaragoza tomorrow."

"Do we really have to go through Aquila Colorada?" Menendez wanted to know.

Before Maggio could respond, Giancarlo said, "You can drop me off in Zaragoza. I can get a bus from there."

"None of that," Maggio decreed. "I gave my word that I would take you to Aquila Colorada. I don't make a habit of breaking my promises. Tomorrow at six o'clock sharp."

Turning back to Menendez, he said, "And you, Sancho, you're obviously going to have to get out of bed earlier. The dogs aren't used to traveling on an empty stomach, you know that."

Menendez said nothing.

That night after dinner, Giancarlo went outside to consort with the stars. It was a nice night and whisper quiet. Michel's house, located in a neighborhood south of Avignon, had a shrub garden that ended at a pool on the side of the house.

Meandering around the shrubs, Giancarlo suddenly stopped, as he could hear Michel speaking in a low voice.

"So, you're saying he doesn't remember anything from the dream other than *remembering means nothing without doing?*"

"He... he's going through a hard time, Michel. We have to understand that. First, he loses his dad and then on the same day he discovers that his *nonno* was made homeless by his own son twenty-five years ago. Let's face it, that's a pretty heavy burden to handle. But when you add the dream on top of that... well, dreams can have many explanations and sometimes they take time to surface. One good way out of that is to learn to control dreams."

"What is your degree of effectiveness there, Master?"

"Almost total—except the odd ones due to indigestion, of course."

They both laughed.

"What about when you have nightmares on an empty stomach? I sometimes have them. They're terrible."

Maggio hesitated before responding, "Well, those arise from old wounds... perhaps highly emotionally impactful traumas we suffer when being expelled—or extracted—from our mother's womb. Do you agree? But let's talk about nicer things. This trip is going to do me a world of good. I've been needing to get out of Genoa for a while now."

"What about your business? How are you handling that in your absence?"

"I have great staff and business is going very well. In fact, I've never made as much as I did over the last year. And this year I was able to expand with twelve more franchises. Have I already told you about my plans to invest in South America, specifically Brazil? The spiritual potential of Brazil is very great, and it's where I get the raw material for my business—the crystals."

Giancarlo thought that he probably shouldn't stay hidden any longer. He walked the rest of the way around the bush he had been circumnavigating.

"I thought I heard someone say business is going well," he said.

"Oh, Gian, take a seat," Amaro Maggio invited him with a smile. "We're talking about the trip. It's going to be great."

The three of them conversed for half an hour. Then they all went up to bed.

From the window in his room, Maggio could see the dogs by the shed. They weren't barking, but they were far from relaxed. The scene brought others to mind. The nightmare from a few days ago came back to Maggio again. *Vallencantado*—the name returned to his thoughts. Just the name itself made him forget about the nightmare. Vallencantado was already synonymous with peace and safety.

Maggio then turned to practicing the steps of channeling. But despite trying for some time, he strangely had no success. For the first time in the past fifteen years, he was unable to establish a channel with *him*—with his spirit guide. But he attributed it all to his excessive anxiety.

That night sleep also did not come easily.

The next day's trip to Zaragoza was uneventful. They arrived by sunset and spent the night.

The morning after that, at exactly seven o'clock, they set off for Aquila Colorada.

Six

Eight hundred miles to Villavieja del Campo! That's a lot of ground to cover, *Signor* Dante!"

Jill closed the road map.

"Are you thinking of giving up, *Signorina?*"

Jill said nothing in response. She was distracted watching the numbers tick by on the pump as she filled the car up with gas."

"Why don't you talk to your mother, *Signorina?*" Dante suggested.

"Good idea. I'll call home."

Replacing the cap on the gas tank, Jill walked over to a payphone. She was quickly made aware that her *nonno*'s health was still stable.

"*Tuo nonno* is strong, *figliola*. I spoke with the doctor. He is impressed but told me not to get my hopes up. At any time, your *nonno* could... so, what I'll say to you, Jill, is: keep going. And be quick. There's nothing you can do here."

"That's true, *Mamma*. But I'll put *Signor* Dante on a train and send him back. I'll go on alone. It'll be cheaper too. And *Signor* Dante is of more use to you at the villa."

Maddalena Heston didn't disagree.

"Take care of yourself, Jill. And bring us back the help we so badly need. I pray to God your *nonno* will hold on until you get back."

Sitting nearby, Dante overheard part of the conversation, so he already knew that he would be headed back home in less than an hour.

Not far away and with his back turned, Tonelli was standing beside his car as he filled it up. He too was looking at a road map of Europe and calculating the approximate cost of a nearly two-thousand-mile round trip.

Shortly after that, he tried to convince Isabella to go back to Naples on her own. She put her foot down and insisted that either they both go to Spain or they both go home together. The problem came down to money. They only had enough on hand to pay for half of the trip for one person—and even then, that person would have to go hungry. They were at an impasse.

While Tonelli crunched the numbers, Isabella went into the gas station minimarket, obviously being careful not to raise Jill's suspicion. She returned crunching on potato chips and carrying a few more little bags for later. She also had a magazine.

She got into the vehicle, then popped her head back outside and whispered, "*Amore!* I already know what you should do. Come in here."

After paying for the fuel, Tonelli got in. He discreetly watched as Jill asked the attendant to check something under the hood of her car.

Isabella handed Tonelli the cellphone and said, softly, "Call the newspaper and talk to your boss."

"Gasparetto? And what should I say, Bella?"

"Shh! Don't yell. Tell him you want to do a report on the sacred paths of the world—starting with the Camino de Santiago."

"What? Where'd you get that crazy idea?"

"Here."

Isabella opened the magazine for him to read:

◆ ◆ ◆

THE ALLURE OF THE UNKNOWN. A modern man rediscovers the hallowed grounds of the world: The Ganges River in India, the Church of the Holy Sepulchre in Jerusalem and the Way of St. James in Spain.

◆ ◆ ◆

"Bella!" Tonelli dismissed. "I'm looking for a million dollars—and not...

not some mystics!"

"Not so loud, *Amore!*" his fiancée whispered. "Listen to me. I've already studied the road map. You could write that story and stay on Jill's tail at the same time. And she will never suspect a thing. *Capisci?* The city of Villavieja del Campo is right on the medieval Way of Saint James, which ends in Santiago de Compostela, where there is a sepulcher containing the bones of Saint James."

"Hmmm! I see what you're getting at. It would be a way of traveling with the newspaper footing the bill."

"Of course, *Amore!* Go call up your boss for a little chat."

Tonelli did as she said. But it all got a bit mixed up. Starting with the bones.

"What? You wanna interview some two-thousand-year-old bones? Have you lost your mind, Tonelli?"

"Who said anything about interviewing the bones, Sir? I was talking about following the tourists who come from all over the world to walk the Camino and see the sepulcher containing the bones of Saint James."

Isabella whispered, "Tell him that there are even scientists trying to measure the energy vibrations from the medieval path. And parapsychologists, too. And famous poets."

Tonelli repeated what Isabella said about the scientists, parapsychologists, and poets. Then came a string of unintelligible words.

Isolated clangs of Gasparetto's metallic voice reached Isabella's ear. She could tell the plan was floundering.

"Come clean," she whispered.

Tonelli covered the phone with his hand. "What are you talking about, Bella?"

"Not so loud! Come clean—say that you've dug up some names and that you're on the trail of a million dollars. He isn't a buffoon; he'll be interested. Then ask for an extra allowance to keep up the search—and at the same time you can also write a story about the Way of Saint James."

"Good idea, Bella."

"Hey, Tonelli, *sei ancora vivo?* Did you hear me?"

"Yes, I heard everything. But let me explain, Sir."

"When did I ask for explanations? You didn't understand one bit of what I said."

"Of course I did. The thing is I'm actually looking into the late Consul

Heston's million dollars."

"What? You're still wasting your time on that? I think I'm gonna cancel your ordinary per diem too."

"It just so happens, Sir, that I have a recording made by the Consul and that I am hot on the trail of those dollars. The money came to Italy and just disappeared. There are some political shenanigans mixed up in the whole thing."

"What? Are you serious? Where did the money end up? Have you found anything? And what does this have to do with Saint James? Do you have any names?"

The distinct volley of questions made Tonelli feel confident that his boss was interested.

"I have two names and I've already asked Vaccaro to look into them."

"Ah, so you're finally learning to do your job, Tonelli. And why the Camino de Santiago?"

"I'm following the late Consul's daughter. She's involved in the scam somehow."

"Consul Heston's daughter? Hmmm… okay!"

"And she's going to Villavieja del Campo, Sir. It's a village in the northwest of Spain. The con is very sophisticated. That's where the money will enter circulation."

"Hmmm! And how much time do you think you'll need for this hunt?"

"I should be back in one week."

"*Va bene*! One week. I'll authorize an extraordinary allowance for your search. But, Tonelli, you'll come to regret it if you go making stuff up like that case with Sheikh Muhalamud's son."

Gasparetto told him the size of the extraordinary allowance.

"How much?!" Tonelli shrieked. "But, Sir, that's very basic… that's only gonna pay for fuel, hotels and two skimpy meals a day."

"Well, you're pretty fat. Why not use this week to start a new diet? But if you can dig up any dirt on the million dollars, I'll cover all your expenses. And I'll give you a bonus, too. I'm hanging up now. I have lots to do. Ah, and don't forget about the story."

"What story?"

"About the pilgrims going to Santiago de Compostela, what else?!"

"Ah, *sì, sì*. I won't forget."

After ending the call, Tonelli flipped his phone shut. He took a deep breath. Isabella looked discreetly out of the window.

"Start the car, *Amore*, and drive forward a bit. Then stop and act inconspicuous. Jill is leaving."

"*E dopo*, Bella?"

"And then? Then don't let her out of your sight. Don't you want your name to be known all over the world?"

"*Sì*," replied Tonelli, quite disheartened. Going on a one-week diet had never been part of his plans. Just thinking about it was already making him suffer.

"Because I want my round-the-world trip—with a wedding ring on my finger. *Capisci?* Let's keep going. To Spain. Even if we have to go hungry and sleep in the car."

Tonelli groaned, totally unaware that Isabella's words actually foretold the future.

Seven

It was eleven in the morning on a fairly hot day. Giancarlo was trying to explain who he was and what he was doing in Aquila Colorada but his heavily Calabrian-accented Spanish left the octogenarian man he was speaking to puzzled. He repeated himself, this time trying to use simpler words.

"*Señor*, I come from the south of Italy, from Vigneto. I came here because... well, I wanted to know if maybe you knew a man by the name of Enrico Bertinezzi. I am his grandson."

His little eyes were scrunched up into a squint, revealing endless grooves in his face. The old man just shook his head lethargically. From his window, he asked, "Your *abuelo* lived here in Aquila Colorada?"

"It's very possible."

"Okay, I know a few people from Italy. But Bertinezzi... Your *abuelo*, did he have any nicknames?"

"Not that I know of, no."

Giancarlo looked from side to side.

"Why don't you ask on the corner, at that bakery?" the old man suggested. "It's owned by an Italian family. Who knows?"

Thanking him, Giancarlo went back to the truck. He spoke with Amaro Maggio and then left on foot to the bakery.

The family—a married couple with two young daughters—had come from a town near Ancona ten years ago. They assured him that, in those ten years, no Italian by the name of Enrico Bertinezzi had spent time in Aquila Colorada.

"Why don't you ask around by the bridge? That's the older part of town."

Minutes later, the truck made its way slowly down an old cobblestone alley. In ten minutes, they were at the western end of a medieval bridge. Maggio stopped again and Giancarlo got out to ask the same questions of residents of the three old buildings there. None of them had ever heard of an Italian by the name of Enrico Bertinezzi.

When he asked in a tavern, the woman who owned it said, "I have met an Enrico before, but I don't know if he was a Bertinezzi. How old was this Enrico you're looking for?"

"Seventy-two."

"Ah, nope. The Enrico I'm talking about is just a kid, thirty years old."

"*Gracias, Señora.*"

"But why don't you go talk to Neno?" the woman asked.

"Neno? Could you tell me where I might find him?"

"The cemetery, of course."

"The c-emetery?"

"Neno is the undertaker. He had another burial today. Go there, he should be finishing up."

That provoked a negative reaction in Giancarlo, an awkward feeling.

"My grandfather isn't that old, *Señora*. I know he's alive."

"I didn't say he wasn't. But just so you know, I once had a husband who was strong as an ox. And he left this world before he hit thirty-five. But anyway, I only mentioned Neno because he was born here in Aquila Colorada. He learned the trade from his father. He's been making urns and burying people since he was eleven."

Before she got back to mopping and drying the floor, the woman added, "Neno might make his living burying the dead, but it's the living who pay his bills. Go look for him. Neno knows everyone who ever lived in this area."

"And where... where might I find the cemetery, *Señora*?"

◆ ◆ ◆

A SHORT TIME LATER, Menendez parked the truck in front of the old cemetery of Aquila Colorada. Giancarlo went in alone.

Neno couldn't have been older than forty. Giancarlo found him at work laying someone to rest. He was scrawny, with a sunken chest, thin arms and small hands that somehow made the bricks look light as feathers as he used them to seal up the family tomb. Giancarlo waited for him to finish the job. Then he waited another few minutes for the rest of the deceased's relatives to leave.

He asked Neno his question. The undertaker scratched his thin neck and wiped away some sweat. He was still holding a trowel.

"Enrico Bertinezzi..." he repeated as if he might have been recalling something. "I've seen that name before. Enrico..." Suddenly, he asked, "What year did your *abuelo* die?"

"I never said he died."

"But then... then why'd you come to a cemetery?"

Neno nudged his bucket of mortar with his foot.

"That's enough for now," he said, referring to the work. "It's almost lunch time."

He scratched his neck again.

"Enrico... where have I seen that name before?"

All the undertaker's mental exertions seemed inextricably drawn to six feet under—and that wasn't what Giancarlo had been hoping for. Neno seemed to remember having seen a name—and not a man.

"Where would I have...? Now I know! Now I remember where I saw this Enrico. Come with me. Your *abuelo* is in the old section. The pilgrims' section."

◆ ◆ ◆

CROUCHING DOWN, Giancarlo ran his fingers over the recesses carved into the gravestone.

ENRICO SMILZO

Livorno, Italia, 1921 — Aquila Colorada, España, 1979

"This isn't my grandfather," he said with relief as he stood up.

"Well, this is the only Enrico in my cemetery."

Neno made another reference to it being *his* cemetery and walked away saying it was lunchtime.

Giancarlo was about to leave too but he suddenly felt the presence of someone else and turned to look.+

"Hello!" said the man with a broad smile.

He could have been a pilgrim on his way to Santiago de Compostela if not for the lack of scallop shells, medieval costume, or other obvious clues. He could also be some modern hiker... an eccentric wayfarer. Who could say? Maybe he was just a nature lover—or a poet. Giancarlo took him for no older than forty-five. His hair, already starting to gray, was half hidden beneath a sea-blue cap with ventilation holes on the sides. His overgrown beard was in desperate need of an expert trim, but the man's expression was far from stern. Two straps held a bulging backpack on his shoulders, and his white shirt and jeans... well, they could really have used some soap and water. His sneakers were yellowed and damaged as well.

Standing next to Giancarlo, the man looked at the gravestone, which was partially covered with grass.

"Enrico Smilzo... Did you know him?" the man asked in Italian.

Giancarlo turned his gaze back to the inscription.

"No, no I didn't. I'm looking for my grandfather—who was also named Enrico... I'm just happy he isn't buried here."

After a brief silence, the man said, "You know, I don't much care for legends. But some were made just to expand our language. I remember one about the revelation given to the Three Magi. And then their discouragement when they lost sight of the Morning Star. From that point on, they wandered aimlessly in the desert. One day, exhausted and parched, they stopped at a well to drink some water. And they saw the Star reflected at the bottom of the well. Awestruck, they looked up. And there was the Morning Star. Then they looked ahead. And they discovered that they were in front of the grotto where the Son of God had been born."

"*Stella Mattutina...*" Giancarlo repeated, remembering his father's fevered delusions. But he didn't elaborate. Instead, he asked, "Are you a pilgrim or a... a poet?"

The man smiled. "Maybe both... and maybe neither." His gaze steady on

Giancarlo, he emphasized, "We have to look at everything as a lesson. At times we feel empty... lost, but we can still find the Morning Star reflected in the water at the bottom of a well. If we let ourselves be moved by revelation, the path *always* leads us in the right direction."

"Revelation?"

"It is that perfect quality that makes a dream true."

While he thought that over, Giancarlo's mind was cast to the dream of the mountain lake. Seconds later, something made him raise his head and look toward the dividing line between the new and old parts of the cemetery. He spotted Amaro Maggio. He was coming to see how Giancarlo's search was going, perhaps impatient at the delay.

Turning around, Giancarlo saw that he was alone again.

"What are you looking for, Gian?" Maggio asked, already quite nearby. "You looked startled."

"A man... a pilgrim, I think. He was here a moment ago."

"I didn't see anyone. Just the undertaker out front."

Maggio's eyes hit upon the inscription on the gravestone.

"But this isn't your grandfather..."

"No, it isn't."

"Well, at least you can always keep hoping he's still alive, right?"

Giancarlo thought about the man he had just spent a few minutes with. And thought about his words... about the Morning Star reflected in the bottom of the well. *If we let ourselves be moved by revelation, the path always leads us in the right direction.*

Something inside of him moved him to say, "I have decided to go with you, Master."

"How wonderful! That makes me so happy, Gian!" Patting him on the shoulders, Maggio concluded, "*Avanti, caro*! We have a long road ahead of us."

Eight

The first four hundred miles from Monte Carlo passed without incident. Jill had made just one stop that whole time to refuel her car and eat lunch—the latter something Tonelli and Isabella ended up forgoing. Their car got fuel. But not their stomachs.

"*E adesso*, Bella?" Tonelli asked with despair. He had just tried to make a withdrawal from an ATM. Gasparetto had yet to release the meager extra funds from the newspaper.

"What now?" Isabella repeated. "Now buckle your seatbelt, and let's go."

"But Bella. Bella *mia*... why don't you make a withdrawal from your account?"

"Never! I already told you, *Amore*. I won't take one cent more from my savings. It's all I have left for a few last-minute expenses."

"Last-minute expenses? What are you talking about?"

"Our wedding, of course. What else?"

As it was, the little money they had left was reserved for fuel, maybe a couple of sandwiches and two meals. Isabella had decided that those meals should be had in the evenings.

"*Va bene!*" Tonelli relented. He swallowed the dry crust of yesterday's sandwich he had found in his pocket and they went back to the car. They sat waiting there for Jill to get back on the road.

♦ ♦ ♦

They stopped again near Lleida, in front of the hotel that Jill seemed to have picked for spending the night.

"*E adesso*, Bella?" Tonelli queried again.

"What do you prefer: a full stomach or a good night's sleep?"

"I'm famished."

"Then it's decided: we'll sleep right here in the car and take care of our stomachs instead."

As they went into the restaurant of the hotel Jill had checked into, Isabella suggested that he give the newspaper in Rome another call to ask about the extraordinary allowance.

"That *bandito* Gasparetto forgot about me!" Tonelli grumbled.

"Or else he changed his mind. Call and then we'll know for sure. If he doesn't release the extraordinary allowance as promised, we'll turn around right now and go back to Naples."

"Okay. But first let's eat dinner."

They sat at the most secluded table. In any case, Tonelli could not afford to be seen by Jill. But they needn't have worried, as she never appeared. They figured Jill must have ordered room service.

An hour later, on the way back to the car, Tonelli took his cell phone off his belt and dialed the newsroom of the paper in Rome.

"It's Tonelli, Mila. Put me through to accounts."

"Tonelli? *Grazie a Dio*! It's actually a good thing you called. The Boss told me to get in touch with you at lunchtime. Why is your cell phone turned off?"

"I didn't realize it was off. But tell me, what's going on? Did he cancel my extra allowance?"

"I don't know. I know the boss wants to talk with you, and it's urgent. I'll go see if he's left yet. Stay on the line."

"Hey!" yelled Gasparetto, picking up shortly. "What did I give you a cell phone for if you're just gonna turn it off?"

"It wasn't on purpose, Sir. The hunger is affecting my senses."

"Lucky for your belly you called today. If not, you'd have had to return to

Naples on an empty stomach."

"An empty stomach?" Tonelli groaned. "Is it really that bad, Sir? Did somebody die? Or..."

"Don't act cute. For me, this is a very serious matter."

For Gasparetto, a "very serious matter" always meant something to do with finances and expediency. Tonelli was sure his boss was setting him up for a shakedown.

"Tomorrow, I want you in... let me check that fancy name. Ah, here it is: Pasonuevo. It's on the Camino de Santiago. You're gonna have to get your hands dirty."

"But how am I going to do that? I'm also tracking Jill."

"And so what? Villavieja del Campo is not far from there. You have no excuse—and I have commitments. I want you in Pasonuevo tomorrow. And what's more, I still don't know if I believe this million-dollar story of yours."

Tonelli thought it best to accept Gasparetto's conditions.

"*Va bene*, Sir. And what's happening out in Pasonuevo? Is it a G-8 summit?"

"Ha! That's a good one. Maybe the world leaders will drop by Pasonuevo to learn some medieval magic from the witches and warlocks too."

"Witches?"

"Looks like it's another New Age Festival. Get some information, look around, but find some way to get to Pasonuevo tomorrow before noon. The mystics will be there. I want you to cover it in depth. This order comes straight from the top. Does your stomach understand that, Tonelli?"

"Yes, Boss."

"Okay then, and be quick about it."

"And what about my extraordinary allowance? What happened to that?"

"I'll authorize the electronic transfer right now. You should be able to make a withdrawal within fifteen minutes. I was only withholding it because there was no other way to get in touch with you. But from now on make sure you keep your cell phone on."

Tonelli only risked looking Isabella in the face when his phone was already back on his belt. He took a deep sigh.

"We've fallen into our own trap, Bella."

Isabella had an incredible aptitude for understanding half conversations.

She had already turned on the interior light of the car and was now consulting a road map.

"So, what exactly is the problem?" she asked. "We'll just do things the other way around."

"What do you mean, Bella?"

"We'll get ahead of Jill. We can leave for this Pasonuevo place right now." Isabella checked on the map. "It's a village next to the N-120 highway—the road to Villavieja. Tomorrow you can quickly cover the New Age Festival, speak to a couple of pilgrims on the Camino de Santiago, and then we just sit there and wait for Jill. When she drives past, we zip out after her. Well? What do you say?"

"It means we're gonna have to drive all night," said Tonelli with a touch of trepidation.

"I don't think it matters. We weren't going to be able to sleep in this sardine can anyway. *Nevvero?*"

With that, they got back on the road. Forty minutes later, having withdrawn the paltry extraordinary allowance and stashed it in Isabella's bag, they carried on toward Pasonuevo.

Nine

After two hours of travel, they stopped at a roadside café so Menendez could take Caesar and Nero out of the back of the truck for some shade under a nearby tree. He waited for the barman to bring out a dish with some nice chunks of meat for them. Then Menendez, crouching down, fed the dogs with his own fingers. The waiter left.

A few minutes later, Menendez came back to join the others. The three—Maggio, Michel, and Giancarlo—were still sitting at the table where they had eaten lunch. Obviously, the discussion was still centered on Michel and Giancarlo. Menendez found himself a spot.

"Well?" Maggio asked. "Did they eat?"

Menendez waited a moment to respond, "They ate everything. And they would have eaten more if I'd given it to them."

"Ah, Sancho! You and your balancing act! Give the poor things as much as they want. You're only thinking of your own growing paunch there."

They laughed at Menendez. And he smiled, but it was a distinctly forced smile. He filled his wine glass and drank half. It was a way of blowing off some steam. He hated being the butt of the joke—always the comic relief, they had even nicknamed him Sancho, after Don Quixote's squire.

Twelve years ago, the ex-mechanic Javier Menendez had made a frustrated attempt at discipleship under Amaro Maggio. In the end, his master simply advised him to go back to the grease of his auto shop in Salamanca.

These days, the squat Menendez had been reduced to something of a perennial candidate for a jack-of-all-trades mystic. His day-to-day prose was normally curt and dry—the total opposite of the real Sancho Panza, who was quite the chatterbox. But there was still a certain affinity between their thick skulls: every time Menendez tried to set off down the paths of the occult, he did so in a syntax that mixed washers, screws and indigestible theories concerning the philosopher's stone. He would never reach the level of master—he knew that very well. But neither would he go back to the grease in Salamanca. He adored the wine from the cellar of his boss Amaro Maggio's country house too much.

"Well, Sancho, what's it going to be like?" Maggio said, his laugh still trailing off. He was asking about the weather outside.

"Very sunny all day, Boss," Menendez responded with a neutral expression. "And it's supposed to be even hotter tonight than last night."

"But it wasn't hot in Zaragoza yesterday, Sancho. You just thought so because you drank too much wine."

Everyone laughed—including Menendez. Everyone, that is, except Giancarlo. Maggio turned back to Michel.

Michel, a thirty-one-year-old Frenchman, taught French literature in Avignon. A smooth talker and always clearheaded, he was dead set on climbing the ranks of all the mystical orders that could possibly exist in the universe. But he had a fault that sometimes got on Maggio's nerves: he would ask questions and then he would jump in to answer them himself before anyone had a chance to speak.

"Michel, Michel! Take it easy," Amaro Maggio counselled. "Humility is the foundation of everything."

It was a veiled warning given around the flash of a toothy smile. These wake-up calls always managed to somewhat curtail the quickness of the Frenchman's wit—even though he knew Maggio didn't always practice what he preached.

In this dynamic, Giancarlo was withdrawing. No one had yet noticed his growing alienation—except for Amaro Maggio.

"I haven't heard you speak yet, Gian," Maggio said at a certain point.

Half surprised, Giancarlo said the first thing that came to mind, "That's because I'm learning to listen, Master."

"Very praiseworthy. It's just that you and Michel reached the stage at which your voices needed to be heard some time ago. The Order is demanding. The moment of your consecration is nigh, and they will accept only one answer to their questions."

"Okay, I think I'm ready. And I think Michel is, too."

"Do you agree, Michel?"

"I do, Master."

"Great. Then we can start rehearsing some of the steps of the final stage. I consider it the most important one: meeting your spirit guide. Let's review it. In many orders, there's no euphemism. They call the guides exactly what they are: demons. I prefer to call them mentors. But I ask you: what is a demon?"

"Well..." Michel took the lead, "in my holistic studies, I..."

"Forget about holism, Michel. What they claim to be *in effect* we know personally through experiences and exercises. All existing orders offer the same explanation: demons are not all bad and not all good. If handled properly, they can be of use to us."

"And what will mine be able to do for me, Master?"

"I'll tell you upfront: anything, Michel. It all depends on the deal you make."

Standing up, Amaro Maggio beckoned for the pair to accompany him to a small nearby grove of trees. Menendez was excluded.

"Go take your usual siesta, Sancho," Maggio said to him. "Use it to sleep off all that wine. We'll be back on the road within an hour."

The group of three left, walking behind the rest stop café. Minutes later, they were at a path leading into the woods.

"I like this place," Maggio said. "It's tranquil. Tranquil and time-honored. People have been passing through and resting here for centuries—and they have all left their mark. Is that not what we are all looking for in this life? To leave the mark of our passing on the stairway of existence?"

Giancarlo was under the impression the three of them would be going together but Maggio said, "You wait, Gian. I have some instructions to give Michel first. You'll understand later."

Giancarlo waited for the two of them to disappear into the woods. Then he went off in search of some shade he could sit in.

At the far-left side of the grove, Giancarlo could see a huge pinkish rock. He headed toward it. The view from there was spectacular. Beyond the stream that lapped at the base of the pink rock, a steep rise ended in what seemed to be an extensive vineyard. And after that strip of homogenous green came a mountain range, its heights lost in the hazy blue horizon.

"Wonderful, isn't it?" Giancarlo heard. He turned around.

"You?! How did you get here?"

"It's a spectacular view."

Giancarlo just stared at him, mouth agape.

"Don't look so startled," said the man, softly laughing as he lowered his backpack. "I forgot to tell you my name in the cemetery in Aquila Colorada. You can call me Nicodemus."

"My name is Giancarlo. So, you aren't Italian?"

Nicodemus smiled.

"What makes you say that? Is my pronunciation really that bad? Would you like a pear?"

Nicodemus took a piece of fruit from his bag.

"If that's all you have, I'll take half."

"I have two. Here."

He handed the pear over and Giancarlo took it. After that, another pear already in hand, Nicodemus sat down on the grass next to the stream with his back up against the pink rock. Giancarlo did the same. It was a nice place. They began eating the fruit.

"You know," said Nicodemus, "if this little river could talk, it would have many stories to tell. But as the waters of a river are never the same, its stories would forever be embellished into incredible foam. Do you agree? Isn't it true that a man weaves his legends only to later be beholden to them?"

"What's wrong with legends? In Aquila Colorada you told me one about the Three Magi."

"That's true. Some of the very few that have redeemed themselves are merely... symbolic. The others are the fruit of our spiritual poverty. But what I was trying to say with the story of the Three Magi, Giancarlo, is that our feet do not make the path: the path of revelation is already there. Did it ever occur to you that your grandfather might have had a revelation in a dream? And that may have been why he left—to follow the Morning Star?"

"A dream could have led him to die far away from his family?"

"That depends on how you understand death."

Giancarlo said nothing. He was thinking of his *nonno*, of the forced pilgrimage his son made him take. The memory of his grandfather brought him back to the death of his father. Finally, he returned again to the dream he'd had in the Apennine mountains.

"What are you thinking about?" Nicodemus asked.

Giancarlo breathed a small sigh.

"Everything that has happened to me in the past few days."

"Would it ease your mind to tell me?"

"Well, the thing is... I'm traveling with friends I've known for a while now; however, they've started to feel like strangers."

"Maybe you're the stranger. Maybe you're going through some... some yet-unexplained interior transformation. At first, such things can generate confusion in the mind. The trouble is inside you—and not in your relationship with your friends, Gian. There is a constant war between your mind and spirit."

"I don't know. All I know is that, minute by minute, I feel like... like I'm being split in two. I can feel two forces, hear two voices... see two different paths. But I don't know. I don't know how to tell which one is best."

"Gian, when there is only *one* way out, whether it is better or worse fades away. In Aquila Colorada, I got the impression that you weren't going to continue the journey with your companions. What made you change your mind about your initiation ritual?"

"It was what you told me—the story of the Three Magi. I decided to let the path guide me to the well of the Star. Who knows? Maybe after my initiation, I'll also find my grandfather."

"So then why are you so worried? The Morning Star will be at the bottom of the well waiting for you—as long as you truly believe."

Giancarlo thought for a moment.

"The thing is that I... Sometimes I want to be here, and other times I think of leaving it all and going back home. I think I'm giving this dream too much credit. It was a very strange dream, by the way."

"That's great. A dream you haven't yet understood could be the blueprints for your personal miracle."

"Personal miracle?"

"You might call it the Great Miracle of your life. It's up to you to build on those blueprints, Gian."

Giancarlo spent a few seconds contemplating. He repeated,

"My Great Miracle... blueprints... I don't get it."

"We can always take enough to get by from our surroundings, Gian—as the Three Magi did before they reached the Savior. On our own, we don't walk a single step in the perfect direction. Because, whenever we think we know something, we never really know what we ought to know. Go back over everything that has happened to you since you awoke from that dream."

"That's what I've been doing more than anything."

"Why not tell me about it?"

Giancarlo told him. And he told him everything that happened to him since the dream. At no point was he interrupted.

When he finished, Nicodemus said, "That was a revelation dream, Gian. It immediately bore positive fruit: it made you ashamed of your lie. And that, in its turn, produced another positive result: you learned the truth about your grandfather. It's like a chain to which more and more links are being added. Rejoice, young man! Soon you'll be free from the legends that bind you to tradition. We can only see the truth when we have cast aside the lies."

Giancarlo stopped.

"I think... I think I've heard that before... maybe in my dream."

"Then what are you afraid of?"

"*Paura? Io?*"

"Look, let me tell you something. Don't judge me on my current appearance... looking like a drifter with no home or family. Don't think about it from that perspective. Think that everything is in motion. You're on the right path—the only one that exists: the path of return."

"The path of return?"

"Gian... one day God *dreamed* the universe and He *dreamed* of having someone in His likeness who He could spend time with and talk to in the garden, which was also something He dreamed. We are the essence of that

Greater Dream. And your revelation dream, Gian, set you in motion toward the Great Miracle of your life: returning to the garden of the Father who *dreamed* you. Didn't I say it's like a chain? A never-ending chain. Nothing, Gian, nothing and no one can stop you from building on the blueprints of your miracle—as long as you keep searching."

Nicodemus concluded, "Your Great Miracle will find you, Gian. Believe me. One day or another. And it will change everything."

"But then... then should I just sit here and wait for it all to happen? Is that it? Wait for my dream come true to find me—like the Morning Star did for the Three Magi?"

Nicodemus shot Giancarlo a grin.

"No, young man. That's not how it works. The Three Magi were lost—but they were thirsty. You have to keep going. You have to keep looking for the place that will quench your thirst. The day will come, Gian, when your thirst will show you the Holy Grotto of Rest. Because our Great Miracle only finds us when we are already on its path."

What Nicodemus said after that left another indelible mark on Giancarlo's soul.

"As I just said to you: rejoice! Worry decays the countenance and dries out the bones. Rejoice! The Greater Dream exists."

Giancarlo heard voices and looked behind him. He stood up to get a better view. It was Maggio and Michel coming back from the woods. His turn had come.

When he spun around, Giancarlo could no longer see Nicodemus anywhere. He was alone next to the stream with the big pinkish rock.

"Oh, no! Not again?!"

Ten

Later that same afternoon, Menendez pulled the truck over twice to perform his own kind of ritual. Without saying anything to his companions, he would get out of the cab and go back to where the dogs were.

He always brought with him a thermos containing cool water, with which he would refill their bowl. This time, Nero gave him two licks, Caesar none.

"Tired, Caesar?" said Menendez, patting the dog's head. After a brief faint howl, Caesar finally licked Menendez's fist. Nero imitated him. "What's going on with you two? You've been like this ever since we left. Not liking the trip?"

"I don't think the trip is the problem, Menendez."

Menendez turned around to find he was looking Amaro Maggio in the face.

"What do you think it is, Boss?"

Maggio had no response. He started petting Caesar's head. He was the older of the two Dobermans.

"It's Giancarlo. Isn't it, Caesar?"

The dog gave a high-pitched howl, almost a whine. Maggio then stroked Nero's face.

"I know it's him. He came back very strange. But when the time comes,

I'll figure out why."

Turning toward Menendez, he said, "No one can know what I just said, Sancho."

With that, Amaro Maggio got back in the truck. Menendez retrieved the thermos and did the same.

"Problem with the dogs, Master?" Michel wanted to know from the back seat.

"No. Everything is fine. It's just the heat and the exhaustion of the trip. I'm feeling it, too. It's been a pretty hot day."

Menendez got the truck moving again. He asked Maggio,

"Should we stop now to spend the night, Boss? I know a good place near here."

"No. We have to keep going. We'll be spending the night in a certain *casa rural* near Pasonuevo."

"Will Gian and I be taking part in the Pasonuevo Festival, Master?" Michel asked.

"Not necessarily. I will. I have my talk, but you can use the time to make your final preparations for the initiation."

"And where will that be? I'm curious."

"You will know when the time is right." Looking at Giancarlo, Maggio finished, "And as for you, Gian, this is my advice: try to get any and all outside disturbances out of your head. I sense that you are still somewhat... somewhat conflicted. From now on, the only thing you need take from the world around you is the air you breathe."

Maggio returned to watching the road. Giancarlo was now instinctively examining the details of the passing landscape. Far in the distance, he saw a group of young farmers working in a vineyard and nearby, a frantic dog ran barking at the Dobermans. For some time, Giancarlo mulled over Amaro Maggio's words.

But then a few memories washed over him. They were flashes—patchwork memories of everything that had happened to him since he set foot in Maggio's country house three days ago. He again sensed the strong presence of two antagonistic situations—almost enemies: on the one side was Maggio with his experience, his success in business... his mystical culture—and above all his enthusiasm to enjoy this vacation, which had been delayed several times.

On the other side was the strange and unfathomable figure of Nicodemus. And something was telling him that Nicodemus was also a master—a person with profound understanding of the mysteries that enshroud the human soul.

So then why the antagonism? Who was right? Who was wrong? Was it possible for two such distinct forms of good to exist?

But the questions running through Giancarlo's mind stopped there. He had run headfirst into a wall. He felt steeped in an atmosphere that was, to say the least, bizarre. What he was experiencing was something completely different. Different and at the same time fascinating.

Noticing Giancarlo's introspection, Michel poked him in the knee.

"Relax," the Frenchman whispered. "Keeping up this silent war isn't doing you any good. Remember what we learned in the forest. Exercise passive submission. Try to wish for the spiritual world to come closer to you. Try to desire reunion with your guide."

"Reunion?"

"So, you didn't have your first experience in the forest?"

"Nope."

Michel couldn't hide his surprise. He said very softly, "You didn't meet your spirit guide, Gian? You still don't know his name?"

Giancarlo responded in his ear, "No, I already told you. Do you know yours?"

"Of course! Then what happened to you in the woods?"

"Nothing. Master Maggio talked the whole time. And you know something, Michel? I'm not bothered by that. Maybe the thing that worries me most is the exact opposite: meeting my spirit guide... my... demon. I don't know if I want to."

"What? Have you lost it? After two years of apprenticeship, now you're scared? Just like that?"

Amaro Maggio's ears picked up on the conversation in the back. He glanced over his shoulder and then turned back to his own introspection.

Giancarlo then whispered to Michel, "I didn't say I was scared. But theory is one thing. I don't think I'm ready for the practice yet."

That ended the conversation.

An hour and a half later, it was noticeably cooler. Now Amaro Maggio, half turned toward the back seat, was conversing with Michel about something that didn't interest Giancarlo. He sank back a bit deeper in his seat. In his mind he replayed everything he had heard from Nicodemus.

Giancarlo was almost spellbound. He has begun to accept the idea that his life was on the cusp of great change.

Eleven

A new day dawned.

The temperature was quickly rising from the cool of the early morning. With not a cloud in the sky, the day threatened to be sweltering. Bit by bit, the stony plains to the east were lit up brighter and brighter. And somewhere out there, Isabella and Tonelli were now looking down from a hilltop. Bella was squeezing Tonelli's right arm. Apart from two stops for a quick nap, they had traveled the whole night. They were both tired.

But it wasn't lack of sleep making Isabella support herself on her fiancé's arm. It was her heart. She felt weak and needy.

Though somewhat harder to read, the same seemed to be happening to Tonelli: he cupped both of his fiancée's hands with his left hand. He wrapped his other arm around her shoulders.

"Tired, Bella?" he whispered in a rare moment of sentimentality.

"*Sì, caro.* Very."

She sighed. Her gaze was lost in the plains to the southeast.

"*Amore...*" she said, putting her head on his right shoulder, "one day we'll be done with all of this, right?"

It was an odd moment—even Tonelli's difficult brain yielded to the undeniable calm.

"*Sì, cara.* This will all be over soon... and we will live our lives at ease... and have a nice bed where we'll sleep every night..."

"...and have our children," Isabella added.

"*Sì.*"

It was a muffled yes. Nevertheless, Isabella flashed a smile. She took a deep breath of morning air. Her blue eyes glimmered. The sleep and exhaustion now weighed much less heavily.

They had parked the car near a road sign that stated that Pasonuevo was two and a half miles away. But there was no more road: just a narrow track—a path really. Quite a well-worn path.

Isabella glanced at an arrow painted in yellow on a rock and went over to it.

"The arrow is pointing to the path, *Amore.* What does that mean? Do you think the only way to reach Pasonuevo is on foot?"

There wasn't enough time to respond: suddenly, three men emerged. They were walking on the trail. They didn't look like Spaniards.

"*Mi scusi, parla italiano?*" Tonelli asked one of them.

"*Sì.* I'm Danish, but I speak a bit of Italian. What would you like to know?"

"Pasonuevo... how do you get there by car?"

"The only way is on foot. Or bicycle, or horse. Just follow the yellow arrows of the Camino de Santiago."

"Hmmm! So, this is the famous Way of Saint James! And are you pilgrims?"

"No, no we're not."

Tonelli looked at the path, which was already being pummeled by the hot sun. He started sweating just thinking about walking two and a half miles.

"So, there's no way to get to Pasonuevo by car?"

"Not unless you want to make a twenty-five-mile detour on a bumpy road. Can I ask what you are planning to do in Pasonuevo?"

Tonelli explained about his story on the witches and warlocks and the New Age Festival. The man scratched his chin.

"Okay, well, maybe I can spare you the effort. We're taking part in the Festival, and I can assure you the campsite in Pasonuevo is now totally deserted.

We're all going to the gathering. Why don't you go gather information for your story there?"

"Great," Tonelli said, wiping his brow with a handkerchief, "and where is this gathering going to take place?"

"Do you know the *casa rural El Rincón*?"

"No, we've never been to this area before."

"It's not far away." The Dane raised an arm and pointed. "You see that gas station? There's a little road fifty feet to the right. It'll take you straight there. In a hundred yards you'll be in front of *El Rincón*."

Tonelli breathed a sigh of relief. That was better than great. He offered to drive the three men.

"*Grazie.* But today we're supposed to go there on foot. Now we have to get going. *Buona giornata.*"

The three men walked away.

"Are those guys crazy, Bella? Walking two and a half miles in this sun?"

They got back in the car. Tonelli had already hatched a plan.

Minutes later, they were rolling down the ancient paving stones of the road. They passed the three Danes, nodded at them, and went the rest of the way to *El Rincón*. Three minutes later, Tonelli went into the *casa rural* and came back out carrying a business card with the phone number.

"Take the cell, Bella. Anything happens, you call me. You never know when that girl might drive past. Now hand me the recorder in the glove box."

Isabella took the card and the cell phone. Then handed her fiancé the mini recorder.

"Make sure to do your work quickly," she said.

"I'll call when I'm done. Bye, Bella."

"Bye, *Amore. Un bacio.*"

♦ ♦ ♦

A REMOTE FARM, the *casa rural El Rincón* had a two-story main house with three shorter and smaller outbuildings. A succession of renovations and add-ons had done nothing to detract from its authentic look as a Spanish country house. This was the first year the owners had competed in the hotel business in the northwest of Spain and they were making a good show of it.

"So," concluded Don Alberto González, the manager, "now we're trying to get the *casa*'s name out there. And that's our story, *Señor*... what did you say your name was?"

"Tonelli. Massimo Tonelli."

"Ah, yes. And so that is the story of *El Rincón*, *Señor* Tonelli."

"Hmm," replied Tonelli, shifting his weight on the leather-seated stool he was perched on. He turned and took another glance around at everything. The front desk was located at the back of an attractive and spacious lobby. The place had been renovated, but the original old stone walls and some woodwork were still exposed. Out back, the broad leaves of the shrubs in the small internal garden were taking in the diffuse sunlight let through by a wooden arbor. On the other side of a large pane of glass, Tonelli saw an ample veranda.

And finally, straight to his left, Tonelli gleefully spotted a double door giving access to a set of tables. It smelled delicious. It was the restaurant. He inhaled deeply.

"It's all very pretty, Don Alberto," he said in his smooth Spanish. "That restaurant is beautiful!"

But what he wanted to know about was the sorcerers. Where were they?

Bald, hook-nosed and with cultured diction, Don Alberto González crossed his arms atop the counter. He was holding back laughter at the Italian reporter's anxious and, to a certain extent, funny face. He explained that only ten or twelve of them were actually staying at the *casa*.

"In fact, *Señor*, we are mostly only providing the space for their gathering today. The others came from Pasonuevo and soon will be going back to the campground. But as we speak, they are all behind that door."

González motioned with his eyes. Tonelli turned aside to look at the large wooden door, all carved with pagan arabesques.

"There are a hundred and ten of them altogether, maybe a hundred and fifteen, *Señor*."

Tonelli whistled in amazement.

"That many sorcerers, really?"

Tonelli soon started thinking of infiltrating the gathering. It would be great to hear a debate between a hundred and fifteen mystics. It would make his job easier. He made a move toward the large door, but the manager said, "*No se puede, Señor*. We have express orders: only people with a nametag can enter."

"A nametag?" Tonelli repeated with dismay.

That seemed to settle the matter. However, leaning over the counter, the manager said in confidence, "*Pero*, someone left this one lying around, *Señor...* *y* it's blank."

Tonelli batted his eyelids at the nametag González's hand was pulling from a drawer. He calculated that it would almost certainly come with a price.

"How much will it cost me, Don Alberto?"

As if indignant, the man composed himself.

"Please, Mr. Tonelli...! What's the harm in cooperating with a reporter from Rome?"

In a half whisper, he added, "*Pero*... I suppose your paper might like to mention *nuestra casa*'s name. *Entonces*... then it just so happens that we have some excellent photos, and I..."

The proposition came as a relief to Tonelli. He smiled.

"We have a deal, Don Alberto. Set the photos aside for me. I'll come by for them later."

Quickly grabbing the nametag, Tonelli filled it in with his own name. Next, thanking the manager with a nod of the head, he walked toward the large carved door.

◆ ◆ ◆

"... AND NO SACRED PATH IN THE WORLD has enough charm on its own to change a man's direction—unless he falls in an unexpected pothole and breaks both of his legs."

The large hall exploded in laughter. Closing the door behind him, Tonelli adjusted his glasses and swept his gaze over the room. Next, having chosen a landing site, he slipped over to it. Everyone was facing away from him, and they were all standing. They were still laughing and testing one another's wit.

"... that we have the sacred inside of us. Meanwhile, walking a remote path like this one... you can experience the smells and sounds of the centuries and generations that passed this way before you. This might be even more than just extrasensory perception. Who among you can say for sure that they didn't make the pilgrimage to Santiago de Compostela in another era? Who would doubt that they might be retracing their own steps from two ... or even nine hundred years ago? For my part, in one of my..."

Tonelli took out a handkerchief and dabbed the sweat off his forehead. He smiled at the fellow next to him. There was no going back.

"... and what greater miracle could happen to a man than... than to cross paths with his past lives and his destiny in the Great Work? It is a world in transition, in which..."

"Nice speech!" Tonelli whispered to the mystic next to him. He wanted to get his attention. But the man just shot him a look requesting silence and went back to listening to the speaker.

"... and because of that, my darlings, I must tell you of an opportunity, which is that all of us..."

His attention scattering again, Tonelli moved elsewhere. He took shelter in the far-left part of the large room. From there he started to run his eyes and curiosity over the group. It was as if they were all hypnotized by the speaker. Tonelli looked at the time. 10:32 AM. He was growing impatient. He felt like he was wasting time. He breathed a deep sigh and went back to looking from side to side in search of somebody he could talk to. He saw no opportunities.

"... we got delayed, the day was moved, and I beg your forgiveness. But within twenty or twenty-five minutes at most we will all walk the Camino de Santiago together to the campground in Pasonuevo. It will be a short two- or three-mile stretch, but I believe that we should all avail ourselves of the energies concentrated there. In Pasonuevo, we will have a spiritual celebration... and an unforgettable finale."

"Twenty minutes?" Tonelli whispered to himself. He groaned and a chill ran down his spine. He had just twenty minutes to interview the chief warlock—unless he wanted to face a two-and-a-half-mile hike. He was terrified at the thought of it.

Then he saw the Dane he had spoken to at the start of the trail. He walked over to him. He told him his plight, but the man had no way of helping. He explained that he was just a novice, practically just a spectator at the Festival. He didn't have the status to approach the speaker. His two companions said the same.

The Dane looked around him at the other attendees.

"Try talking to that guy. He's in the speaker's inner circle."

Tonelli went over. As he had done with the Dane, he started in a clean and leisurely Italian. He first said his name. And that he was a reporter from *Il Faro* in Rome.

"I'm Italian, too."

"Ah! *Benissimo*! What's your name?"

"Giancarlo."

"And your guys' boss, the guy who's surrounded by mystics?"

"Amaro Maggio."

"Ah, Maggio! I've heard the name before."

Tonelli grabbed Giancarlo's right hand.

"*Per favore*, help me out. I have no time... I need to keep going, but first I have to interview one of the leaders. Maybe this Maggio fellow. Could you help me out with that, Giancarlo? Ten minutes would be plenty. Or twenty, if you can manage it."

Tonelli continued stating his case. He finished by saying he needed to quickly slap a story together—whatever he could get. Anything would do.

"It would be nice if you could walk to Pasonuevo with everyone," Giancarlo suggested to Tonelli's dismay.

"Eh! Walk two and a half miles? I'd fall down dead after the first quarter mile, *amico*!"

"It's going to be a spiritual walk, laid-back."

"*Sì, sì*, I understand. The thing is just that my spirit is already a bit too laid-back."

Giancarlo stifled a laugh.

"Okay then. I'll see what I can do."

With that, he went over to the crush of people around Maggio. He would come to regret it.

"What? Have you lost your mind, Gian?" Maggio jumped on Giancarlo as soon as he mentioned it. "How could you think a little ten-minute talk with a journalist could give him enough to write a proper story? Frankly, Gian...!"

After spitting these words out, Amaro Maggio went back to the middle of the group. He still had a few books to autograph.

Disconcerted, Giancarlo shook his head "no" at Tonelli and stayed put. But Tonelli beckoned him back over with his hand. Giancarlo obeyed.

"Okay, forget about your boss," Tonelli said as soon as Giancarlo returned.

A tiny procession of beads of sweat had cropped up on Tonelli's forehead. Starting the mini-recorder in his pocket, he proceeded, "How about you answer my questions: What is provoking this wave of occult festivals all over the world? What kind of people are drawn to these things? And why did you choose Pasonuevo for your Witchcraft Festival?"

Giancarlo wanted to laugh. Not at the Italian journalist's questions—but at the reporter himself. He looked like he was worried he was going to miss the last bus.

"New Age Festival," Giancarlo corrected him.

"*Sì, sì*, of course. New Age Festival. But what about my questions?"

Giancarlo hesitated.

"Why don't you answer them for me, Gian?"

Recorder still in hand, Tonelli looked over his shoulder. Then he turned to Giancarlo again, who said, "I think you'd be better at this, Michel."

"Oh, is that right, Michel?" Tonelli asked.

With a few of his characteristic hand gestures, Michel acquiesced.

"Only my Italian isn't very good. I'm a professor of French literature..."

"What I've heard so far is great, Professor Michel. *Su, Andiamo*."

Tonelli latched onto Michel's arm and they both went to sit down at one of the tables.

Twenty minutes later, the Frenchman ended the interview. Tonelli didn't look too pleased.

In groups and pairs, laughing and gesticulating in a carefree manner, the Festival participants started to leave the big hall.

The two-and-a-half-mile walk to Pasonuevo was about to begin.

Twelve

None of them had yet reached the front door of *El Rincón*. Don Alberto González was there dispensing smiles, his hands folded atop the counter. He saw Tonelli and signaled to him. Tonelli walked over.

"The photos of *El Rincón*, Mr. Tonelli," the manager said, handing him a brown envelope. He thanked him with a broad smile.

Despondent and lost in the throng of people, Giancarlo was feeling very strange. Laughing teeth swam through his vision and in their wake were staring eyes and disembodied hands being employed to various effects. In the middle of this whirlpool, he began to feel unwell. He needed to get out.

That was when it happened.

As if touched on the shoulder, he lifted his head to see the front door of *El Rincón* being opened from the outside. And he saw a young and attractive woman standing in the doorway. She came in, stopped, and held the door ajar. She seemed startled by all the commotion. The lobby was practically full.

Attracted, they met each other's gaze. Giancarlo felt like everything froze around him: the laughter, the conversations, the hands, the people—everything except this woman. Her tousled hair... her eyes... she was everything...!

Giancarlo was spellbound.

Suddenly a huge piece of plaster came crashing down between them on the floor. Then a long bolt of lightning flickered. Thunder. Strong wind and rain. The window shutters battered against their frames and Don Alberto González ran over to close them.

Little by little, the small and silent crowd started chirping again. They were all shocked. There hadn't been even a hint of rain, the sun had been blazing down and then… this thunderstorm. But not everyone was paying attention to the storm that had been unleashed outside: Amaro Maggio was standing right in front of Giancarlo. And he was staring at the reflection in his eyes of the woman who had just walked through the door.

Regaining her composure, she ran a hand through her hair. She shot Giancarlo a smile. Taking two steps forward, she examined the pieces of plaster on the ground. And then she looked back at Giancarlo.

"Whew! That really caught me off guard!" she finally said. And smiled. "How unbelievable! It was such a nice day out!"

Giancarlo remained frozen. Embarrassed, she poked through her hair again, then adjusted the strap of the bag that hung on her left shoulder. She glanced at him again and then turned away. Half disconcerted she walked up to the front desk of *El Rincón*, where Don Alberto González was using a white handkerchief to dry his rain-soaked arms.

Giancarlo was still immobile. Wrapped up in tracing the woman's footsteps, his eyes didn't notice Amaro Maggio's approach.

"Gian," said his master, touching his arm. Giancarlo was a bit startled. He turned around to face Maggio. "Looks like this rain is gonna ruin everything… we have no way of getting to the campground now. We need to rethink our plans. Get Michel and go upstairs. I'll be waiting there."

This caught Giancarlo off guard. The problem was surely something the Festival's organizer, McDowell, had to deal with… it had nothing to do with him or Michel.

"Something the matter, Gian?" Maggio asked.

"N-no, everything is fine. I'll go look for Michel."

Maggio disappeared into the small crowd of spiritualists. Giancarlo took two steps aside and stopped.

Little by little, the Festival participants were filtering back into the large hall. Giancarlo followed, but as slowly as possible. He couldn't help lingering to listen to the conversation between the beautiful stranger and the manager of *El Rincón*. She needed a mechanic. Her car had broken down and she had left it on the highway.

"I couldn't find anyone at the gas station, and they told me to come here. They said your chef's son is a mechanic."

"Indeed, *Señorita*," said Don Alberto González. "Manuelito does know a thing or two about cars. But it just so happens he went to Madrid this morning."

"Oh no! That's what I need."

"Where did you leave your car, *Señorita*?"

"Four or five miles from here. I hitchhiked here, and I never would have thought it would be so difficult to find a mechanic. Do you know of anyone else, sir?"

"Only in Leon."

"Is that far from here?"

"Seventy-five miles, *Señorita*."

"I might be able to help."

She turned.

"My name is Giancarlo."

"Hi! I'm Jill. How nice! So, are you a mechanic?"

"No, I'm not. But one of my companions used to have an auto repair shop in Salamanca."

Jill felt relieved. Their eyes met for a fraction of a second. Both sets seemed frightened.

"How wonderful. And where can I find him?"

"Wait here. I'll go find Menendez."

◆ ◆ ◆

THE DOGS GROWLED when Giancarlo opened the door to the hotel room.

"Shush!" Maggio said. The Dobermans settled down on a rug five feet from the door.

Giancarlo repeated what he told Menendez about helping the woman downstairs. Menendez had agreed to do it but only with his boss's permission.

Amaro Maggio reflected for two seconds before he said, "It's fine. Menendez can take the truck. But you stay, Gian."

"I'm going to need help," Menendez said.

"Take someone else with you. Go down and talk to McDowell. I'm sure he can spare someone. There's enough rope in the back of the truck if you end up having to tow the car."

Giancarlo chose not to argue with Maggio. He followed Menendez out of the room.

"Gian," Amaro Maggio called, "let Sancho take care of everything. I need to talk to you."

"Now? I'm just gonna walk Menendez back down to the woman."

"Now, Gian. Sancho is not blind. And he has a mouth."

Giancarlo retraced his steps. Menendez left. Maggio walked over to the door and turned the key.

"Why don't you sit down for a bit? Did you go get Michel like I asked?"

"N-no. You want me to do that now?"

"Sit, Gian."

Giancarlo sat down. Amaro Maggio held a brief silence. His eyes sought Giancarlo's, but they were subtly averted.

"I've been a bit hard on you, but you brought it on yourself, Gian. You're creating a solitary world for yourself, you know? You haven't been the same since you came back to my house. Am I wrong? And it would be foolish to say it's your father's spirit that's attached itself to you. It is not your father's spirit—the two of you did not have much in common, as far as I know."

Giancarlo was now unable to escape his gaze.

"It is your grandfather's spirit, Gian. That's what's gotten into you. You, with your emotions, have ripped your grandfather's soul from its rest. Why not leave him in peace? Or do you still believe you might find him alive?"

Maggio wasn't asking—he just wanted to show Giancarlo the absurdity of going after someone who disappeared twenty-five years ago.

"It's hampering your progress, Gian. Practically bringing it to a standstill. Doing this... giving space to this familial spirit... if you do this, you will never be able to maintain contact with your spirit guide. No. He will leave you. He will not accept sharing you with another. And the thing that did not happen yesterday in the forest cannot be repeated. You did not establish a channel with your guide, and without that, the initiation ritual makes no sense—it will be nothing but a farce. And our work does not accept farces. It is serious. You know that."

Giancarlo listened in silence.

"But bear in mind that the one who can help you find what you're looking for—dominion over any and all situations—is not your grandfather: it is your guide. Make it easier on yourself. Don't dispel these forces with cheap emotions."

Amaro Maggio repeated one of his most common phrases,

"The only thing you need take from the world around you is the air you breathe. Never forget this. That was all I wanted to tell you. Now let's go. I need to find out what everyone has decided. The rain is already letting up, but I doubt anyone will want to walk the muddy path to Pasonuevo now."

Giancarlo left first. The dogs started growling again.

"Shush," Maggio said. And the Dobermans quieted down.

Thirteen

I n the end, there was only one thing they agreed on. The Festival attendees were eating lunch. One group felt strongly about moving the walk to Pasonuevo to the next day. The majority wished to stay where they were and finish their work right on the premises of *El Rincón*. If this were the case, a group of volunteers would have to drive back to the campsite and retrieve everyone's belongings. It was that road that took a twenty-five-mile detour and was all dirt, but the idea was gaining traction. The final say was with Scotsman Richard McDowell, the coordinator of the Festival.

Giancarlo didn't eat much and quickly left the group. He began walking aimlessly. Distracted, he breezed into the garden with its worn stones paving its narrow and ancient paths. Moss and weeds sprouted from every crack in the dry-stone walls surrounding the internal courtyard.

At a certain point, he heard, "Well then?"

Giancarlo cracked a smile. It was Nicodemus.

Nicodemus was sitting on a rustic stone bench. He returned Giancarlo's smile as he approached.

"You disappeared again yesterday. How do you do that? What's your secret?"

"Take a seat and I'll tell you."

Giancarlo sat down.

Nicodemus continued, "I know these places like the back of my hand, Gian. Is that enough for you? Anyway, don't you think I'm a pilgrim?"

"Well, I've never met a pilgrim who does tricks like that."

Nicodemus laughed.

"Well? What can you tell me about this journey of yours?"

Giancarlo flashed a smile. His eyes came to life.

"I think it happened, Nicodemus."

"What happened? Tell me about the enthusiasm I see in your eyes."

"It was unbelievable!"

"Ah, I think I understand. The woman in the rainstorm. Did I guess right?"

"Yes, you did. Her name is Jill."

"Jill."

"What do you think of her, Nicodemus?"

"Hey! Am I really the guy you should be asking?"

Giancarlo laughed.

"She's... she's beautiful, Nicodemus. I can't keep my eyes off her," Giancarlo continued.

"It isn't good for a man to walk alone, young man. Isn't that what's written? Nicodemus replied.

Giancarlo answered with only a smile.

"Exactly. Do you believe that? You should. Or do you think her car breaking down just five miles from here was a mere and happy coincidence? Well, there's no such thing as coincidence. In this world there is only providence—for better or for worse."

What Nicodemus said was exactly what Giancarlo wanted to hear. It transformed him into a giddy child. After a slight gasp, with a certain glint in his eyes, he said, "It was incredible! Out of nowhere she comes through the door... that thing falls down between us... the lightning... the thunder... and that downpour...! Oh my! Nicodemus. She is beautiful!"

Giancarlo savored the moment.

"You know, I'm starting to think our meeting really was ordained by the providence of God."

"Your meeting—yes. But the plaster crashing down from the ceiling... and that sudden storm and everything else... probably not."

"Why? It was like... a bugle sounding... an extraordinary event... a commemoration. That's how I see it."

"Well, those are not the kind of signals God tends to use, Gian."

"Okay, but if there are no coincidences, then what caused all that?"

Nicodemus's gaze sharpened.

"The right question would be *who* caused it. Listen, Gian. There is an invisible battle being fought all around us. Invisible and deadly. You have to face it in earnest. This isn't just a fantasy. What happened was a... an ebullition of evil."

Giancarlo sat there in expectation.

"The spiritual battle is the only battle there is—the battle to own us. All these blood feuds... these lines that divide us... love and hate... suffering—all of those things are no more than the stitches of a single tapestry. They are little scenes of day-to-day life fit snugly inside a greater, invisible scene—the main scene."

Giancarlo reflected for a moment.

"Then... then what you're trying to say is that there is an unseen force fighting against me and... and against that girl, Jill? Against us meeting?"

"The struggle is not against you two: it is against the scent of God. There is a darkness lingering in the air and working against this Greater Love... a conspiracy older than mankind itself. It's a powerful conspiracy, terrible, deadly... and it's all wrapped up with a pretty little bow to charm the human eye."

Giancarlo reflected a moment and then said, "Maggio is always telling me that the whole universe conspires in our favor. And that is what I've learned from books as well. But... this seems to contrast with what you just said. How can the universe *conspire in our favor*—if you say the same universe is haunted by a deadly conspiracy against us?"

"Gian, lies are never beneficial: they are always extracted from the truth. They are distortions, deviations. And they can be taken from the transient laws of Earth... or the Eternal Laws of the Heavens. Doctored copies. Everything cooperates for the good of those who love God and are called to pursue His aims. Everything beyond that is a spiritual *conspiracy* of the world of darkness to lead man away from his true calling. And, like I said, it's a nice-sounding conspiracy, elegant... full of false altruism. But, using men as puppets, these spiritual conspirators rob, kill and destroy."

Nicodemus stood up from the bench.

"You two... perhaps you and that woman could be united side by side in this fight, Gian. That is what I see in your eyes. And there is no spiritual conspiracy in the universe that can separate that which God has brought together in these celestial spheres. And now I suggest that you go. Someone is looking for you."

Giancarlo turned his head. On the other side of the garden, just beyond the glass-paned door, he spotted Michel.

When he turned around again, he found himself alone.

Fourteen

Jill's arrival at the *casa rural* was a huge relief for Tonelli. He called Isabella and told her the good news.

Not long after, once the storm had passed, Isabella caught up to her fiancé at *El Rincón* and together they headed for the diner attached to the gas station.

Isabella allowed a few coins to escape her tight purse, which they spent on two meatball sandwiches. Half an hour later, a third of their daily battle with hunger had been won.

Tonelli went back to his old song and dance. "But, Bella, why not just take some money from your account?"

"Never!"

They were still sitting at the diner. Tonelli glanced at his wristwatch.

"*E adesso*, Bella? They left an hour and a half ago. They must be back by now. I heard that her car broke down just five miles from here."

"*Oddio!*" replied Isabella, annoyed. "Stop looking at your watch! Half an hour more, half an hour less... what difference does it make? We have to think about leaving, of course. But now her car has broken down and she has to stay here. What about us? Are we going to be able to stand to spend another night in that sardine can? We can't afford to spend another dime. What time is it?"

"Ah, so now you want to know what time it is, too? One fifteen. Don't act so annoyed, Bella."

"Who said I'm annoyed?"

Isabella let out a sigh.

"It would be so easy to end our suffering," Tonelli deplored. "You just have to use your bank card."

Her response was a sideways glance. "We could both be dying of hunger and lack of sleep for all I care, but not a single cent more is leaving my account. What I want, *Amore*, is for all of this to finally be over."

Just then, they both saw a truck pulling into the gas station. It was towing Jill's car. Once it had been untied, Jill locked the car and got into the truck. They then headed for *El Rincón*.

"Looks like her car still hasn't been fixed, *Amore*."

"What now?"

"*Adesso?* Now we need to think of a way out."

Tonelli considered it.

"I think they went to eat lunch. And after lunch, the mechanic will take a look at her car. And speaking of lunch, Bella..."

"No! Let's get out of here. We have to feel things out and figure out what's going on."

◆ ◆ ◆

DON ALBERTO GONZÁLEZ bent over backwards to handle the emergency: the eighteen women and ninety-four men, still unable to reach an agreement, were all famished and sitting around. It was the fallout from the storm. *El Rincón*, with its thirty-two rooms, now seemed small with all those people in it. Its wine cellar even more so.

Sitting on a sofa in the lobby, Isabella distracted herself by flipping through a magazine. Tonelli walked up to the *casa's* manager.

"What a day we've had, *Señor* Tonelli...!" González griped, wiping his forehead with a white handkerchief. He was trying to organize some files on the reception desk. "I can't remember it ever raining so hard this time of year before. Thankfully, it passed quickly."

An echo of laughter came from the annex.

"It's them," said González, shuffling the packet of files into a small wooden box. "They're going to ask for more wine soon, and I'll have to tell them we're out."

"But I should be thanking *Dios*," González went on to say, crossing his arms over the counter. "That big rain shower ended the day with excellent profit for the *casa*."

Tonelli flashed a smile.

"But how is it possible? A hundred and some witches and warlocks gathered together... and none of them could predict a storm?"

"They never predict anything. Not even yesterday's date. The demons do it all for them."

The voice came from behind. Tonelli turned to see who it was. The man smelled so strongly of wine the vapors of alcohol were actually visible. He was thin, with a small bowed chest, hollow cheeks, and a severe mouth. He seemed to be in his mid-fifties. He looked serious—possibly incapable of laughter. Either that or he had a problem with his dental work. Tonelli thought that maybe his lower dentures were new—or the wrong size.

"Don García, please!" González pleaded.

Don Alberto González was still quite polished, but his voice now took on an unpleasant tone. Tonelli could tell it was because of the little man now in the lobby of *El Rincón*.

"Please, Don García. You know what my orders are, *Señor*. I'm very sorry."

Obviously, it was a polite way of asking him to leave. And Don García did so. His sharp eyes and hermetically sealed mouth unchanged, he made a half turn and left *El Rincón*.

"What a strange man..." Tonelli pondered with his elbow supported on the counter. Through a large pane of glass, he watched Don García's retreat. "Who is he, a retired tax collector?"

González didn't find the joke funny.

"A nuisance. That's what he is." Quickly, González added, "Well... deep down Don García is not a bad person. But here and there...! *Dios*! I don't like to speak ill of the clergy—or former clergy. But frankly...! That was the last thing I needed! The last thing I needed was for Don García to intrude on this group of people. It could have sparked a war. *Dios nos libre*."

Tonelli freed himself from the counter and looked at the manager.

"So, he's a priest, huh?"

"Don García was a priest. And he was also a... a *brujo*."

"A sorcerer?"

"*Sí*. But he used to live in a monastery. He caused less harm there."

Now Tonelli crossed his arms on top of the counter.

"Anyway, Don Alberto, what's that guy's problem?"

González summed it up a few words and made his excuse to leave.

"I have to see how things are going with our guests, *Señor* Tonelli. Excuse me."

González left and Tonelli walked over to the glass of the window. He saw Don García walking up to the road. He was headed for the gas station—or back to the tavern he had come from.

Returning to Isabella's side, he said, "Try to figure out what's going on with Jill's car."

Isabella put down the magazine.

"And where are you going, *Amore*?"

"I'm going to finish that story for Gasparetto."

And he went after Don García.

◆ ◆ ◆

THE SAME CARICATURE OF A MAN now revealed himself, before Tonelli's surprised eyes, to be the proud owner of an implacable sense of dark humor. He was simultaneously joyful and acrid, highly critical and terribly scathing. And Don García also didn't actually have a single bad fitting fake tooth in his mouth. Now nothing was stopping him from constructing meaningful expressions or stretching his lips wide. Maybe the wine had finally loosened his tongue—Tonelli considered.

Serving himself another glass, Don García returned to the matter at hand,

"*La humanidad* has the incredible tendency to worship legends, *Señor* Tonelli. And it is always a fetish, like a pagan who sculpts a piece of wood and kneels before his own work of art. It happens in every part of the world. But I don't want to talk any more about the bones of Saint James... or his remarkable sword."

Don García upturned the glass and drank half the wine in it. He placed it back down on the table and stuck his left pointer finger up to Tonelli's nose.

"Am I boring you, *Señor*?"

Tonelli was a bit startled. He smiled.

"Absolutely not, Don García. I'm appreciating the conversation."

"Hmm. In that case our meeting wasn't pointless—unlike others I've had. You know, *Señor* Tonelli... anyone who is willing to listen to what I have to say comes away saying they've been given a... a treasure."

"I feel the same way, Don García."

Tonelli had a question locked and loaded. The time had come to ask it.

"Don García... what can you tell me about this Festival that attracted sorcerers from all over the world?"

Don García burst out laughing. Then turned serious.

"*Señor* Tonelli...! There is no established intellectual consensus on a way to discern those *who are not* what they claim to be. Nor is there a scale that can weigh the many pounds of nonsense carried by the wave of occult consumerism currently sweeping the globe. To others, *Señor* Tonelli, we are what we wish to be. Do you understand? We lie between the naivety... and astuteness of every person."

"I don't think I understand, Don García."

"No one challenges anyone, *Señor* Tonelli. No one debunks anything. India is an excellent example. Everyone likes to consume ideas from people who have made a pilgrimage to the Ganges—or who *say* they made a pilgrimage to the Ganges. Do you understand? Months later, you come back and you're a renowned mystic in the media. You gather followers, write a book and the world buys it. Of course you've just memorized a bunch of clichés... many of them stolen from books like the Bible—or stolen in part, as the case may be. From that point on, *Señor* Tonelli, every grain of salt that comes out of your mouth tastes like honey."

Don García filled his lungs with air and let it out slowly. "I have vast experience there, *Señor* Tonelli. I was also a *brujo* once—and one of the most obstinate of them."

"And what happened, Don García? Why did you leave the occult behind?"

"Well... I started to challenge some of their traditional concepts, and I made enemies... mostly from the other world. Do you understand me, *Señor*?"

Don García stretched out his neck for emphasis.

"Demons, *Señor* Tonelli."

Sitting normally again, he continued, "I have a very strong Christian background, and that made my spirit guide quite uncomfortable. I was... we were fire and water. Do you understand me, *Señor* Tonelli? I prayed my masses and... and afterward I would go channel spirits behind the parish house."

"So, you were torn, Don García."

"Exactly. Torn. So *they*... the demons led me to commit some foolish acts. I was taken for a madman. And that's why I ended up on the mystics' blacklist. All the orders consider me a Dark Sorcerer, *Señor* Tonelli."

Now Tonelli could understand why the manager of *El Rincón* wanted to get rid of the man. Don García had an esoteric bone stuck in his craw. He may have already tried to rid himself of it in front of some other group of occult guests—and that could have launched an infernal war. And caused a dip in profits, of course.

Soon Don García confirmed Tonelli's suspicions.

"In part, Don Alberto is right. I have already caused many problems for him. Sometimes I lose my cool, *Señor* Tonelli. Sometimes I feel like... like *they* will never truly leave me alone. And they're only waiting until I die to harvest my soul."

Don García's speech was fading. Maybe it was the effect of the wine and the intellectual purging—or perhaps it was fear. He was reduced to nothing. Tonelli felt mildly vexed their conversation had ended.

Adjusting his glasses, Tonelli picked up his mini-recorder and switched it off. He stood up. Don García was now resting his head on his arms and the table. He may have already fallen asleep.

Even though he knew he couldn't spare a cent, Tonelli paid for the bottle of wine and left the tavern.

◆ ◆ ◆

Minutes later, as he opened the door of *El Rincón,* he ran straight into Isabella coming out.

"Where have you been, *Amore?* I've been looking for you everywhere."

"Wrapping up my story. And so, what did you find out about the girl?"

"I found out that her car won't be able to go anywhere until the mechanic is able to get a new alternator from Leon. And that should be happening early tomorrow. You know what that means, don't you?"

Tonelli let all the air out of his lungs. They were now both outside the *casa.*

"I know. We'll be spending another night in the car."

"Oh, *Amore...*! I can't go another day without a shower. What are we going to do?"

"Well, you could use your bank card, Bella... and pay for a room in the hotel. And, of course, a proper dinner."

This time Isabella didn't shout. But the look she gave him said it all.

"Okay," Tonelli resigned himself. "I'll try to make another deal with Don Alberto. Who knows? Maybe he has an idea."

"Another deal? What are you talking about?"

Tonelli told her about trading the photos for the name tag. Then he added everything he had heard from Don García.

"Do you think all of this might lead to something?" he asked.

Isabella's eyelashes were already surrendering to the weight of exhaustion.

"What are you thinking about, Bella? Whatever your plan is, make sure it includes a nice dinner."

When Tonelli heard the scheme, he raised his eyebrows.

"Great idea, Bella *mia*! *Fatti dare un bacio*!" he said and deposited a kiss on his fiancée's forehead. "Let's get on that right now. And tonight, we'll have real beds to sleep in. And a nice dinner too, of course."

They went into *El Rincón*. Isabella looked for the sofa with the magazines. Tonelli walked right up to the front desk. He waited for Don Alberto González to finish talking to a guest. Then he said to him, "Don Alberto... what a colorful character that ex-clergyman is!"

The man had already finished what he was doing. Tonelli got as comfortable as he could on one of the small stools. He held the manager of *El Rincón* in his sights. Don Alberto's face had started changing color.

"I don't understand, *Señor*."

"I'm talking about Don García. He was a big help... enormous really. And very polite... thanks to him, I can already start wrapping up my story."

Under cover behind a magazine, Isabella saw the effect these words were having on Don Alberto González. His expression started to crumble, but only for an instant, as his broad smile—nearly a scowl—was quickly plastered back on.

"What did you say, *Señor*?" he asked indignantly. "Don García?!"

"Yes," Tonelli responded, pretending to wipe his glasses. "Don García was a big help, Don Alberto... he saved me a lot of time. He was great. Really nice. I'm lucky to have met such an... erudite man... with such a profound understanding of the centuries-old history of the Camino de Santiago—and of sorcerers, of course. I think I can draw up a series of stories about the truth behind the legend of Saint James' bones... the two skulls that were displayed here and there... and of the remarkable sword that decapitated sixty thousand Moors in one fell swoop."

Don Alberto González's face looked flustered. Coming out from behind the counter, he grabbed Tonelli's arm and frog marched him to the far-right side of the sofa. However, they didn't go far enough to prevent Isabella from hearing.

"Let me tell you something, *Señor* Tonelli," said Don Alberto González with pursed lips. "Don García is a... a *borracho*. How can you trust a drunk?"

"Many kings have been overthrown by drunks, Don Alberto. And the literature he cited, what about that? And what about what Erasmus said when he returned from his pilgrimage to Santiago de Compostela?"

Anger gritted González's teeth. He continued, "*Señor* Tonelli... I cannot allow you to be deceived in such a fashion. You have to trust me. Yes... I agree there is some nonsense in the story... some exaggerations with regard to the bones. But the faith in Santiago's sword is greater than that. The Spanish people were fighting for an ideal... and that was how Spain was taken back from the hands of the Moors."

"Okay, Don Alberto, I am familiar with the history of Spain. It's glorious. But what can I do? I'm a reporter, Don Alberto, and reporters seek the facts— and people who know the facts."

"I'll tell you what Don García knows! *Nada*! He's a failed clergyman... a *borracho*! And a *brujo*!"

"Well..." Tonelli mused, toying with the cuticle on one of his fingers, "if we had more time... at least another day... then maybe we'd be able to hear from other people. There must be someone else I could talk to."

"Without a doubt, *Señor* Tonelli. *Yo mismo soy uno*. And I could introduce you to the mayor of Puebla Rosada... and the magistrate of Siete Fuentes... and Bishop Buendia... Anyway, many distinguished men—and all of them intimately familiar with our history."

González put both of his hands on Tonelli's left arm to plead,

"I beg you, stay! Please, find some way to stay one more day. If you do, I will take the greatest pleasure in exposing that... that *borracho*."

Tonelli breathed a furtive sigh of relief. The first battle was already won. He launched into the second,

"Well, it would be great if my partner and I could stay. But you must understand, Don Alberto, Italian newspapers are strict... and we have to stick to our timetable. Isn't that right, Isabella?"

That was the signal for Isabella to join in. She set the magazine aside and went to join them. But she remained standing and did not sit down next to them.

"This is Isabella, my coworker."

"Charmed, *Señorita*."

"The pleasure is all mine, Don Alberto. But it's true. We have to get going to Villavieja del Campo. And even though we'd like to stay, we have a problem, Don Alberto."

"A problem? And what might that be?"

"Our per diems are thoroughly accounted for. *Il Faro* is a serious newspaper."

"It's true," Tonelli joined in, hammering the point home.

Isabella continued,

"Our internal regulations do not allow for any funding that is not preapproved, Don Alberto."

Tonelli gave the manager fifteen seconds to pick up on the subtle appeal. He did not.

"Well, what are you going to do then?" was all Don Alberto González said.

Wilted, sensing that their boat was sinking, Tonelli looked at Isabella, begging for rescue.

"However, ..." she said, addressing her fiancé, "if you'd like to stay... if you want to collect this important testimony from Don Alberto and his friends... for my part, out of devotion to the truth, I agree to sleep in the car... in that sardine can."

"Would you really do that for Don Alberto, Isabella?"

Isabella's voice sashayed out in a swooning, "*Sì*."

A sudden movement startled them both. It was Don Alberto González bursting out of his seat.

"By no means, *Señorita*! I cannot allow such a sacrifice! You must stay at

El Rincón! And at our expense. It would be our pleasure."

Tonelli and Isabella's eyes were already celebrating when they saw that Don Alberto's enthusiasm had been derailed.

"*Qué lástima*!" he said, all exhausted by the impetus that had launched him up off the couch. "I forgot that we don't have any vacancies! *El Rincón* is completely booked. *Qué lástima*!"

But the plan was flawless. Isabella said, "Don Alberto... what about the suite at the end of the hall?"

"What? Ah, that is a special suite... it's reserved for the *casa's* proprietors, *Señorita*."

"But... where are the owners now? I heard they're on a tour of Paris."

"Well... that's true, *Señorita*."

The man was at an impasse.

Taking advantage of this weakness, Tonelli got up off the couch to say, "All right then... we still have the recording I made of the interview with Don García... We'll have to go with what he told us, Isabella."

González thought for only half a second before declaring with renewed vigor, "Absolutely not! It's decided! You will stay at *El Rincón hasta mañana*. I can spare you the special suite. I'll order another bed to be brought in at once."

"As long as there's a fold-out sofa, there's no need," said Isabella.

"*Sí*. There's a double bed in the bedroom and a sofa in the living room."

"That will be plenty, Don Alberto."

"As you like. Now you'll have to excuse me. I have to go find someone to clean the suite."

He was already leaving, but then he stopped.

"Ah, yes, *Señor* Tonelli. I'll schedule us a meeting for tomorrow morning."

"Perfect, Don Alberto. After breakfast would be great."

Finally, he left. Tonelli let out a sigh of relief. Then he wiped the sweat off his forehead.

"What a struggle, Bella *mia*! But we got what we wanted. Now let's go grab the suitcases."

◆ ◆ ◆

Twenty minutes later, they were all checked in. Tonelli looked everything over. It was an excellent suite. Returning to the living room, he found Isabella looking downcast. He sat down next to her on the sofa.

"Bella... Bella *mia*... are you in pain or something? Are you maybe so hungry your stomach hurts?"

"No!" his fiancée wailed. "My stomach isn't what hurts! The pain I feel is here!" She pointed at her head.

"*Oddio!* What could it be? You've never had headaches before, Bella."

"Don't play the fool. It isn't my head that hurts—it's my conscience."

"Conscience? *Ma che succede?*"

"What's going on? What's going on is that you're corrupting me!"

"*I-io*, Bella?"

"*Sì, tu.* You made me lie... I said things that weren't true."

"*Io?*" said Tonelli, placing his hand reverently on his chest.

"*Sì! Sì!*"

"But it was your idea!"

Tonelli got to his feet.

"What about your part? Didn't you say you wanted to take a shower? Well? Why don't you stop your complaining and go take that shower?"

Pacing from one end of the room to the other, Tonelli continued to talk for at least seven minutes. He unfurled an infinite number of reasons he judged as satisfactory for doing what they did.

"Let me take all the guilt," was the way out he finally found. "And I'll come to terms with my conscience. *D'accordo?*"

Isabella looked at her fiancé, defeated. Her conscience relented and she felt like taking that nice cold shower.

Fifteen

A pleasant breeze was blowing in from the north. The harbinger of a cooler night.

It was twenty minutes to seven, still too early for dinner in Spain. Leaving the key to her suite at the front desk, Jill went out onto the side veranda.

It was a nice place. The ancient stone walls were enhanced by the reddish light of the setting sun. On the opposite side, the cooler part of the veranda, the drooping leaves of the hanging ferns all glistened with droplets of water, bidding the day a graceful farewell.

Jill liked the veranda. As she sat down at one of its little tables, she thought it would be the perfect place to eat dinner. She asked a waiter if that would be possible.

"Unfortunately not, *Señorita*. We do not serve dinner in this section."

"What a pity," Jill lamented. "It's fantastic out here."

"What would you like to drink, *Señorita*?"

"Nothing, thank you. I'm just going to sit here for a few minutes. Until the sun goes down. It's pretty."

"Make yourself at home, *Señorita*."

The waiter left and Jill sat back to take in the magnificent sunset. Then she saw a woman. She was sitting at one of the little tables at the end of the veranda. She seemed to be admiring the sunset as well.

Ten minutes passed and the sun went down. The gray of night began its work, pulling a blanket of darkness over everything. But the other woman hadn't moved a muscle. She was still staring at a sun that was no longer there.

Taking a pen and notepad from her bag, Jill jotted down a few lines. Then she signaled to the waiter, who came over. She handed him the folded paper.

"Please," she said, "bring this to that woman."

The waiter did as he was told. He gave the note to the woman and disappeared through the access door to the dining room.

◆ ◆ ◆

"JILL."

Ever since he had seen the woman from the rainstorm sitting on the veranda fifteen minutes earlier, Giancarlo had totally forgotten he was at the table with Menendez and Michel. The ex-mechanic had already told them everything that had happened over the nearly two hours that he, Jill, and another of the Festival attendees had spent on the side of the highway. Menendez had tried his best to fix the car, but to no avail.

"Jill," Giancarlo almost said out loud. He couldn't get the name out of his head. And now Menendez and Michel's voices were nothing more than distant muffled background noise.

The other two were sitting with their backs to the veranda. So, sitting across from them, Giancarlo could see her on the other side of the large pane of glass. He saw her writing on a piece of paper. He watched her give the note to the waiter. He saw the other woman's face when she received the note. And he saw that woman, in a sudden movement, lower her face and cry into her hands.

What Giancarlo didn't notice was that Michel, looking sidelong, had also seen Jill. And was also watching her.

Then Michel mentioned Giancarlo's name.

"What did you say, Michel?"

"Hey! Where have you been? Was it nice?"

"Sorry, I was distracted. What was it that you asked?"

"I didn't ask you anything. I was just asking Menendez if he knows where we're going tomorrow. He doesn't. Anyway, what can you tell me?"

"I can't tell you anything either. You're the one who's close to our master, not me."

"Oh! It looks like I must have stepped on your toes—or your eyes," Michel mocked, turning his body, and casting a suggestive gaze through the glass. "Beware of strong emotions, hey? Remember the lesson we learned yesterday in the forest."

"What is it, Michel? Are you a spy now?"

Giancarlo didn't want to talk anymore. Shooting a significant glance at the Frenchman, he turned and left.

As he walked away, Giancarlo was still able to watch the scene unraveling outside: the woman came over to Jill and gave her a hug.

But although he was intending to go out and meet Jill on the veranda, Giancarlo chose the longest route to get there. He didn't see when Michel left, nor when he entered the outside area through the back door. But he did see when Michel came up to Jill.

Then, feeling a passing insecurity, Giancarlo changed direction.

◆ ◆ ◆

ISABELLA HAD ALREADY TAKEN HER SHOWER. The headache was gone, but at no point had she exercised her mezzo-soprano as she usually did in the shower. She left the bathroom with her mouth closed and saw her fiancé dozing off on the sofa in the living room. She felt sorry for him—or a renewed sense of love. Poor *Amore*! He was doing everything he could to seem like a... a bad guy. But it wasn't working.

She went over to shake him.

"Wake up, *Amore*!"

Tonelli opened his eyes, afraid.

"What? What's happening, Bella?"

Isabella went to grab some clothes from her suitcase.

"Leave the sleep for after dinner. And you should go shower too."

Tonelli yawned happily. *Dinner* was an incredibly nice word. But Isabella brought his enthusiasm crashing down to earth,

"We got a free night's stay, but we shouldn't abuse it. A bowl of soup each will be just fine."

Tonelli jumped up off the sofa.

"You can't be serious… Can you?"

Isabella hung a dress on one of the hangers from the wardrobe. She returned to her suitcase and pulled out a blouse. She said, "Just in case, we should be careful and save as much as possible. You never know what tomorrow may bring."

"But when I get my hands on that money…!"

Tonelli wished he could take back what he said. But it was too late, Isabella stopped styling her hair.

"Money? What are you talking about?"

Tonelli tried to wriggle his way out of it.

"Now, okay. I think I'll follow your advice. I'll go take a shower."

"No, you won't!" Isabella said, clinging to her fiancé's arm. "You're going to tell me everything that's going through that little mind of yours. That's what you're gonna do!"

"Bella *mia*… Let me explain."

Isabella backed off. She released her fiancé's arm.

"You know, Nezzo Bologna…"

"No, no! I can't believe what I'm hearing again! You promised me you weren't in this because of that man! *Nevvero?*"

"Bella, let me explain."

"I can't believe you're being paid by Nezzo Bologna to dig up some dirt on that cocky old politician Francesco Ricotta!"

"No, Bella, let me explain…"

She wrinkled her brow right in Tonelli's face.

"*Amore*… I can't believe you've accepted a commission for that kind of piece! I can't believe you dragged me into this mess!"

"I didn't drag anyone into anything!" Tonelli yelled, extracting himself from his fiancée's gaze. "Wasn't it you who insisted on coming? Did you already forget that?"

Exhausted, they both fell to the sofa. The brief argument had been a small battle. Seconds later, Isabella's face crumpled. Her eyes glistened. She was going to cry.

"I knew you never told me the whole truth about anything, *Amore*. I always knew that. And I never cared. But now…! How long are you going to keep pulling the wool over my eyes, can you tell me?"

They were both still on the sofa. Tonelli moved closer to her.

"*Io*?!" he raised his left hand reverently to his breast. "Me pull the wool over your eyes, Bella *mia*? Now I'm the one who's upset. And to think that this whole... this war... started over two meatball sandwiches—that have long been chewed and swallowed—and two future bowls of *minestra*. Ridiculous."

Tonelli lifted his fiancée's chin. Then embraced her. Now Isabella's tears streamed out and onto his cheek, burning it as they ran down.

"Bella *mia*... dry your eyes, *per favore*. Everything is fine. You can trust me. I'll write my big story... and then the two of us are gonna take a cruise around the world."

"As husband and wife?"

"Of course!"

They hugged again and traded a kiss. But the end of that kiss brought restlessness back to Isabella's blue eyes. And another idea, more distrust.

"*Amore*... the money you were talking about... when you got your hands on it... what money?"

Tonelli escaped from his fiancée's arms and the sofa. The war had started again. She went after him.

"Would it happen to be from Nezzo Bologna, *Amore*? How much did he promise to pay you to find that the money from America had ended up in Ricotta's campaign fund? Tell me!"

Tonelli took a towel, clothes, and a bar of soap from his bag.

"I've already explained everything, Bella," he said to the suitcase.

"Then look at me and tell me I'm wrong."

Straightening up, Tonelli took off his glasses and looked at his fiancée.

"Not without glasses! You can't see my eyes that way."

He put his glasses back on. Put his towel on his shoulder. He picked up the clothes and soap. Then he looked at his fiancée.

"Is this good enough, Bella? Of course you're wrong. I'm on my way to writing a big international story—the scoop of a lifetime. It's just a question of time. Trust me."

Tonelli's face was touchingly sincere.

He finished, "Now I'll go take my shower. Then we can go for that bowl of soup. I agree with you."

Blowing a kiss from six feet away, he went to the bathroom. Isabella threw herself back down on the sofa. Suspicion was still weighing heavily on her.

◆ ◆ ◆

AT THE SAME TIME, Michel was walking up to Jill and putting on his best and most trustworthy smile.

"Hi. I'm impressed with what I've seen. Congratulations. I'm a professor of French Literature in Avignon, but I studied psychology for three years before that. You should pursue it as a career, you know? You're a natural. My name is Michel. You're Jill, right?"

Based on his smile and confidence, Jill expected the guy to take a seat. He did. Then she said, "At my university in Atlanta, where I finished my doctorate in Clinical Psychology, men don't sit down next to a strange woman without being invited."

Michel turned pale. He wasn't sure whether to get up or just smile and ignore it. He did neither.

"But today is different. You can stay. *Oui*, my name is Jill. Who told you, was it the mechanic Menendez? Do you want to keep speaking French, or can we switch to Italian?"

Now Michel smiled. He thought she was breaking the ice in her own way.

"*Allora*, I'll beg your forgiveness in Italian. I think I behaved like a fool, Dr.… Jill?"

"All right. I forgive you. And you don't need to call me Dr. Heston, call me Jill. But tell me, were you trying to say you were spying on me, Michel?"

"Well, I couldn't help watching. You know, I felt that woman's hopelessness after she read your note. And I saw how much she cried. I bet she was crying out of remorse... out of true soul searching. Am I right? It was an incredible change. What did you write to make her give you that hug and leave with her head held so high?"

"Do you really want to know?"

"Of course."

"Well, it's a professional secret. I'm very sorry."

Now much more relaxed, Michel came closer, crossing his arms on the table.

"You are incredible, you know that?"

"Well, it's already landed me one lawsuit. Did you know that?"

Michel laughed alone. He heard Menendez calling.

"Calm down, Menendez," he said, looking back. When he saw that it was because Maggio had arrived for dinner, he dropped the cheerful façade. He turned back. "Sorry, Jill. I have to go."

"Be my guest, kid. But first tell me this: why did that friend of yours not come with you?"

"Who, Menendez?"

"No, the other one who was sitting with you and the mechanic at that table."

Begrudgingly, Michel said, "Ah, Gian. I don't know... he just disappeared."

"I saw him leave."

Michel left without saying another word.

When he got to the table, Menendez was by himself.

"Where's Master Maggio?"

"He only came to say he was eating dinner with McDowell. They need to talk."

"Then why did you call me, Menendez?"

"His orders. He also asked about Gian and I said he ran off somewhere. He didn't like that. It seems he doesn't want to see either one of you get mixed up with that woman over there."

Those words made Michel, as he sat down at the table, glance back at the veranda.

But Jill had already left.

♦ ♦ ♦

RICHARD MCDOWELL sipped the last of the wine from his glass, right to the very last drop. Then, placing it on the table, he stared in silence at Amaro Maggio's face.

Moments later, he repeated,

"Vallencantado... And why does it have to be there? Just give me one reason and I'll accept it."

"Let me give two. The first is that it is entirely my own business, and you know what I'm trying to say, McDowell. You were my master, and it was with you that I learned how crucial it is to keep what happens between a person and their spirit guide a secret."

"Correct."

"Second, Michel and Giancarlo are ready for the initiation ritual."

"But I thought the campground there in Pasonuevo would be ideal, and it's much easier to access than Vallencantado castle. I went there many years ago—six or seven. It's in ruins."

"But it has to be there, McDowell. I beg you to accept it. For me and my two disciples."

McDowell reflected for a moment. Then he asked a question that somewhat bewildered Amaro Maggio, "Tell me something, Maggio... what exactly is your problem?"

Maggio wanted to burst out laughing. "Problem? Me? What makes you say that?"

"Your eyes are saying it. But forget I asked. It's your business, as you say. I just wanted to remind you of the thing I exhaustively explained to you fifteen years ago before your own consecration."

Maggio blinked.

"Let me refresh your memory: your previous involvement with inferior forms of spiritism when you were younger."

"Ah, McDowell! That was so many years ago. I've already forgotten the spiritual connections I had in the past. There are many forms of engagement with the other world, you know—and endless categories of spirits. I've made my choice. I moved on... I evolved. The spirit *Sete Flechas* is only a name from my past. You're the one who taught me that it's a mistake to look back. In our tradition, we deal with a much higher level of spirits, isn't that right? It's as if I separated out the desirable friendships from the chaff."

Dinner arrived. While the waiter was serving them, they didn't exchange a single word. The waiter was soon gone, and McDowell said, "All right. I'll do as you like, Maggio. I'll teach you the way to Vallencantado."

"But I need you to be there, McDowell. You and at least three others."

"We will come too. Tomorrow, before six in the evening, we will be in the village near Vallencantado. After dinner, I will make you a map of the route. Now let's eat. I'm hungry."

Sixteen

Leaving the night-cloaked veranda, Jill went up to her room and placed a phone call to Villa Piomondo. Genoveffa answered and went to get Maddalena Heston. It seemed that her grandfather was still going strong.

"Maybe the doctors were wrong, *figliola*. Your *nonno* doesn't even look sick."

"He hasn't had any more coughing fits like that one the other day?"

"Not even one. And he's eating better than ever before. Thank God. But Jill... you know who called yesterday from New York?"

"Who, *Mamma*?" Jill asked wryly. "And what does Mike want? To catch the next plane to Italy?"

Her mother laughed.

"I think so. But I told him you went on a trip to Spain and were going to be gone for a week. He urged me to tell you he called if you got in touch with me. Well, I've told you."

"That's fine, *Mamma*. Message received. But if he calls again, tell him that... that I've met someone amazing."

"What? If I tell him that, he'll come shooting out of his tenth-story office and fly right over. What's the story? Who is this *amazing* person you've met in the past three days?"

"It was a joke, *Mamma*. Forget it."

"Jill…! I know you too well. Who's been stealing your heart? Some *torero* from Seville?"

"Mom, what nonsense! I already said I was just joking. But I'm hanging up now. I'm hungry."

"You haven't had dinner yet?"

"Not yet."

"And he… your *someone amazing*… is he waiting to share a candlelight dinner with you?"

"Bye, *Mamma*. *Un bacio* for you, and more for *Nonno*."

"Bye, *figliola*. And beware of sudden infatuations."

"Bye, *Mamma*."

♦ ♦ ♦

As Jill was walking back to her room, Giancarlo was leaving the room he had taken refuge in so he wouldn't have to share a dinner table with Michel. The two nearly collided at the door of the small lobby.

"Hi!" she said, smiling to conceal her slight shock.

"Hi!" he responded, also smiling to hide his pleasant surprise.

They looked at one another without a word. The first to find something to say was Jill.

"Um… thanks for the help today, it all turned out okay—or almost. I should be getting a new alternator early tomorrow. I'm counting on your friend Menendez to change it for me."

It was a high-traffic area. People were passing by—some that Giancarlo knew from the festival. He felt like he was being watched.

"You wanna get out of here?" Jill asked. "Where can we hide from your boss?"

Giancarlo heard her devious tone. He smiled. She also smiled. They were already out of the danger zone.

"I was joking. It's just that, not long ago, I saw your friend Michel looking a bit flustered when he saw… what's your boss's name actually?"

"Maggio. Amaro Maggio."

"I don't know him. But he must be a big deal from what I've seen."

They kept walking.

"Was he the one who didn't let you come back with *Señor* Menendez?"

"When?"

"After that rainstorm, when you left saying you were going to get me a mechanic."

Giancarlo was left with no response.

"This Maggio... who is he?"

"He's an initiate."

"Ah, a sorcerer, hey? I should have known. He has a dual gaze."

Giancarlo almost laughed. "Dual gaze? What does that mean?"

"Gaze number one is for everyday use, but the other is like a trench periscope. Who is he hiding from?"

Now he laughed.

"What a crazy idea! We need to establish some sort of code."

"For what?"

"So, I can know when you're being serious."

They stopped in front of the restaurant door. Jill noticed Giancarlo's eyes sweeping the tables.

"Well? Is the coast clear?" she asked.

He smiled again. "You really are incredible!"

"Who told you, Michel? And did he also tell you I've gotten into a lawsuit over that stuff before?"

"No, he didn't say anything. What kind of lawsuit?"

"Hmmm... it's complicated."

"Where?"

"Have you eaten dinner yet?"

"Not yet. You?"

She shook her head, saying, "You can pick the most secluded table in the house."

"Hey, are you sure you want to eat dinner with me?"

"Why not? I'm a black belt."

Maybe she really was, and it wasn't just another joke—thought Giancarlo. But the expression on her cute little face was like a challenge. And her constant half-smile even more so.

They laughed and went into the restaurant.

◆ ◆ ◆

THE TABLE THEY CHOSE was at the back of the restaurant. There weren't many people eating dinner there yet.

"Hey," said Jill, "what happened to the huge crowd that welcomed me when I arrived?"

"More than half of them left. And you were to blame."

"Me?"

"Didn't you bring the rain? The plans for the closing ceremony of the festival were completely ruined."

"Festival? What festival?"

"The Third Pasonuevo New Age Festival. Ever heard of it?"

"So, you're saying that… the people in that crowd were actually sorcerers?"

"Mystics. Alchemists. The ones who stayed finally decided to walk back to the Pasonuevo campground tomorrow morning."

"Ah. And you and Michel will go with them. Right?"

"No. We have a different destination."

Jill brushed her hair out of her face with her left hand. Giancarlo laughed.

"What happened? Are you laughing at my hair or my hand?"

After he got his laughter under control, Giancarlo said, "I'm remembering Michel's face when he came into the room upstairs. He was furious."

"With me or your master?"

"With himself—but it was your fault."

"Thanks."

"But I'm not interested in talking about Michel. I'm curious about that woman."

"Ah, I see. Even there you and Michel are evenly matched. What do you want to know?"

"Had you two met before?"

"I've never seen that woman in my life. Trust me."

"I do. But then who told you her problem? Or, rather, her former problem because she left here in a great mood."

"Don't exaggerate. She just forgave herself. She was somewhere between leaving with another man and… throwing herself off a cliff. She has a three-year-old daughter. And she was cheating on her husband."

"Who told you that?"

"She did, before she left."

They looked briefly into one another's eyes.

"Trust me."

"I do. But tell me one thing, I'm curious."

The waiter brought over two menus.

"Just leave them, thanks. We'll order in a minute."

"As you wish, *Señorita*."

The waiter left and Giancarlo insisted,

"I'm curious. Explain to me how you do this magic."

"Hasn't your master taught you yet?"

"Not yet."

"I see. You haven't gotten your diploma yet. You know, I've been reading that you guys usually find exotic locales for your mystical consecration rituals. Is that why you're here?"

"Hey! We were talking about you and that woman."

"That's true."

"How did you know about her life?"

"By looking into my portable crystal ball, of course."

"I'm being serious, Jill. Why are you being so... so...?"

"So what?"

"Just so!"

"Hmm…" she smiled. "Okay, you've won me over with that so very eloquent poem about me. I accept your gallantry. I didn't respond to your question because... because I thought you were going to say the same thing your friend Michel did."

"And what was that?"

"That I should have been a psychologist like him."

"Oh yeah? I didn't know Michel was a psychologist. I thought he was just a teacher."

"... of French Literature in Avignon," Jill finished. "He is that as well. And he was very pampered by his father, who seems to be a very rich French industrialist."

"Is that so? I didn't know."

"Neither did I. I was only just hearing about it now."

Giancarlo wanted to laugh.

"You're pulling my leg, Jill. Who told you about Michel?"

"No, seriously! Someone whispered it in my ear just now. But let's go back to your friend. It turns out he's not a psychologist. He dropped out halfway through the course."

"Ah, I see."

"So, I guess he's *part* French literature professor... *part* rich... and *part* warlock. Maybe he also flies on only *part* of a broomstick."

Now Giancarlo laughed freely. It wasn't so much what Jill said—it was the serious look on her face when she spoke. Her little face was sharp and candid at the same time. And enchanting.

"Tell me something: what order do you belong to?"

"Order?"

"Yes, there are many affiliated with the tradition."

"Ah, you're asking if I'm a witch too."

"More or less."

"Who knows? Maybe I'm a witch who doesn't belong to any order—especially considering what happened to me in Atlanta."

Giancarlo moved forward a bit to ask, "How do you say *streghetta incredibile* in English?"

Jill's response was a musical giggle.

"We've gone too far."

"I agree. Let's go back. You still haven't told me about that woman... and what you said about Michel. How did you come to know those things? Leave the crystal ball out of it and tell me."

Jill turned serious.

"You know, I... I don't exactly know how these things happen to me. And they don't always happen. I feel like someone... like a voice is whispering in my ear telling me intimate details about other people. Sometimes I hear pure criticism... and other times messages of support."

"So, there are two voices."

"Two voices? Interesting, I've never thought about it like that. But I don't think it's very likely because I know I'm hearing my own subconscious. It's

140

sharing universal knowledge."

"Okay… so you're saying that a voice told you about that woman's problems."

"More or less, yeah. I see it as a revelation, something that just suddenly comes to me."

"So, in this woman's case, you picked up a pen and paper and just… sent her a note?"

"I did."

"And what did you write?"

"I don't even remember exactly. Words."

"Was it something like '*Where are those who wish to throw stones at you? Forgive yourself for your wrongdoing; go and sin no more.*'"

Jill looked Giancarlo dead in the eyes.

"H-how did you know? Even I couldn't remember…!"

Giancarlo laughed at the expression Jill was pulling.

"I thought you were still at the beginning of your discipleship, Gian. I see that I was mistaken. Congratulations to your master."

"It's nothing like that, silly," he said, still laughing. "I ran after the woman. Look what she gave me."

Giancarlo placed the paper from the notepad on the table.

"My note?! You're terrible!"

"We are."

They both chuckled.

"Are you mad about my trick?" he wanted to know.

"Of course not. I'm a good sport. And you got me good. But I don't think you'll ever make a good sorcerer. You're too practical."

After a brief silence, Jill started laughing again.

"I'm thinking back to when I got here…"

The virulent laugh spread to Giancarlo.

"And I'm seeing that piece of plaster crashing to the ground!" he said.

They cackled, but at a half whisper.

"And that storm that came out of nowhere!" she said.

"And the lightning!"

"The thunder!"

"And the manager running around like a chicken with his head cut off to close the windows!"

Jill took a breath and added,

"And the faces on that the crowd of mystics! I think they were more astonished by me and you than the sudden storm."

"I think so too."

They fell silent. There was no longer any sound at all in the universe. They looked at each other. They gazed into one another's eyes for an interminable amount of time. Then Giancarlo put on a serious air.

"Someone told me that was a demonic manifestation, Jill."

"What?" she wanted to laugh again. "Demonic? Ah, Gian, be serious! There's no such thing as demons. The Greeks made them up... they're just a figment of our imaginations—or the fantasy of a brilliant filmmaker."

Then she added, "I think it was God."

"Ah, so you do believe in God."

"Why the surprise? Don't the mystics believe in Him?"

Giancarlo ignored Jill's question and said quite seriously, "I believe that we met because of God, yes. But I also believe that there is... there's another entity that didn't like it."

Jill laughed.

"An entity? Do you mean a demon? Goodness! But what an idea...! Who's putting these ideas in your head?"

"His name is Nicodemus."

"Nicodemus was a man of the Law. Out of fear of society, he went to seek Jesus in the darkness of the night."

"Well, this one is a drifter."

"What? A drifter?" Jill put her hand to her mouth. She laughed. "A drifter named Nicodemus? He must be a real character."

"You could say that. He appears... talks to me... tells me profound things... and when I look again, he's gone."

"Then maybe he's an angel."

"You know what he told me, Jill? That nothing... nothing and nobody can stop you from building upon the blueprints of a miracle—if you are truly determined. I'm trying to live by those words."

"Incredible positivity—coming from a drifter. And what exactly are the 'blueprints of a miracle?' Did he tell you that?"

"Are you asking because you want to know, or just for your own amusement?"

"Because I want to know, of course. Why do you ask? Because I'm laughing?"

"Hard to say."

They laughed.

"Yes, he told me. Every time we dream with an objective in mind, we are drawing up the blueprints of a miracle."

"Mm-hm. It does work, in theory."

"And you know what else he told me?" Now Giancarlo placed his elbows on the table to support his chin on his interlaced fingers. It was a way of bringing his head closer to that of Jill. "He said that everything exists because of the Greater Dream of God."

"Ah, how beautiful! Another poem!" exclaimed Jill, putting up a little performance. "See, maybe this drifter friend of yours is a poet. Or better yet an angel-poet?"

"An angel? Nicodemus? What an idea. Angels don't take bites out of pears."

"Did that happen?"

"What? Him eating a pear?"

"No. Him having a pear to eat."

"Of course. He also gave me one. He had two."

"And you still think he's a drifter?"

"Could he be an angel?"

"Well... considering what you told me, that he appears and disappears... yes. I think it's easier to find an angel that eats pears than a drifter carrying two in his backpack."

"You're terrible!"

"Why? Did I say something foolish? I think you'll find that he's not an angel nor a drifter: he's some eccentric millionaire making the pilgrimage to Santiago de Compostela."

Their eyes exchanged a few more brief flickers of light.

"It was nice to meet you, Jill."

"Thanks."

"And even... even if I don't get what I'm looking for... even if I still don't find the well of the Star... this very long journey was still worth it."

"Well of the Star? What's the story there?"

"The Morning Star. It's a legend about the Three Magi, how they got lost in the desert and ended up finding the Holy Grotto. They saw the Morning Star reflected in the bottom of a well when they stopped for a drink of water."

"And the moral of the story," said Jill, "is that the success of a search is proportional to the thirst of the person searching. Good logic. Was it the drifter-poet who told you that tale?"

"Yes, it was."

"Then I'm inclined to believe he's some financial genius enjoying a little time off."

"By the way, Jill, where are you going?"

People were now starting to arrive for dinner, and Giancarlo waited for them to pass.

After that he asked, "Tell me about you. Where are you going?"

"Villavieja del Campo."

"Where is that?"

"According to my map, a hundred and twenty miles from here."

"And what are you going there to do? Visit relatives?"

"No. I'm looking for a man."

"A man? How old is he?"

Jill laughed.

"Why the face? Over seventy. His name is Giovanni. *Signor* Giovanni di Stefano. I need his help."

Giancarlo crossed his arms on top of the table.

"What type of help are you looking for?"

"Money."

"Money?"

"Well, it's a special case. It isn't for me. It just so happens that I have thirty-three orphaned children to take care of."

"What? Thirty-three... orphaned children? I never would have taken you for someone who runs a daycare center."

"Who said I was? I have thirty-three children to shelter, dress and feed. And educate."

"Thirty-three *bambini*?"

"They are victims of turf wars between rebel groups in Kurmania."

Giancarlo furrowed his brow.

"Jill... are you kidding me?"

"Hey! Why would I joke about something like this? I can see on your face that you don't believe a single word I just said."

"I wasn't trying to say I don't believe you. I'm just surprised. Such a young woman with that big of a burden? Why don't you tell me everything?"

◆ ◆ ◆

Six feet away from their table, conveniently hidden by an exotic vase containing white peace lilies, Tonelli and Bella were staring at each other. He raised his head over the table.

"What luck, Bella!" he whispered to his fiancée. "We came at the right time. Pay attention to what she says."

"You make sure you don't raise any red flags," Isabella went back to whispering. "And eat your soup. It's getting cold."

But Tonelli wasn't going to be able to eat the soup. Returning to his previous position, he stopped like a paused video. Listening attentively, Isabella went on gingerly savoring her bowl of soup as if it were the last meal on the planet.

◆ ◆ ◆

Jill began by talking about Missionary Benny Marshall.

"He was forced to flee the village in Kurmania where he was living with his wife. There they were taking care of children orphaned in intra-factional fighting. It just so happens that Missionary Benny Marshall was an old friend of my father's. They fought together in Vietnam. Twenty-one years later, my father was made Consul here in Italy. Then Missionary Marshall got in contact with him and asked for help getting the children out of Kurmania. If not, they would have all starved to death in no time—including the missionary and his wife."

"This distress call went out four months ago. At the time, I was still in Atlanta. My mom says my dad just couldn't say no. You know, Gian, he and Missionary Marshall, when they fought in Vietnam, they worked together disarming landmines in Cambodia. And the whole world knows what's been happening there for the past twenty years... all those innocent victims... peasants with their children about to plant their rice and... all of a sudden, they're sent flying into the air."

"How do you think my father felt when Missionary Marshall called him from Africa asking for help? My dad spent nights on end unable to sleep. It was his past coming back to haunt him. And he felt like he needed to do something… something to ease his conscience. So he promised help to Missionary Marshall."

"Two and a half months ago, my father arranged for a small boat to ferry Missionary Marshall, his wife Mary and the children to somewhere near Berbera."

Giancarlo was listening with rapt attention.

After a brief pause, Jill resumed, "As it happened, my father took the initiative because he was counting on some financial aid that was supposed to arrive from America."

"The help never came," said Giancarlo.

"Well… it didn't. But then my dad died unexpectedly, and we were lost, without knowing who to turn to for help. Not even Missionary Marshall knew exactly who was helping my father. He thought it was a US Senator, but this could not be confirmed after my dad's death. And all I know now is that I must carry on the work that my dad started."

"I'm very sorry, Jill. I really am. I can appreciate what you and your mother are going through. I also… I just lost my father. I loved him so much…unfortunately, I didn't get the chance to settle some things between us…"

"Oh, Gian…!"

"It's okay. I'm coming to terms with it."

"And your mother? Tell me about her."

"She is a Calabrian woman and strong in every sense of the word."

"My mom is from Salerno. Ever since she came back from America with my dad ten years ago, they've been living at my grandfather Vittorino's villa."

"How did they meet?"

"Well, it was right after Vietnam, in '75. My dad's mom was from the north of Italy, near Treviso. My paternal grandfather was from Toledo, Michigan and my dad was born in the middle of the Atlantic."

Jill gave a somewhat sad smile.

"He had dual nationality. Then, after the end of the Vietnam War, he decided to stay here in Italy. That was when he met my mom."

"Do you have any siblings?"

"No, I'm an only child. My mother's pregnancy was rough, and she couldn't have more children. What about you? How many siblings do you have?"

"I have one, Tullio. He's two years older than me."

Giancarlo wanted to go back to the previous topic.

"But tell me... what about those kids? Where are they?"

"I have to keep that secret. But I have to get them out of there quickly, otherwise they'll be sent back to Kurmania."

"And what about Italian law? What does it say about war refugees, have you looked into that?"

Jill sighed.

"Yes, I still have that problem too. There are so many of them! My mother got in touch with a friend of the family. He knows influential people in Rome. We'll see. But right now, the most important thing is getting the kids out of where they are."

"And what are your plans for them?"

"I have a few. But first I have to find them a safe place to stay."

"And what are you thinking? Buy a farm or..."

"That was my father's idea... buy a farm in the far south of Italy. But his death changed everything. Then we decided to take the children to my grandfather's villa. And now it just so happens that my grandfather... ah, Gian, there are so many problems...!"

Jill told him about the situation at Villa Piomondo and its relation to her grandfather Vittorino's severe health problem. Giancarlo kept putting his hand to his head in sympathy.

"I understand why you're looking for money. If your *nonno* dies, goodbye Villa Piomondo."

"That's right, Gian."

Jill stopped talking.

"And what were you saying about a lawsuit in Atlanta? Are you a fugitive from America?"

Giancarlo threatened to laugh. But it was Jill who did.

"You guessed right."

"Hey! I was asking a serious question, *ragazza.*"

"Hey! I gave you a serious answer, *ragazzo.* Trust me."

And with a serious air, she added,

"But I don't want to talk about it."

"Why not?"

"Well... among other things, it makes me think of people who let me down."

"Hmm," Giancarlo said while he mused. "And was one of these people... a single man?"

Jill was taken by surprise.

"Where'd you get that idea?"

"I figured women were only let down by men—and vice versa. That's all."

"Hmm..." it was Jill's turn to muse. "The logic is sound, but I am not sure if it is always true. And I won't deny it, though: it was a man who let me down badly."

"And does... does he have a name?"

"Mike. Five foot eleven. Size 9 shoe. And 15 inches at the collar."

They caught each other's gaze. Then two chuckles exploded out of them.

"That's fine," said Giancarlo, "let's forget about this size-nine-shoe guy."

"I agree. Now tell me about you."

♦ ♦ ♦

EMERGING FROM HIS PHYSICAL FREEZE, Tonelli's brain decided to open his mouth. And he used his napkin as a barrier to whisper to his fiancée,

"Bella...! Did you hear what I heard?"

"*Sì, caro.*"

"Then let's go. I need to make a phone call."

"But aren't you going to finish your *minestra, Amore?*"

"I won't be able to finish this cold soup. Let's go."

Tonelli instantly shot to his feet—keeping his back turned to Giancarlo and Jill's table the whole time.

"What about the bill?" Isabella asked.

"I'll drop by the register and sign for it. Let's go, Bella. *Sbrighiamoci.*"

Ten minutes later, they were back in their suite. Isabella said she was dead tired—and was afraid that if she didn't get to sleep soon the hunger would be back. She said good night and went to the bedroom.

Making himself comfortable on the living room sofa, Tonelli took out his cell phone and called the newspaper in Rome.

"Mila? It's Tonelli. Do you have a pen handy?"

"Go ahead."

"Jill Heston. I want you to find everything you can on her—newspapers, etc. Start with the Atlanta police department."

"Did you say Atlanta? In America?"

"*Sì*. And I also want to know what Francesco Ricotta's been up to recently. Ricotta is her uncle. You got that down?"

"*Sì, carissimo.*"

"Do you have any news from Vaccaro?"

"He isn't back from Sicily yet."

"If you get in touch with him, tell that jerk I'm still waiting. He knows what for. *Ciao*, Mila."

Tonelli closed his cell phone and put it down on the side table, which was topped by a round mirror. He looked at himself. *Great job, Massimo Tonelli! You're getting there. That girl is shrewd; she doesn't deny who her parents are. She said the money was coming but didn't arrive—and you know what that means, don't you? That* BAM! *someone else got their hands on the money from America. Soon you'll catch that clever vixen with her hand in the cookie jar. And then... the two hundred thousand dollars are yours! And that's just the beginning. You're going to be famous, Tonelli.*

Then he went into the bathroom to put on his PJs. He was running on forty hours of no sleep and just many without eating a decent meal. Lying prone on the sofa, he attempted to squash the hunger out of his stomach. In ten minutes, he was snoring.

Seventeen

They had already finished dinner. The conversation carried on, but at no point did Giancarlo mention his dream from the Apennine mountains. He didn't talk about the graduation ring he gave back to his mother either. He told her about his father's death and his grandfather Enrico's one-way trip. He didn't mention the circumstances though, much less the stones buried at the farm in Vigneto.

They spent a few moments in silence. Giancarlo used the pause to pull a folded piece of paper out of his shirt pocket. When he unfolded it, Jill was astonished. It was a charcoal drawing.

"But...! That's me! Incredible! Did you draw that? When did you do it without me noticing?"

"An observation here, another there."

"It's great! You're good at that! Wow!"

It was a stylized portrait with nuanced streaks of gray and white on top of a darker base. Jill was full of enthusiasm.

"Do you do oil painting, too, Gian?"

He took some time to respond, "Well... I used to dabble. I sold my work at markets in Venice. But that was four and a half years ago now. I've given up the canvases and brushes since then."

"But why? You have talent. You can tell it's me by just three or four details, and that's not something any camera could do. Your style is impressionistic and fantastic. I'm imagining it as if it were oil on canvas. Why did you stop painting?"

"My subject was landscapes... ordinary rural landscapes. Maybe I'll go back to painting one day."

"You didn't answer me. Why did you stop? Did you get discouraged?"

He didn't want to talk about attending art classes and how he had to abandon it all to please his father.

"I just had a change of heart."

The response didn't convince Jill.

"I'm sure something must have happened."

"Well, let's say it all started when I read a certain book. Have you ever read a book that made you reconsider your life?"

"I read many books in graduate school and I'm still reconsidering my life. I think changes happen gradually—at least the ones that stick."

"With me it was different. I was struck. I'd found the answers to all my questions."

"Maybe those were the exact answers you were looking for. But it must be quite the book. Who's the author?"

"Fernando Sierra."

"No, no! That's trash, Gian. Wasn't he the one who wrote... what was it called? *Awaken the Mystic... something-something?*"

"*Awaken the Mystic Inside You.* That's the one. Have you read it?"

"No, no I haven't—and I don't think I want to. But a friend of mine from Atlanta, Sue, read it and told me a little bit about it. I didn't see anything amazing change in her life."

"Well, that book blew my mind. That, Jill, was when I started becoming interested in mankind's magical pathways. And when I started to practice transpersonal regression."

"Transpersonal regression? Ah, at least we have something in common again now. I did an extension course in metaphysics. Something about it caught my interest, and I intend to revisit the topic one day."

152

"In one of the sessions, I learned that my work... the rural landscapes I enjoyed painting so much... were nothing more than memories, vestiges of memories from other lives I had lived."

"Interesting. Then your soul was expressing itself through painting."

"Exactly. But I had this experience alone, you see. I followed the steps in Fernando Sierra's book religiously."

"And one day you realized that you'd left the paintbrushes behind."

"That was how it happened. Painting mere vestiges of past lives no longer made any sense. I had to keep moving forward. I needed to find my identity in the universe. Then I discovered that Fernando Sierra had been a disciple of Amaro Maggio."

"Ah, got it," Jill said with a hint of spice. "Let's take it back to the beginning, to your master. I saw quite the scene before dinner, and it starred the teacher from Avignon. When your master came by, poor little Michel just freaked. You know, Gian, this afternoon I almost sent him a note. But I held back."

"Sent who a note? Me or Michel?"

"Don't kid, Gian. I'm being serious. You know who. Do you want to see the note?"

"Of course I do."

Taking the paper out of the bag, Jill handed it to Giancarlo. He read it silently.

"For the thing I greatly feared has come upon me,
And what I dreaded has happened to me."

"Just that? Is it from some Biblical prophet?"

"I don't know, could be. You don't think much of it, then? What happens depends on how afraid someone is. And from what I was able to see this afternoon, your master has quite the anxious look about him. Have you never noticed? What's he running from?"

At that exact moment, Giancarlo saw Michel standing next to the restaurant door. The Frenchman shot him a discrete signal. Giancarlo understood that Michel had been sent by Maggio.

It was hard, but he had to say it, "Jill... I... I have to go."

"Of course. But can I tell you what I'm reading in your eyes?"

"Tell me."

"That you just saw someone—possibly Michel—making a signal for you to go back. Want me to turn around and check?"

Giancarlo was already on his feet. He turned serious.

"No, don't turn around. I... I'll pay the bill on the way out."

"Just half, please."

"Okay then."

Taking a step aside, Giancarlo tried to minimize the awkwardness.

"Jill, listen. I... I'd like to talk with you a bit more, but I have to go. Excuse me. Good night."

She didn't say anything in response.

"Good night, Jill," Giancarlo said again. "Please don't be annoyed. I'll see you tomorrow."

He left. He signed the bill the waiter handed him and left with Michel.

Jill remained seated for another few minutes, keeping her back turned to the door. She picked up the drawing on top of the table. And she found it unsettling. Even so, she folded the piece of paper and put it in her pocket.

Only then did she decide to go up to her room.

◆ ◆ ◆

THE DOGS WERE SLEEPING when Giancarlo walked in with Michel—but they woke up. They started howling, barely audibly at first, but they got louder. And their eyes were fixed on Giancarlo. Michel noticed.

"Shush," said Maggio. Falling silent, the dogs put their heads back down. But they didn't close their eyes.

Maggio asked Michel and Giancarlo to sit down. Giancarlo was ready to hear a lecture. But it didn't come.

Maggio went over to the closet. He opened a drawer and took out three eight-inch candles. One by one, he tried to get them to stand upright in a niche in the wardrobe. He gave it three good attempts and succeeded. Next, he sat in one of the armchairs. Giancarlo was in another and Michel on a three-seater sofa.

"You two are just one step away from a very big day, maybe the biggest in your lives," said Maggio. "Fifteen years ago, I went through this experience. It's unforgettable. I must confess that you are causing me to relive it."

He stopped talking. His right elbow supported on the arm of the sofa, Maggio raised his hand to his temple and touched it with the tips of three fingers. He closed his eyes. Around thirty seconds passed. Then he opened his eyes and stared at the three candles. The one on the left caught fire. Then the other two also lit themselves spontaneously.

"I just wanted to remind you," Amaro Maggio began, "that we can control any type of power however we like—and whenever we like. It's a question of discipline—and submission."

At that point, Maggio swept the air in front of him with his extended right arm. This made the three flames atop the candles go out. Then he sat watching his disciples in silence for a moment.

This was the first time Giancarlo detected something inexplicable in Maggio's eyes, an apprehension of some kind —a weakness born out of the hope to prove himself strong. That might have been why he felt the need to exhibit his powers. He thought back on what Jill had said.

Standing up from the armchair, Maggio took a few steps around the room. He paced while speaking.

"The language of the universe is written in two words: coincidence and luck. Turning them both in our favor is the task performed by our mentors—or demons. Do not fear this word: demon. In fact, from now on you should be trying to become comfortable with it. Since ancient times, *demons* have been the inspiring *geniuses* that preside over the character and destiny of each one of us. The secret is not faith: it is the pact. Only through the pacts we make with these geniuses can we overcome obstacles—and perform miracles that boggle the imagination. But keep one thing in mind: the upcoming initiation ritual will not add anything to what you can already do. The ritual is just a party—a celebration of the pact. Any questions?"

Giancarlo lowered his head. But Michel had some questions. While he asked them and got his answers, Giancarlo thought over Jill's observations about Maggio. Giancarlo was not worried about how easily she could sense other peoples' tensions and feelings: he was concerned about Maggio. He had never seen him looking so vulnerable before.

The constant presence of the dogs in his suite confirmed this. And Giancarlo knew that they were only able to be there because of a bribe. One of the employees of *El Rincón* had offered to open the door to a disused stairwell in the back of the hotel so the dogs could come in.

Apparently satisfied with the result of the short meeting, Maggio said, "Get everything ready tonight, because we will be leaving early tomorrow morning."

"Where are we going, Master?" Michel wanted to know.

"Have you heard of Vallencantado castle before?"

"No."

"Okay, well it's actually the ruins of a castle. It's a completely abandoned place. That's where we're going."

Giancarlo was worried about the time.

"How early?" he asked.

Maggio shot him a sharp gaze.

"Why does that concern you, Gian? That woman's car troubles are her own problem—not yours. Be ready to leave at eight-thirty."

Maggio opened the door for them.

"Sleep well, Michel. Good night, Gian."

As soon as the door was closed, Maggio's eyes were drawn to the three candles. Without any movement or thought on his part, one by one they lit up. Maggio's face turned pale.

Seven minutes later, the flames had fully consumed the candles.

Over the next half hour, Maggio made several attempts to achieve a hypnagogic state to contact his guide. He was not able to escape consciousness. Nor his growing anxiety.

He fell asleep quite late.

◆ ◆ ◆

He could not tell if he was dreaming.

For some time already, he had been restlessly staring at Michel sleeping on the next bed over, the same as Menendez by the other wall. They were both still sleeping deeply. The room was immersed in shadow and, through the slits in the venetian blinds, he could see traces of dawn. He decided he was not asleep.

But slowly, through the fog, the point of light came closer until it transformed into a quasi-human figure—like a sort of blurry projection.

It's *him*—was the first thought that occurred to him. It was his personal guide. And *he* cracked a smile.

156

"I come bearing a message from your grandfather. Isn't he the one you're so worried about?"

"Y-yes."

"Your grandfather has suffered a great deal, but today he is a spirit of light. He is doing fine. He is reunited with the ancients and sent me to say that you should move forward with your progress. I will be your friend if you will be mine. And I can reveal many paths unto you."

"What is your name?"

"Think and my name will come to your mind."

He thought. And the name came. At the same time, the fog dissipated, scattering the blurry image.

In a burst, Giancarlo sat up in bed. He'd had his first contact with his guide. Without seeking him, he came. He felt a mixture of satisfaction and fear.

Eighteen

It was six-thirty in the morning.

His pack already on his back, Giancarlo headed for the restaurant of *El Rincón*. He was not looking for coffee—but rather Jill. Maggio's spur-of-the-moment change of plans, rescheduling their departure for 8:30 AM, made it impossible for Menendez to fix Jill's car. Menendez didn't even try to warn her. Giancarlo, though, intended to do that.

"*Señorita* Heston has not yet come down for breakfast, *Señor*," the waiter informed him.

Thinking of calling up to Jill's room, Giancarlo left the restaurant and went toward the front desk. Halfway there, he saw Nicodemus. He was standing beneath a palm tree at the back of the garden. He walked over to him.

"I thought about you when I woke up this morning," said Giancarlo. "We're leaving, Nicodemus."

"I can see the bag on your shoulder. Your big day is coming up, isn't that right? And how are you? Feeling confident?"

They started walking leisurely through the far part of the garden.

Giancarlo hesitated a moment before responding, "To be frank... I don't think so."

"And why not?"

"I don't know... it's personal. Something inside of me. I don't know how to explain it."

"Fear?"

"No, not fear."

"Doubt," Nicodemus affirmed.

"Doubt? It must be something like that."

"Then your master is failing, Gian. Did he not explain to you that the initiation ritual is just a seal—a seal that adds nothing to what you already have?"

"Wow! That was exactly what he said last night. And he said that my power would be proportional to the relationship I establish with my guide."

"Correct. With your exclusive demon guide. I imagined your master had told you that. The thing about that is, this exclusivity is only for him, the demon."

"What do you mean? I don't get it."

"Your demon guide will have free access to you, and also to many others. It isn't you who will invoke him: he will suggest that you do it."

Giancarlo felt strangely frustrated.

"Last night I had my first contact."

"Ah, then it's begun. At first, he opens a dialogue with you... he draws you in... he's obliging. Right?"

"That's exactly right. I didn't ask him anything, but he told me that *Nonno* Enrico is doing fine and that he is a spirit of light. He said that one day we would meet."

"That is true."

Giancarlo understood that Nicodemus was giving the guide some credit.

But Nicodemus had more to say, "Gian... demons build lies on top of truth—but they cannot alter the truth. It is true, your grandfather is in the best of company, and the two of you really will meet. All that is true. But you need to understand what I'm really telling you."

Giancarlo looked at Nicodemus.

"Are you trying to say that I'm going to meet my grandfather... alive?"

Nicodemus didn't want to respond, but he said, "At the stage you're at now, the demon guide presents himself as a *genius*—a genius who is prepared to remove obstacles that he himself put in your way—he or others of his ilk. Then... then he begins to dominate you with suggestions... with amazing feats. He will lead you to believe that you are capable of true miracles. Miracles such as changing the color of a rose... or starting things on fire spontaneously with the power of your mind—or what he wants you to think is your mind. Of course, you won't be seeing your guide do this though: isn't he invisible?"

Nicodemus carried on, "But the total possession will come when you least expect it, Gian. With no preparation or warning, you will suddenly start collecting minutes and hours you can't remember whatsoever. In the end, he will come and go from your mind whenever he sees fit—and when he is within you, you are less than nothing. Until one day he comes to collect on every one of the feats he performed for you. And while they pile the earth over your dead body, he will carry your soul to a second death. That is the true price of the pact between you two."

Giancarlo held a profound silence. After a brief moment had passed, Nicodemus asked, "Do you think it's bad for me to say that Gian?"

"N-no. I'm just a bit... a bit confused. But can I ask you a question?"

"Of course."

"It's funny... I've listened to you speak for a while now, and I've deduced that you don't approve of what I'm doing. So then why... why keep playing coy? Why not tell me I'm making a mistake?"

"I can't. You are the one who must become aware of this for yourself—I can't tell you what to do. And you know something else? Within an hour, you might not recall a single word I told you. Your mind has been shaped to repel this type of message."

"But then... then do I have no way out?"

"Only when your thirst causes you to gaze into the well inside yourself."

They stepped back onto the garden path. Giancarlo's expression was troubled.

"What are you thinking about, Gian?"

"I don't know why... but I'm thinking about Maggio's dogs. They used to be friendly to me, but lately they've been *acting strange*."

"Maybe they aren't acting strange toward you, but rather someone accompanying you—and protecting you."

Giancarlo's lips traced a laugh. "Could it be an angel with a glowing sword, maybe, Nicodemus?"

"Why not? There might be someone calling for you."

After that, Nicodemus changed the topic.

"But tell me... what about the woman?"

Giancarlo let out a slight sigh.

"She's incredible. She's fighting a good fight that few people would see through to the end."

Giancarlo recounted some details of the Kurmanian orphan children's plight. Nicodemus listened in silence.

"I've never met a woman like Jill before. It's a pretty name, isn't it?"

"And what does she think of your name?"

Giancarlo smiled.

"I don't know what she thinks of me. Maybe nothing. I actually think she likes some guy back in America. All I know for sure is that she's keeping me up at night."

"And today you got out of bed early."

"Well, the thing is, I needed to talk to her about the car. And bring her a book."

"What book?"

As he unzipped his backpack, Giancarlo said, "I hope Maggio doesn't see me doing this. He is insanely jealous of Fernando Sierra."

"Fernando... Sierra? Did you say Fernando Sierra, the Spanish writer who lives in Málaga?"

"The very same. Do you know his books?"

"Y-yes, of course. And I know him, too."

"Fernando Sierra? Personally?"

"Mm-hm."

"Wow! That's a surprise to me. Which of his books do you like most?"

"The most recent one. It was a big departure. The Spanish edition just came out."

"What's it called?"

"*The Death of a Mystic.*"

"What a name! Is it fiction?"

"It's based on a true story. You have to read it. You'll like it."

"I always keep this one on my nightstand," said Giancarlo, passing the book to Nicodemus.

"Awaken the Mystic Inside You."

"It was because the book was dedicated to Maggio that I went looking for him in Genoa. Fernando Sierra was a disciple of Maggio, but now Maggio can't even stand hearing Sierra's name. Do you see what I mean? He's a foolish man. He refuses to accept that the disciple could surpass the master. Now and again, he quotes the words of Jesus to me."

Nicodemus gave the book back to Giancarlo.

"Gian, listen. Man cannot go without reading, but he must know the origin of what he is reading. There are people with good intentions who end up falling into the hands of unclean spirits. They write what the demons want—and they write beautifully. And thus, they sow toxic seeds in the earth. And those seeds come to bear fruit that kills the human spirit."

Now Nicodemus looked over Giancarlo's shoulder.

"If you have to warn the woman about her car, you'd better go quickly. Your friend Menendez has already started bringing the bags down."

Giancarlo looked behind him and confirmed this was true.

"Okay then. Will we see each other again?"

"Of course, Gian. We will see each other again."

Giancarlo walked over to the front desk and called Jill's room.

"Jill? It's Giancarlo."

"Hi, Gian. Your call startled me."

"I'm sorry. Did you sleep well?"

"More or less. I couldn't fall asleep right away."

"I have to tell you: we're leaving."

"What? But what about... about *Señor* Menendez. Is he going too?"

"Yes, of course. He's our driver. And that's why I'm calling."

There was a moment of indecision.

"But are you leaving already?"

"We're leaving within half an hour. Maggio is very punctual."

"I'm on my way down."

"I'll be waiting here at the front desk."

Michel emerged exactly when Giancarlo hung up the phone. Maggio wanted to see them both up in his room.

◆ ◆ ◆

TEN MINUTES LATER, Jill came downstairs. She didn't see Giancarlo at the front desk, so she peeked into the restaurant. Then, she went out to the patio. Giancarlo was nowhere to be found. But she saw Menendez maneuvering the truck outside.

Cutting a path through the pedestrian entrance, she reached the hotel's drop-off area at the same time the truck did.

"I'm very sorry, *Señorita*," Menendez said in the face of Jill's expectation, "but there was a change of plans and we have to get going."

"But what am I supposed to do, *Señor* Menendez? The alternator should be arriving within an hour. Who will change it for me?"

Menendez shrugged his shoulders.

"There has to be a mechanic somewhere around here. Did you ask at the gas station?"

"I did, *Señor* Menendez."

"Okay, well my advice is to go back there. Maybe somebody who knows how to fix your car will stop when passing through. I'm very sorry, *Señorita*. And now I have to go, I have to get the rest of our bags."

He was already leaving when Jill asked, "What about Giancarlo, have you seen him?"

"I left him and Michel up in the room with Maggio."

Jill felt annoyed. Not knowing what else to do, she decided to go over to her parked car at the gas station.

◆ ◆ ◆

AT THE SAME TIME, Tonelli and Isabella were sneaking into the restaurant for breakfast. It was included in the nightly rate—and so they intended to eat as much as they could, as they were allowed to do so.

They were literally choking with hunger. Two waiters looked on, astonished, as they gorged themselves. Isabella chose what she wanted to eat and drink and ate it all with gusto. Tonelli went back several times to try everything on the abundant buffet table—including some white beans with *morcilla*, which he found nearly inedible.

Their bellies finally satiated, the two left the restaurant dishing out smiles and waving their thanks.

"What time did Don Alberto set the meeting, *Amore?*"

"I'll go find out right now."

Suddenly, they overheard about Jill's renewed troubles from two passing *El Rincón* cleaning ladies. She was again left without a mechanic.

"*Oddio!*" Tonelli was alarmed. "If this is true, Bella, what will become of us? What are we going to do for lunch? And dinner? What if we have to spend another night here? Who will come to our rescue?"

"Control yourself, *Amore,*" Isabella whispered to him. "You're too anxious. Try and relax a bit."

"*E come faccio?* Where is a mechanic going to come from, huh? How long are we going to have to endure this suffering? Did you ever think that we might have to spend a week here? For her, it's no problem... she has a fortune waiting for her. *Ma noi due?*"

"You should have thought about that before you started."

"And you? Why don't you withdraw some money from your account?"

"How many times have I told you that it's *my* savings for *our* wedding?"

"*Va bene.* Then I'll have to think of another arrangement with Don Alberto... maybe change the meeting to tomorrow morning. It's always good to be a step ahead. Help me think of a way out of this."

"Count me out!" She yelled in a forced whisper. "Enough scheming! I'm going up to the room. I can feel that terrible headache coming back."

◆ ◆ ◆

Jill was sitting in her car with her feet out on the ground. She was quite upset. She didn't even notice when Giancarlo walked up.

"I ran here, Jill. We're leaving now. Have you found another mechanic?"

"Can't you see it on my happy face, Gian?" she attacked. "I can't believe it, Gian! You call me, wake me up, and then slink off with your master!"

Giancarlo stayed silent. She took a deep sigh.

"Forgive me. The thing is that sometimes I feel like I should drop everything and go back home." She almost added, "*...and call Mike and set the date for our wedding. That would be a comprehensive solution.*"

"Don't do that, Jill. The difficulties are a sign we're on the right path."

"Oh, I know. I suppose you heard that from your master. Or maybe that drifter. They don't know anything, Gian. They only know how to construct hollow phrases."

Setting his suitcase on the ground, Giancarlo crouched down next to Jill. She didn't move an inch.

"Okay then. You can offload your rage on me. After all, you should be asking yourself what kind of friend I am. I didn't even talk to Maggio about Menendez fixing your car. Isn't that right? You trusted Menendez."

"It isn't your fault. If you didn't talk to... to that half-broomstick-riding warlock, it's because you knew what his response would be. I understand. There's just one thing I don't get, Gian."

"And what is that?"

"How could you have allowed a man like that to ensnare you like this?"

"It isn't just him, Jill, it's the Order. Only when we learn to be slaves to the Order do we truly attain our freedom."

"Slaves? Freedom? There you go again with your set phrases. They make no logical sense. Why don't you compile a collection of them and publish it under the title *Superficial Gibberish*?"

Jill pursed her lips. Opening his backpack, Giancarlo took out the Fernando Sierra book.

"I wanted you to have this. I'd like you to read it."

"What for? So I can be *enlightened* like your master—who is so great he cannot allow a person to change a broken alternator in someone else's car?"

Self-conscious, Giancarlo opened the backpack again to put the book back inside. But Jill took it from him.

"It's fine. I'll keep it."

Jill stuck the book in her glove box. Then, returning to her previous position, she sat facing the gas station. Giancarlo didn't mind. He felt like she was struggling with her thoughts.

"Beyond not having a mechanic, Jill, what else is worrying you?"

"That guy."

"Who?"

Giancarlo followed the line of sight from Jill's eyes.

"He's pretending to check something in his car," she said.

Giancarlo recognized Tonelli.

"Ah, he's from Rome. He works for a newspaper."

"I know. He's from *Il Faro*. And his companion doesn't understand the first thing about journalism. She was the one who called me at the villa wanting to schedule an interview. She asked about the children, and I gave her an answer to match the tone of her gossip."

"But she's very sharp, Gian," Jill continued after a brief silence. She was still looking at Tonelli. "She knows I dodged the subject—just like I know that they are following me. And I know that they are not only interested in a story about the children. There is more."

"Like what?"

"Maybe my problem in Atlanta... I don't know. Maybe they know everything."

The word Atlanta carried with it another association: Mike. Giancarlo didn't know how to hide his predicament,

"No matter what happened to you in Atlanta, I think you're mistaken. They came to write a story about the Way of Saint James and the New Age Festival that ended yesterday."

"I have my doubts. But I'll keep my guard up around them. I don't believe they're covering the sacred path. They don't have anything spiritual about them."

Fifteen seconds later, Jill continued,

"The man left. He noticed I was watching him."

Jill went back to examining the road map next to her. She wanted to see exactly how many miles were left to Villavieja del Campo. That caught Giancarlo's attention. He put a finger on the map.

"Hey! Villavieja del Campo is right next to Vallencantado."

"And what is that supposed to mean?"

"That's where we're going."

"Is Vallencantado where you're going to transform into a warlock?"

"How nice to have you back to your normal self, Jill. It's much better this way. But that's exactly right. It's just that I don't know exactly where yet. I only know that it will be near a village called Vallencantado. That's great, don't you think?"

She lifted her eyes off the map.

"Great? Great why? What could happen there that didn't happen here?"

"Well... I was thinking of our friendship."

"Ah. And you… have you been duly authorized to cultivate friendships, Gian?"

It was a barb. But soon a shout broke the impasse,

"*Señorita!*"

Getting up from the car seat, Jill saw that it was someone from *El Rincón*. The man came closer.

"*Señorita*, Don Alberto González told me to say that Manuelito will be getting in from Madrid today. He just called his father to say so."

"So, who is this Manuelito?"

"He's chef Ricardo's son. Manuelito is a mechanic, *Señorita*."

The clouds obscuring Jill's facial expression cleared.

"Ah, yes. When will he be arriving?"

"On the eleven o'clock bus."

"*Muchas gracias, Señor.*"

The man went back into *El Rincón*. Giancarlo noticed that Jill was still not too pleased.

"Looks like you didn't like that news."

They avoided each other's eyes.

"Not exactly, no. It's looking like I'll only be able to get back on the road later today."

Just then they heard the truck honking. It was Menendez, still outside. Michel was also there. Only Maggio was missing.

Giancarlo also didn't seem cheered. Slightly disgruntled, he said, "Well… the time has come. Now we go our separate ways."

He waited for Jill to react in some way. But she didn't. Speechless, she sat back in the car seat and closed the car door. Giancarlo straightened the backpack strap on his shoulder.

"Bye, Jill," he said, stepping aside.

"Bye," she responded evasively.

Then Jill sat and watched Giancarlo's every step to the truck. She felt a tightness in her heart but didn't get up. She stayed and watched the chief sorcerer arrive with his inseparable dogs.

Ten minutes later, the truck was already hitting the main road. Only then did Jill get out of the car. She slammed the door, locked it, and walked back to *El Rincón*.

On the way, she needed a handkerchief and opened her bag. Her fingers touched a folded piece of paper inside. She took it out. She unfolded it. For four seconds, she stared at Giancarlo's drawing.

Then, shoving it back into her bag angrily, she kept walking.

◆ ◆ ◆

WALKING INTO THE SUITE, Tonelli found Isabella sitting on the living room sofa. She was filing her fingernails. She seemed to be deliberately making slow, meditative work of it—back and forth with the nail file. Tonelli understood. The terrible headache was back.

"You know, *Amore...*" she lamented without taking her eyes off the file on her nail, "sometimes I hate myself. Sometimes I berate myself for being so... so cheap. I sell myself out for so little. At times like that, I wish I could just press a button and make myself disappear."

This time Tonelli did not sit on the sofa. It would have been foolish to start this argument over again. He stayed firmly planted where he was.

"Lies disgust me," Isabella continued. She didn't stop filing her nails nor did she look up from her hands. "How long will *noi due* have to lie for such petty things as... as a bowl of soup? Or a soft bed? When will *noi due* use our creativity for something better than... than tricking other people? We are no better than the people who pass crazy rumors on. I think liars like us are all cut from the same cloth."

"Enough, Bella! Enough."

Tonelli's screech was accompanied by a screech from the cell phone on his belt.

It was Vaccaro. Tonelli's world was about to come crashing down.

Nineteen

"**A** boat?!" he shouted.

"Vaccaro, you jerk! What are you telling me? You're saying there's no such person as Domenico Sbroggio Pellegrino and that *Pellegrino* is the name of a boat? What about Domenico Sbroggio?"

"Domenico Sbroggio is the captain of the *Pellegrino*. Where did this whole mix-up start? Someone's taken you for a ride. The *Pellegrino* is a small ship, and it's anchored in the Bay of Naples—for now. But it will soon have to leave."

Miro Vaccaro's search had uncovered more: that thirty-three children orphaned in turf wars between rebel groups in Kurmania were in the *Pellegrino*'s hold. And that an American missionary couple, Benny and Mary Marshall, were coordinating the whole operation.

Tonelli felt stunned by the news. The children did exist. The idea that the late Consul was orchestrating some grand con came crashing down—and that completely destroyed several of Tonelli's dreams. He almost lost his breath.

Abruptly turning off the device, Tonelli left the room, dragging Isabella after him to the restaurant. He left his cell phone on the sofa in the living room.

"You don't want to wait for lunch, which is in two hours, *Señor*?" suggested the waiter.

"Two hours?! No. Lunch is a completely separate issue now," Tonelli responded. He ordered a pizza.

The waiter left and Tonelli got to it. He didn't want to have to swallow what Miro Vaccaro had uncovered. His fiancée then brought up Nezzo Bologna. And that complicated everything. They started arguing again right there at the restaurant table.

When the pizza arrived, they were still arguing. More Tonelli and less Isabella. He absolutely did not want to accept that the late Consul had, in fact, helped a group of war orphans get out of east Africa.

"Vaccaro was sold a sordid fabrication, Bella. He's fallen victim to a Machiavellian ploy. That's it. Vaccaro is a smug man."

He filled his mouth again and reflected.

"But if those children really do exist... and if they still haven't seen one red cent of the money, then I see only one man to blame: Francesco Ricotta. He got hold of the money. Right Bella? It was his brother-in-law's betrayal that made Consul Heston die from disgust. That must be exactly what happened."

Isabella just chewed—and in no hurry. It was as if she wasn't even there. Tonelli didn't like that.

"When is this headache of yours gonna go away? Can't you see that life is still going on around us?"

There was no response.

"But anyway, I blame Consul Heston. He never should have given Ricotta a chance. Maybe on a deeper level they were in cahoots. Do you agree, Bella?"

Isabella set her cutlery aside. She was finished.

"*Va bene!*" Tonelli contradicted himself again. "Let's go back to the suite. I have to talk to Vaccaro again."

The bill signed, Tonelli took the leftover pizza, and they went upstairs.

Back in the suite, he picked up his cell phone.

"Hey, Tonelli," Vaccaro chided him, "why did you hang up on me? I wasn't done yet."

"Vaccaro, you jerk. Where did you dig up that deceptive information? I don't believe a single thing you told me."

"Tough luck, Tonelli. The source is Nico Sacchi."

"What? That Sicilian with a Mafia-trained nose?"

"The very same."

Miro Vaccaro told him that he had been getting his shoes shined in Palermo when he saw Nico Sacchi. Sacchi said that the *Pellegrino* was in the process of being fined for skirting customs: they had been moored there for two months but still hadn't submitted embarkation or disembarkation forms to the harbormaster.

"And they aren't going to," Miro Vaccaro continued. "That was what Nico Sacchi told me. He told me he has a man on the inside. That was how I learned everything."

"Nico Sacchi…" repeated Tonelli. There was that bucktoothed *mafioso* again. "And what else does Nico Sacchi know?"

"What else does he have to know? Nico earns his keep on shoeshine, it's his thing… and it's where he reads newspapers and hears conversations."

Yet again, Tonelli abruptly hung up on Miro Vaccaro. He threw himself down on the sofa. He tried to combine the old ingredients with the new ones. Talk and think, think and talk. The recipe always came out tasting the same: there still must have been some deception even if the late Consul Heston never lied. He still wanted Heston to be a criminal—that made everything easier. A criminal American Consul and his brother-in-law, a politician from Milan, both colluding behind the scenes—it would make the perfect dish. An internationally famous dish.

"Take the Consul out of this mess," said Isabella, shaking her nail polish bottle all the while. "He was a great man. And he got double crossed."

This isn't so bad, Tonelli. It's not so bad. No matter what, Nezzo Bologna will still be happy to hear that Ricotta—*BAM!* —snatched up the aid money from America.

Tonelli was already swallowing that idea when it occurred to him that Jill Heston was probably just as innocent as her father.

"What now? In that case, what money is she looking for, Bella?"

Isabella was now painting her first fingernail. She didn't look up to respond,

"I always suspected we were on the wrong track. Ever since we met that guy Peppino at Villa Piomondo."

"Peppino? *Perché?*"

Isabella still didn't turn her attention away from what she was doing. She said, "Our obsession limited us—we acted like kids. Except our minds. Our minds were still tainted."

"Enough, Bella! Enough." Tonelli shouted.

It was because of a knock at the door. He went to open up. It was Don Alberto González.

"*Señor* Tonelli, regarding the people I was telling you about. They're all waiting downstairs right now, including Bishop Buendia and the mayor of Puebla Rosada."

"What? Bishop? Mayor?"

"The illustrious men who will debunk everything you heard from that *borracho* Don García, *Señor* Tonelli. Didn't we schedule a meeting for this morning?"

"Ah, yes, yes, of course. That's right. I forgot. Of course, Don Alberto. I'll be down in ten minutes."

"*Muy bien.*"

The door closed and Tonelli tore straight into the pizza box. He ate one piece and picked up another. But only then did he notice that he'd turned off his cell phone again. With his free hand he pressed the button. The second the device turned on, it squealed.

"Is this some kind of joke to you, Tonelli? How long am I meant to sit here waiting for you to turn on your cell phone? Do you have any idea what time it is? I've been off the clock for a while now."

"*Va bene.* You can tell me everything now. Let's try and wrap this up quick. I'm already fed up."

"I didn't even find out this part of the information, but telling you ended up being my problem because they told me I should call you. It's about the American woman Jill Heston. She's half American and half Italian, they say. She got a PhD in Clinical Psychology but left a teaching job to work in a restaurant."

"What? A restaurant?"

"Yeah. But not as a cook or a hostess or anything. She came up with a novel method of bringing in repeat business—and it multiplied the profits of the Atlanta restaurant that hired her. They ended up paying her five times as much as she was earning as a professor—and she was sending her wages to

Italy to pay for her father's restoration project."

"*Davvero?* So, what did she do to attract all those people?"

Vaccaro laughed.

"There has to be some hearsay in all of this, Tonelli. But the news stories say she would analyze the dish a customer ordered, then inspect their face, belly and—get this—most of all how they chewed. Then she would jot something down on a piece of paper and have it sent to the customer. Word is people liked it because you basically got a free session with a talented psychic on top of your meal."

"*Oddio!* What lunacy!" Tonelli muttered, scarcely believing what Vaccaro was telling him.

Miro Vaccaro emphasized, "The thing is, one day she happened to send a note to a bigshot businessman she didn't know. And according to the newspaper, she literally quoted the Book of Job to him "*The eye of the adulterer waits for the twilight, Saying, 'No eye will see me'; And he disguises his face.*" She sent it while the man was having dinner with his wife. She dumped a bowl of hot pea soup right over his head."

"*Oddio!* What a waste!"

"And you know what happened the next morning, Tonelli? She filed for divorce. This destabilized the company's shares and, of course, created major financial shockwaves in Atlanta."

"*E dopo?*" Tonelli asked.

"After that, faced with an imminent lawsuit for libel and moral and pecuniary damages from that businessman, she just up and disappeared. The Board of Psychology was about to expel her. It was chaos. They say she fled to Italy. It was around that time that her father suddenly died."

Miro Vaccaro concluded,

"But do you know how the story ended? That businessman ended up hospitalized with a bullet between his ribs. And guess who shot him?"

"His mistress, of course."

"Close. Only he didn't have a *mistress*. He had a *mister*. And with this new evidence that publicized his extra-marital affair, the businessman lost his case against her. I don't think she's even aware that, if she went back to Atlanta, she could continue her previous work. That's a pretty happy ending, *nevvero?*"

"*Sì*," managed Tonelli, still somewhat stunned by the news. "Bye, Vaccaro."

"Hey, wait a sec, Tonelli. I'm not done yet. Mila told me to say that Francesco Ricotta has given up politics for good. Ran out of steam. Bank debts. Bye, *bello*. And don't forget that you owe me two bottles of whiskey now."

After turning off his cell phone, Tonelli went back to his piece of pizza.

◆ ◆ ◆

It was three o'clock on a hot afternoon.

A stray dog barked in the distance. In the nearby forest, a large group of birds twittered jubilantly. Tonelli was looking out his window, taking in the landscape and the sounds, but his mind was still going over the events of the previous day.

After that, around noon, head pounding, he went down to eat lunch. He had a chicken pie with white beans. He ate alone. Isabella claimed she wasn't hungry.

And now—at three in the afternoon—his shirt soaked with sweat, for a moment Tonelli thought back on his brief meeting with Don Alberto González and his illustrious friends. The three men were outraged by Don García's behavior. Tonelli tallied up how many times the word *borracho* had been used during the meeting: thirteen. Maybe they didn't have any other facts they could use against the ex-priest.

To cut the meeting short, Tonelli ended up accepting that the bones of an apostle of Jesus *might* have been in a tomb in Santiago de Compostela. This new historical revision provoked another flareup of Isabella's headache. And there was no shower that could dampen the heat of her annoyance.

◆ ◆ ◆

It was three-thirty in the afternoon.

Getting up off the sofa, Tonelli turned on his tape recorder for the fourth time that day. And for the fourth time he listened to the recording of the conversation between the late Consul Heston and Senator Frank Borsato.

Tonelli's brain was boiling—and it had nothing to do with Jill Heston's shenanigans in the Atlanta restaurant. No. It was because of everything else Miro Vaccaro had discovered.

But now, he sat as still as a statue while he analyzed the recording again. Suddenly he gave a shout and jumped off the sofa. And his enthusiasm burst forth.

"*Evviva!*" he celebrated, pumping his left fist.

Frightened, Isabella pointed at the front door. She saw that her fiancé was already throwing his belongings into his suitcase.

"We're leaving, Bella! Quick, pack! We aren't stopping until Barcelona!"

"Barcelona?!"

Tonelli closed his suitcase.

"We have to find the *Pellegrino* right away, Bella *mia*! And I want you to take some nice pictures. After that we'll go back to Naples to celebrate."

Tonelli squeezed his fiancée's shoulders.

"Bella! Bella! I knew a miracle would happen to me one day! It had to!"

He pumped his fist in the air again. Skeptical, Isabella asked,

"And where does that man enter into all of this?"

"Bologna? Nowhere. You'll see. He isn't involved! I'm free of Nezzo Bologna!"

"And that cocky old politician?"

"Him too! I'm also free of Francesco Ricotta! I'm free of both of them!"

Squeezing Isabella's shoulders again, he topped it all off,

"I figured everything out, Bella *mia*! Everything! It's a mess! And a big one! How could I be so blind? *Oddio*! I just need one person to confirm it: Missionary Marshall."

Tonelli hugged his fiancée and twirled her in the air.

"Our 'round-the-world trip is right around the corner, Bella *mia*!"

"You can forget that old trick," said a restrained Isabella, wriggling out of her fiancé's arms to go get changed.

"*Ma cosa…!*" went Tonelli. The serious tone of her words spooked him.

On the way to the room, Isabella stopped. Turning around, in a serious tone, she went as far as to say, "I don't know what you intend to do in Barcelona. I don't know what Missionary Marshall knows that could possibly be so important. But I do know that I'm tired of talking about this. Count me out. I'll go my own way from there. I want to get back home as quickly as I can."

Twenty

High on the rugged slope of its eponymous valley, Vallencantado Castle was much more than just some mound of old medieval ruins, like so many others found throughout the northwest of Spain. It was perfect for their needs, as it has the characteristic the tradition prized most: isolation. Like the ancient hard-to-access caverns they also traditionally used, these ruins made it difficult for those not affiliated with the Order to stumble upon their initiation ritual.

This was the focus of the brief lecture given by Amaro Maggio while he, Menendez, Giancarlo, and Michel were busy clearing a passageway into the grand atrium. From it, there were doors leading to innumerable chambers—including circular stone stairways that led to the top of two gigantic cylindrical towers. Both were partially in ruins.

Caesar gave Amaro Maggio's hand a cool lick. It annoyed him.

"Get out of here Caesar! Hey, Sancho! I already told you to keep the dogs tied up."

Menendez set aside the huge dry branch he was carrying and went to the truck. He came back holding two dog collars and long leashes. He took the dogs and tied them to convenient bronze loops on the crumbling remains of a fallen door.

Clearing a path through to the long atrium took more than half an hour. Now all that was left was to prepare one of the chambers for the night's ceremony.

Forty more minutes and everything was satisfactory. Looking down from one of the watchtowers, Maggio filled his lungs with the noble air of the valley.

"It's marvelous out here! Do you think I could buy these ruins? Who knows? Maybe in the future we could have another spiritual retreat center here. The magical ambience of the ancients is present. Don't you feel it?"

Michel had a bit to say about that. Giancarlo just kept to himself, looking out at the landscape from the other watchtower.

A while later, they made their descent and went back into the atrium. Maggio stayed behind to untie the dogs from the bronze ring. Giancarlo and Michel left the castle. They crossed a small bridge—a former drawbridge—over the moat, which was connected to a stream. They reached the truck quickly.

"I've never seen him so... so relaxed, so happy," Michel said to Giancarlo.

Giancarlo couldn't deny it. Maggio seemed like a teenager. But he had to add, "Jill said something strange. She asked who Maggio was hiding from."

"Hiding?" Michel wanted to laugh. "Where'd she get that crazy idea?"

Giancarlo stared into Michel's eyes.

"I think from the same source that told her the truth about the woman who was cheating on her husband."

Michel stayed silent.

Giancarlo continued, "Do you think Maggio was having problems in Genoa that he didn't want to share, Michel?"

"How ridiculous. His business was going very well, you know that. And his ex-wife, who used to give him trouble, is remarried now. She lives in Belgium. I've never seen Maggio looking so confident and carefree."

Amaro Maggio walked over, playing with the Dobermans. Menendez followed. When they reached the truck, Maggio said, "Sancho, leave the materials in a box for me. Did you bring shampoo like I told you?"

"Of course, *Signore*."

"Great. I'm going to give them a bath. Water is one thing this place has plenty of. I want their fur gleaming for tonight."

Amaro Maggio now turned to Michel and Giancarlo. "And I have to be fair, let's face it. Caesar and Nero have been with me since the week after my initiation." Maggio laughed. "They were two cute little puppies then. I remember all the trouble they got into. And they would only drink milk. They were a gift from McDowell, did you know that? So, I think it is only right for them to take part in our celebration."

Maggio looked out at the green valley. He breathed in the pure air.

"It's just so nice here! I'm glad I came. I feel like I'm back in the medieval age, this castle is bustling and I'm dreaming up a million plans to conquer the yet-unsettled world. I feel like I recognize every one of these rocks. Who knows, maybe I'll find out that I used to live here—and that I used to be one of the Knights Templar?"

With a happy expression on his face, he went back to the other two men,

"And I'm glad you came with me. We're going to have some unforgettable experiences in this castle. You'll see."

Menendez took hold of the truck's steering wheel. Maggio himself closed the door.

"What time should we come back?" asked Menendez, starting up the vehicle.

"I think eight o'clock should work. I want to start the ritual before eight-thirty. McDowell said he would be arriving from the village by 6:00 PM at the latest."

Maggio had special instructions for Michel and Giancarlo,

"And you two: try to spend the hours we have left like they're the most important two hours of your lives. Concentrate. Don't waste a single minute on what might be happening around you. Now you can go."

◆ ◆ ◆

It was one-thirty when lunch was served. Giancarlo went to find Don Miguel, the owner of the guesthouse. He had his four-year-old grandson Pedrito on his lap. Giancarlo asked him how to catch the bus on the highway.

"Just drive up to the stop."

"I don't want to. I'd rather walk. I heard you mention a shortcut."

The man took Giancarlo to the door and showed him the way.

"*Gracias*, Don Miguel."

As Giancarlo snuck behind the house to get on the path, Michel appeared in front of him.

"I can't believe you're going after her."

Giancarlo waited a moment to reply,

"What now, Michel? Are you going to run off to the castle and tell our master?"

"Of course not. I'm just finding this absurd, you're... you're shirking your responsibilities."

"Don't worry. I'll be back before eight."

"We're going down to the valley at seven-thirty."

"All right. I'll be here."

With that, Giancarlo stepped around Michel and got back on the path.

Twenty-One

Crossing the Mediterranean Sea south of Corsica and north of Sardinia—deviating from the route the *Navigatore* usually followed between Barcelona and Palermo—was costing almost a third of what Tonelli managed to get for selling his old car. Isabella did a lot of grumbling over that act of lunacy.

Eight hours earlier, still on the docks of Barcelona, they had been at yet another impasse. Isabella wanted to go back to Rome. She was tired of her fiancé's *garbugli*.

But he insisted, "It will all be worth it, Bella. Believe me. Once this is all over, I'll buy you a brand-new car."

"What else are you going to do, pray tell? You want to go find a ship without knowing where it is. And for what? Answer me! I am no longer willing to be an accessory to your schemes. Enough!"

"Bella!"

"Don't you think it's time to come clean? Why did you suddenly become so interested in this Missionary Benny Marshall when we were at *El Rincón?* What do you think you're going to find?"

"I've already found everything, trust me. All that's left is to confirm it. Just give me one more chance. *Per favore*, Bella."

Tonelli was just short of falling to his knees there on the docks of Barcelona. But Isabella was not going to give in—and not just because their old car had accumulated yet more problems during the rest of their trip. Pulling out a spark plug, Tonelli had found one last issue. And that was the deciding blow. They traded the car for a paltry sum.

And now there they were on board a cargo ship called the *Navigatore*. The captain was a formidable man from Taranto.

The problem was the *Pellegrino*'s exact location. The captain of the *Navigatore* was in no mood to scour the whole Mediterranean looking for the ship.

"The *Navigatore* has to arrive in Palermo on schedule," he repeated. "If you do not sight the *Pellegrino* near Sardinia, you two will have to disembark there. Either that or come with me to Palermo. For that I won't add a single cent."

Palermo didn't interest Tonelli. And neither did staying in Sardinia.

"What do you think, Bella?"

"Me? I don't think anything," she responded, holding tight to her unyielding mood. She was only there because she had been overruled.

He cleaned the lenses of his glasses in silence.

"That's the third time you've done that today," she said.

Tonelli put the glasses back on. More silence.

"I don't know what's going on in that crazy head of yours," she started again. "I really don't. And I also don't know why I'm still here with you. All I know is that we're still standing."

"Hmm. If you could just give me an idea of how to locate the *Pellegrino*!"

The ship captain came over to them.

"So? Have you made up your minds? Either get off in Sardinia or stay aboard until Palermo."

With that, he walked away.

"*E ora*, Bella? What are we going to do?"

"We? You, *caro mio*! I'm not saying anything, I already told you. *Niente*! You dragged me out here against my will. And you sold the car against my will. I would have said to fix it, and we'd be getting into Rome by now."

Tonelli couldn't see her rationale. He went to ask the captain if he had any snacks. He did. Dried fish.

Tonelli made a disgusted face.

"*Che schifo!*"

He returned to where Isabella was.

"Bella... I need your help. Why don't you work with me on this? Without you helping me think, I get stuck."

"Count me out—at least as long as I don't know the whole story. Just the fact that you're hiding things from me tells me there is something nasty going on. At *El Rincón*, you said you were free of Nezzo Bologna and Francesco Ricotta. And that's great. But then *who* or *what* came to take their place? Because there must be something else. I know you."

That time, her arguments softened Tonelli.

"*Va bene, mia cara.* But if I tell you, will you make up with me?"

"Maybe."

They walked out of earshot of the captain. And he told her everything—or almost everything. He said as much as he thought she needed to know to help him, anyway.

Nevertheless, it caught her off guard. Isabella said, "All right. If what you told me is true, *Amore*, then we have to act fast."

"*Amore?* You called me *Amore*, Bella?! That's great! *Ma come?* How can we be fast? Will we fly off to find the *Pellegrino?*"

"Listen. If you want to know where a ship is moored, wouldn't the most logical path be to get in touch with the harbormaster and ask?"

Tonelli pumped the fist of his left hand.

"*Brava*, Bella! Vaccaro said that the *Pellegrino* was in the jurisdiction of Naples."

Taking the cell phone off his belt, he looked up the information and found the number he was after.

Three minutes later, he heard, "Try Cagliari, *Signore*. The *Pellegrino* has left the Bay of Naples. I'll give you the number."

"*Grazie, Signorina.*"

A few minutes later, Tonelli heard from the Cagliari harbormaster, "The *Pellegrino* is just setting off, *signore*."

"What? *Oddio!* And where is it heading?"

"One moment, let me check the log."

At his side, Isabella asked what was happening.

"A disaster, Bella! The ship has already left."

Seconds later, their savior was back, "The *Pellegrino* is heading for the Red Sea, *Signore*. But I'm just being told there's been a holdup. It's still in the harbor."

"*Grazie, grazie!*"

Tonelli slammed the phone shut and put it back on his belt. He went off to find the captain.

"How far are we from Cagliari, Captain?"

"Who said I'm going to Cagliari?"

The man's tone was stern. Tonelli rubbed his chin.

"*Per favore*, it's important. Very important. The *Pellegrino* is moored in the port of Cagliari, but it will raise anchor at any moment. I need to get there before it's too late."

Now it was the captain's turn to stroke his beard. Isabella could see in his eyes that he was carrying out some complex mental arithmetic.

 Standing in front of her fiancé, she asked the man, "How much will it cost?"

"*Ebbene...*"

She heard the price. In her head, she quickly performed one division and two subtractions. Then she made a counterproposal. They reached an agreement easily.

In a matter of moments, the ship accelerated to maximum speed.

Twenty-Two

Villavieja del Campo was a small town—two hundred small ancient houses centered around a *plaza*, which was nearly deserted at that time in the afternoon. Except for three boys playing in the corner of the square and two women chatting next to them, Giancarlo was the only person there. He got up off the stone bench when he saw Jill's car. She looked somewhat surprised—happily surprised.

"What are you doing here?"

Giancarlo walked slowly over.

"I thought you'd gotten lost. You took so long."

"Walk around and get in, Gian. It's really hot outside."

He did.

"So, did your master bring you here?"

Giancarlo threatened to laugh.

"What's so funny?"

"I already said I like seeing you this way, Jill. It's more authentic. No, it wasn't Maggio. A bus dropped me off at the village gate."

"And your friends, where are they?"

"We're staying at a guesthouse in Vallencantado. It's an ancient village. I sort of snuck away. I walked to the highway and caught a bus."

"All this fuss just to get here?"

"Not just to get here: to see you. I was starting to miss you."

"Hmm. Who'd have thought?"

"But what about you?" Giancarlo continued. "What have you learned about the man you came here to find?"

"When I got to the village, I asked half a dozen people and none of them had ever heard of Giovanni di Stefano. And all the roads end at this square, so here I am. But do you know what I'm starting to realize? It was crazy to have come on this trip. I put too much faith in the words of a drunk."

Giancarlo saw three men leaving a building on the other side of the *plaza*.

"Wanna try them?" he asked.

She drove around the square and stopped next to the three men. She stuck her head out and asked in Spanish,

"Please, I'm looking for a man by the name of Giovanni di Stefano. He's Italian."

The three kept their heads down. But a fourth man came out. He was thin with sharp features, wearing a big hat, and was probably a bit older than fifty. After asking the others, he squatted on his heels next to the car. He was fiddling with a straw cigarette.

"There's a man called Giovanni near my farm, *Señorita*. He has a little piece of land, a few sheep. I don't know if his surname is di Stefano. But I know he's Italian."

"How old do you think he is?"

"Over seventy."

"Must be the guy. How do I get there?"

"Look, well, it's kinda hard to explain."

"Could you maybe show me the way to your farm, then, *Señor*?"

"Only tomorrow morning. I still have some things to take care of around here today. I'm only going back to the farm tomorrow. But his is right next to mine."

"How many miles?"

"Seven. And the road is pretty bad. When it's raining, you can't get there by car."

Jill looked from side to side.

"Do you think I can find anyone to take me there today?"

"It'll be pretty hard, *Señorita*."

"Okay then. We'll meet up tomorrow morning. Let's agree to meet at eight."

"If you can guarantee you'll be there, *Señorita*, I'll wait. If not, I'll catch the only bus of the day. It's pretty early."

"You can wait for me right here, I'll be here."

"*Bueno*. I'd like to take my niece with me, too. She's ten. Will that be a problem?"

"Not at all."

The man walked away.

"What's your name, sir?"

"Jorge Valverde."

"Okay then, see you tomorrow at eight, *Señor* Valverde."

"*Hasta mañana*."

The man walked away. Giancarlo checked the time.

"I think I have to go," he said. "I was told that the last bus back is in half an hour."

"How many miles is it to Vallencantado from here?"

"Forty on asphalt, but three on dirt."

"How about I take you there?"

"No, Jill, it wouldn't be appropriate."

"Why? Did you run away?"

He squeezed out a laugh.

"More or less."

"I see. Well don't let that stop us: I'll just drop you off before we get into the village. Then I'll come back here. Would that be all right?"

"I... I don't know if it's the right thing to do. I made commitments, and outsiders are not permitted. It's serious, Jill. In fact, I'm supposed to be deep in meditation right now—and not here talking to you."

"Woah, you're risking your neck because of me? Then let me alleviate my conscience, Gian. Let's do what I said. I'll drop you off then I'll leave."

Gazing into her eyes, he asked, "Then it's just a matter of conscience, is that it?"

She maintained eye contact for a few seconds. Then looked away. She seemed spooked.

Giancarlo said, "Well… I think we're starting to intrude into each other's dreams."

She started driving.

"And is that good or bad?"

"I guess it means that we're not in the same dream, right?"

"Then it's bad—according to that drifter friend of yours."

Giancarlo had nothing to add.

◆ ◆ ◆

THEY REACHED THE OUTSKIRTS of the village at exactly 7:20 PM—it was still a bright night, not too dark.

As they wound down the little dirt road, it felt like it would never end. From five hundred yards away, you could see the whole settlement. Giancarlo couldn't see the truck. In fact, he didn't see a single vehicle by the guesthouse.

"What is it?" asked Jill, noticing his apprehension.

"I think we're too late."

"But it isn't even half past seven yet. Well, what should I do now? Stop to let you out or…"

"Keep going. I need to make sure. Maybe Menendez went to bring Michel to the castle and will be coming back to get McDowell and the others."

Giancarlo was mistaken. Don Miguel soon informed him that the truck and another blue car had already left for the castle.

"Oh no! What a mess I've made!" said Jill.

"Don't worry. I knew what I was getting into."

"Show me the way so I can take you closer to the castle."

Giancarlo had to agree.

"Would you be able to drive without the headlights on?"

"I can try."

"You see that big tree?"

"Mm-hm."

"Go that way and take a left."

Twenty-Three

The *Pellegrino*.

It was a small ship. The name, quite faded, was missing half an L and two-thirds of an O. But that didn't diminish Tonelli and Bella's enthusiasm.

The captain of the *Navigatore* came over to them.

"We found it, Captain," Tonelli said.

"Negative. We're five minutes too late. The *Pellegrino* just finished raising anchor."

Tonelli watched the ship leaving a serene wake in the water behind it.

"*Oddio!*" he grumbled. "Just what I needed." Waving his arms, Tonelli ran over to the deck railing.

"Hey! Wait!" he shouted.

Isabella joined him. Desperate, they shouted and flailed their arms.

◆ ◆ ◆

TEN MINUTES EARLIER, when the order had been given to raise anchor, Benny Marshall stood on the bow, leaning on the railing and looking south.

Marshall was a strong, calm man, and he always had a smile on his lips.

He was fifty-four years old. Within seventy hours they would be back where they had come from, and that had left him with the bitter taste of defeat. Nevertheless, he was still tranquil. He had done everything in his power to stop it from happening. He fought with everything he had. Their request to disembark had been denied several times. Consul Heston's death had brought the whole project to a crashing halt.

Was there something he could have done?

"Don't be like that, Benny," said his wife Mary. She had snuck up on him softly as ever. She was a gentle woman and quite youthful despite her forty-six years. She rested her head on her husband's shoulder. "You did the best you could."

A sweet hymn drifted up to the deck.

"Do they know we're going back yet?" asked Marshall.

"No. Not yet. I want them to sing their hearts out now, because later..."

After a few moments, Benny Marshall said, "There was a moment, Mary, when I thought everything would turn out okay... that we would win. That was two months ago. I believed there would be a miracle like the many I've seen before. But now, going back to where we started... I don't know. I don't know what to expect. And I don't mean for us two, Mary."

"I know." Mary ran her hand through her husband's hair. "I know you very well. I know how you suffer for the children."

Domenico Sbroggio, captain of the *Pellegrino*, walked up and anchored his arms to the deck railing. He was as tall and strong as the missionary, but decidedly less meek. He looked at the horizon over the sea following Marshall's example and said, "Finally, I'll be able to sleep at home, Missionary."

Marshall said nothing. What could he say? That they were hanging by a thread because of that long, two-month wait? And all because one day he, Benny Marshall, put his faith in a miracle? What could he say?

Marshall knew very well that Sbroggio was not the owner of the ship. He had people above him and a company behind him. A company that relied on numbers to stay alive. Numbers—and not tears of pity. What was there to say? When he was alive, Consul Heston had friends in high places to help them out. But Heston was dead now.

And with him, the chance for things to turn out right.

Benny Marshall said in shaky Italian, "I'm sorry for all the trouble we've caused, Captain Sbroggio. Mary and I know how much you fought for all of us."

Sbroggio gave a tragicomic click of his tongue. And asked, "How many years did you fight in Vietnam, Missionary?"

"Three and a half."

"Hmm. Maybe now you'll have to spend seven doing forced labor in the salt mines, Missionary Marshall to pay the debt from this charter. And me too."

Only Mary didn't find it funny.

Domenico Sbroggio kept joking around,

"Or maybe they'll put me in prison for the rest of my life for delaying our return so long. Or they might make this my last voyage as captain. But I don't think I care. I've been thinking about retiring. I'm sick of the sea's surprises, Missionary."

The two stayed there, leaning with their arms on the railing, resting their bodies. Mary was still by her husband's side.

"I don't fear the salt mines, Captain," Marshall said. "Our two sons have already graduated and now they're missionaries in South America. My wife Mary and I have learned how to get by on just bread and water over the years. And sometimes even without bread. We aren't thinking of ourselves. We're thinking about the kids, what will become of them. They have nowhere to go, just like many others in the same situation. The two of us didn't intend to stay here. Mary and I were always going to go back to provide emergency services to the people there. Mostly for the innocent victims."

"Maybe a miracle will still happen," said Mary.

"A miracle?" Sbroggio wasn't really mocking the missionary's wife. But he felt the tickle of humor. "It'll be a miracle if I ever get another job—and if you don't go to the salt mines, Missionary. But I never believed in miracles. That's why no more false alarms will be getting in the way of the course I just set for the *Pellegrino*. I think there's been enough of that already. It's above my authority now."

"We understand, captain. And we're grateful. None of us went hungry for two whole months."

"It was like the feeding of the five thousand."

Sbroggio gave a chuckle.

"Are they signaling us from that ship?" asked Mary.

The two men looked to the portside. Sbroggio removed the hat from his head and made it into a visor.

"They actually are," he confirmed. "Either that or they're swatting flies."

"It's a man and a woman," Mary continued.

Sbroggio looked through a pair of binoculars.

"The *Navigatore*. It's a cargo ship. And quite an old one. I don't think it's flies after all. They must want to talk to us. Who knows? Maybe that guy is the angel you've been waiting for all this time."

"But didn't you just say you don't believe in miracles, captain?" Mary Marshall called him out. "I'm about to start laughing now."

Domenico Sbroggio paused a second before replying, "Miracle or not, if I get my money, I promise to believe in it... the money that is."

Turning aside, Sbroggio asked them to give him the megaphone. Moments later, he boomed out, "What is the problem, *Navigatore*?"

But not much dialogue was possible at that distance. They could hear just enough for Benny Marshall to realize they were looking for him. And that the salt air had destroyed the *Navigatore*'s megaphone, and their lifeboat was a bathtub.

"Half a miracle," Sbroggio reproached. Then he gave an order for a dinghy to be let down and told one of his sailors to take Marshall over to the *Navigatore*.

"I'll keep the engines off for forty-five minutes at most, Missionary. Until nightfall. You can't stay here—unless you want to lose your ride back to the salt mines."

When the dinghy had made it halfway over to the other boat, Sbroggio lowered his head.

"Sometimes I feel like I don't recognize myself. I don't know why in the world I stayed here for two months!"

"It wasn't down to you how long the *Pellegrino* stayed here, Captain Sbroggio. It was God's providence."

Sbroggio turned around. And the question came out serious,

"You mean we stayed against my will, *Signora* Mary?"

"Exactly right, Captain. God can bring forth fresh springs from dry land—just to make sure no one goes thirsty."

◆ ◆ ◆

Twenty minutes later, once on board the *Navigatore*, Benny Marshall was talking to Tonelli and Isabella. They found some privacy on the far end of the bow. Their dialogue took place in a mix of Marshall's crude Italian and Tonelli's sorry English. In fits and starts—and always touched up by Isabella—Tonelli recounted the better part of the story. Marshall's silence served as full confirmation of Tonelli's words.

After briefly thinking it over, Benny Marshall asked,

"How did you learn that about Senator Frank Borsato?"

With a certain air of mystery and some vagueness, Tonelli raised his shoulders and showed the palms of his hands.

"Professional secret, Missionary."

"Please," Marshall begged. "This is the kind of thing... there are facts that you cannot put in your newspaper. Would you be able to guarantee that you won't print some things? It's just that the little that I know can't be confirmed. I'm not asking for myself, you know.

"Hmm... I... yes, I promise. I'm just trying to help, Missionary. I'm not looking for a scoop. Trust me."

Tonelli was drawn in by the sparkles in Isabella's eyes. The sparkles were blue, but they contained the following phrases outlined in crimson, "*You lying creep! You'll pay if you break that promise.*"

Tonelli turned to Marshall.

"The thing with the money is practically taken care of, Missionary. Captain Domenico Sbroggio will be happy to know that."

"Definitely. We were already on our way back to Kurmania—or some other part of Africa. I have to say that your arrival at this precise moment is almost a miracle, Mr. Tonelli. It could be a piece of the miracle we were so desperately hoping for. But... the one thing I'm finding strange is that Ms. Heston never contacted me."

"She hasn't had time, Missionary. Trust me. She's traveling around the north of Spain. But she's very, very resourceful. She must be getting in touch with the man who has the money you need right now."

"Who is this man, do you know?"

"Yes, of course. He goes by the name of Giovanni di Stefano. Seems to be quite rich. In the past, this Giovanni and a few other friends received many favors from Jill's grandfather. But now it's payback time, right?"

Marshall looked at Tonelli as if searching for sincerity. Staying firm, Tonelli said, "But let's go back to the subject you're most interested in. The money problem is solved. The issue now is disembarking. And that's why we're here. We want to help—and we can help."

"How?"

"To get the authorization to disembark. My partner and I can take care of it."

Standing not far away, Isabella wrinkled her eyebrows. Another scheme. She seemed to be living in some sort of episodic nightmare.

Marshall, next to him, liked what Tonelli had to say.

"I'll do whatever it takes to make that happen," he said.

"Then we have to go to the *Pellegrino*, Missionary. We have to take some pictures of the Kurmanian children. My newspaper will fight the good fight, but we need proof. We need to move public opinion. With the photos and some other stuff, we can bring the authorities in my country to their senses. I promise you that."

Isabella was on the verge of passing out. That was a pitch and then some—although thankfully brief.

"All right," said the Missionary. "Let's do it right now before it gets dark."

"Great," said Tonelli, rubbing his hands together.

When he turned back to talk to Isabella, he saw that she was leaning on the deck railing, eyes lost in the sea.

Tonelli left the missionary deep in conversation with the captain of the *Navigatore* and approached his fiancée.

"Bella..."

"Don't you dare talk to me, you...!" she whispered with rage, without turning around. "My head is exploding again."

Tonelli joined her at the railing. To outside eyes, they both appeared to be simply admiring the waves of the sea.

"What's on that rotten mind of yours?" Isabella went back to whispering. "How long have you known about the money they need? And how much for the photos of the children? What kind of harebrained scheme are you cooking up now?"

"The paper is gonna need them for..."

"You're lying! You aren't thinking about your paper. Or those kids. What are you trying to do now?"

The rage had sketched Isabella's lips into two pale thin lines in desperate need of lipstick.

Tonelli looked away. He saw the captain leaving the missionary alone. He didn't offer any additional argument. He made his excuses for Isabella as he walked back to join Marshall.

"My partner is... she's not feeling well, Missionary. It's her first time on a ship, *capisce?*"

"Yes, I understand."

"But the two of us can go. I'll go get the camera."

◆ ◆ ◆

IT WAS GETTING DARK.

Captain Domenico Sbroggio didn't ascribe the news he was hearing to a miracle. His opinion was amenable to change, of course, provided he got his hands on the money. Then maybe he would consider it miraculous.

"Just one caveat..." he warned, "I'll only wait until tomorrow at noon. Not a minute longer. Got it?"

"Thank you, Captain," said Marshall.

Tonelli said nothing. His mind wasn't on what Captain Sbroggio was saying—it was on the camera. He had discovered that it had only three shots left on the roll. And no spare film.

"Let's go down," said Marshall, getting them all moving.

Mary Marshall was at the bottom of the stairs linking the double hold to the upper deck. She was waiting for the two men to come down. Benny introduced her to the Italian journalist.

"He has good news, Mary. It's the miracle we were waiting for. The money is coming. And the authorization to disembark."

"Praise be to God!" Mary exulted, clasping her hands together.

Almost buzzing, Tonelli looked around.

"Where are the children?"

"Come with me," said Mary. Tonelli followed. Marshall was close behind.

The *Pellegrino* was a small, twenty-five-year-old merchant ship. Its double hold—the area between the bilge and the deck—was watertight, with no cracks or windows. The only way for air to get in was through two hatches in the deck.

They walked over to a tarp that stretched from floor to ceiling. Mary opened a crack and went through. Inside was a third hatch for light with no ladder. Seconds later, Mary opened the tarp again for Tonelli to come through. He tucked his camera under his arm and went in.

Suddenly, there was sound. It was the children's hymn, smooth, sweet, content, full of warmth. The Italian refrain rang out, *"Blessed be the soles of the feet of the man who brings good tidings."*

Tonelli's jaw felt stiff, his tongue frozen. The camera was shaking in his hands. He tried to take the first shot. The flash didn't go off. He tried a second. The flash didn't work again. He tried a third time, but there were no shots left on the film.

Then, slowly, he set the camera down. He looked at Mary Marshall. Then he turned his gaze back toward the children's gaunt little faces. Their cheeks were somewhat emaciated, and their eyes were big and, incredibly, they smiled at him.

Then he needed to pull his handkerchief out of his bag. And he began wiping the sweat off his forehead.

Twenty-Four

Amaro Maggio's truck and Richard McDowell's four-door sedan were parked in front of Vallencantado Castle. Jill stopped her car just over eighty yards away on a bend in the abysmal gravel road. Surrounded by the darkness of night lit only by the waxing moon, she sat contemplating the walls of the castle with their innumerable lookouts and two partially crumbling central towers.

"You look nervous," she said to Giancarlo. "Could something go wrong?"

"I hope not."

"When do you have to go in?"

"Eight."

"We still have twenty minutes. Tell me about your ritual. Or is that against the rules?"

"Sort of. And the stuff that I *can* tell you is boring."

"I see. Then tell me what you stand to gain from this. The secrets of a spell to transform metal into gold? A sliver of the philosopher's stone? Do you know if the philosopher's stone can actually be broken, Gian?"

She had to laugh.

"It must be something fantastic. Otherwise you wouldn't come this far to meet in a medieval hole like this one. Someone will put their hand on your head... maybe put a gash in your forehead with some ancient dagger and say something like 'Giancarlo, you are consecrated. Now you may go and perform your miracles throughout the world!' Is that it?"

"Jill! Jill...!" Giancarlo held back a laugh. "There is a world beyond ours... a world with hierarchies—a world which is invisible but real. We make associations with guides from that world... mentors. They are distinct and wise spiritual figures with a lot of experience. And they grant us knowledge that we can apply to our practical lives."

"Interesting. Then it's something like an otherworldly advice bureau. There are doctors, legal consultants... financial experts... what else? And how much do they charge?"

Giancarlo didn't judge Jill for her mocking air.

"Nothing. Absolutely nothing."

"There's no such thing. Not even between a loving couple."

"Okay, well they ask only for loyalty."

"Oh, I know this one. Loyalty. Look at me."

He looked.

"You know, Gian, suddenly I see your eyes looking as... as lost as your master's." And then she stressed, "Gian, Gian...! Wake up! Do you really not see the mistake you're making? Do you not see that there are no such things as *distinct and wise spiritual figures with vast experience* that only want to help you? What *happens*—and to be clear, I said *happen*, not *exist*—what happens is the simple possession of your conscious mind by your own subconscious. Do you get the picture? It's all you. It all comes from you. Your guide is in your head."

"How can you be sure that's true?"

"How? Experience, how else? By being rational. It's a question of logic. Pure logic."

Giancarlo thought about that for a bit. Then he said, "If it's all that mechanically simple... if you just take everything you need and more from inside yourself—then what's left over for the occult forces?"

"Occult forces? Oh, Gian...! Please!"

"Well we have to believe in something, Jill. I can't just believe in light switches I flick to make the lights turn on. There has to be more."

Bit by bit, Jill lost her mocking tone. She turned serious.

"You know… I'm not really sure if I believe in anything that isn't rational—and that could be because of my education. Maybe. I've just taken in so much information that I… I feel somewhat lost, incapable of making a decisive decision. And I just let things happen."

Giancarlo looked like he was about to laugh.

"Now I get it. So that's why you always try to find an element of humor in everything."

"Yeah. I think it's my form of escape—the style given to me by my education. But deep down, I think you and I are both in the same dark tunnel. I say this thinking about what I came to Villavieja del Campo to do… about the money I need. Maybe there is an easier way of resolving this situation."

"I already know. The size 9 shoe."

Jill let out a laugh.

"How do you know Mike is rich?"

"I didn't say he was rich. I didn't think it either. I just meant you could share the load."

They spent a few moments in silence.

"It's time for me to go," he said.

"Yeah. It is."

He stepped out of the car but turned around to face it. He bent down to see inside and looked Jill in the face.

"Regardless of him, the size 9 shoe, no matter what happens I'll find a way to go back to that *plaza* in Villavieja tomorrow."

"But what could happen to you? I feel like you're afraid of something."

"It's only natural, I think. And it was just a way of speaking, a figure of speech. I was thinking about time and whether I'd have the opportunity to leave my companions and come meet you. That's all."

"Really?"

"Of course."

That response didn't convince Jill.

"How long do you think the ritual is gonna take?"

"One hour—or three or four. As far as I know, it's unpredictable."

Then she decided she was going to wait. She would stay right there in the car until everything in the castle was over. When she could see that everyone was starting to leave, she would leave ahead of them. But she didn't tell Giancarlo.

"Bye, Jill."

"Bye, Giancarlo."

He was already leaving when she asked,

"What's your shoe size?"

"Ten. Why?"

She responded with a smirk. And added,

"No reason."

◆ ◆ ◆

Giancarlo conquered the eighty yards of road, walked past the parked vehicles, crossed the ruined drawbridge, and made his way into the castle. Shortly after going into the atrium, he saw two burning torches. The second was on the door of one of the chambers. He went over.

But he didn't notice that someone had been watching him ever since he left the car. As soon as Giancarlo entered the castle, Maggio descended from his vantage point.

Before Giancarlo had even made it into the chamber, he heard a dog growling. And another. Standing still, he looked to the left. And he saw Maggio. He was holding the Dobermans by their leashes. The dogs' fur was glinting in the low light. Their eyes too.

Walking two more steps toward him, Maggio stopped when the dogs were right in front of Giancarlo. His features were morbidly accentuated by the yellow torchlight. The dogs started to howl—nearly a whine.

"Shush," said Maggio. The dogs fell silent. Then Maggio turned his gaze back on Giancarlo. "Let me just say that you did everything perfectly incorrectly, Gian. How could you be so irresponsible?"

"Master, I..."

"I'm not asking for explanations. Anything you'd tell me would be a lie anyway. And now I no longer know what will happen to you. I fell flat on my face in front of McDowell, and he blames me for your irresponsible behavior. I agree with him. You are not ready for this. Why don't you just give up?"

Maggio walked to stand in the doorway with his back to Giancarlo. But before going in, he turned to look over his shoulder and said, "Nevertheless, the final say is not with me and it never could be. The one who has to accept and forget your irresponsibility is your guide—not me."

After he said that, Amaro Maggio went into the chamber with the dogs.

◆ ◆ ◆

THE CHAMBER was lit from three angles. One of the torches was near the entrance and the other two were in the corners of the opposite wall. Because of this, the darkest point was the middle of the chamber. And there, in the very center, someone had drawn a large black circle on the ground. To the right, next to the wall, Giancarlo saw Caesar and Nero. The dogs were growling at him again. Menendez retied their leashes and said something. The dogs settled down. Giancarlo felt a sense of relief.

To the left and outside the circle Michel was waiting for the ritual to begin. Giancarlo went over to meet him.

They waited for ten minutes. Then, through a dilapidated door at the back, three men entered dressed in long black-hooded capes. Two more men came in after them wearing medieval religious garb. The first was Amaro Maggio—Giancarlo noticed. The second was Richard McDowell. Based on his positioning, Giancarlo could tell McDowell was going to be acting as high priest for the ceremony.

It was now 8:15 PM.

Suddenly, the overblown and tremulous voice of the high priest echoed in the tower. He began reciting a sequence of strange names—the dozens of names the tradition used for the universal mind. Giancarlo started to feel dizzy. He had a strong sensation of repulsion. He steeled his mind to keep himself from joining the others in their forced trance.

Once the invocation was over, the torches seemed to have dimmed. A wild-smelling odor flooded into the chamber. Soon, however, Giancarlo noticed the smell breaking down into the rotten stink of sulfur. He could barely stand it.

Somewhere beyond the numbness in his limbs and his sudden exhaustion, Giancarlo could hear a wavering voice that said, "Step forward and enter the inner circle, disciple Michel."

Michel went into the middle of the circle. There was a question and answer dialogue. He responded "yes" every time.

Abruptly, Michel was bent down grotesquely to the ground. It looked like an invisible rope was dragging him down by the neck. Seconds later, seemingly released and slowly able to stand up again, Michel's features looked different. It was a Michel Giancarlo had never seen before—with a touch of sinister in the way his mouth had been drawn into an over-thin smile, as well as in the unnatural angle at which his eyebrows had frozen, and in the almost-imperceptible tension rippling under the skin of his neck and hands. He stood that way, still slightly bent forward, like a hunchback, for several minutes.

Then, bit by bit, Michel's facial expression began to return to normal and he was allowed to straighten up. This was his body getting used to the new weight, to the spiritual rider Michel was now carrying. His hands, eyebrows, and the half smile on his face all looked normal now—in every way he was the same Michel as ever. Except for his eyes. His eyes were still static. Cold. Lifeless.

The sequence of phrases uttered by the high priest indicated that Michel had passed the test of complete possession with flying colors. The strange hymn he now chanted, both enthralling and medieval, served as further proof. Once finished, Giancarlo saw Maggio raise his right hand with his index finger cocked. Michel had been confirmed as a full member of the order.

Still in a trance, the high priest raised his voice to proclaim, "You were not given any powers you will not have to answer for, Michel. And every day of your universal existence, your messenger will be your rewarder—or your tormentor."

Giancarlo was surprised by those words. Michel didn't seem able to hear them—he was still possessed by his guide. So, the high priest's words must have been directed at him—at his guide. Michel was about to give himself, via a pact, into the hands of a... of a demon. The words the high priest prayed were in fact the terms of sale. Michel no longer belonged to himself. Michel was a slave—and it was possible he would never be aware of that.

An idea began to etch itself into Giancarlo's mind.

Now Michel's demon jockey steered him out of the circle. Michel's frozen smile was stamped onto his lips as if he were in extasy. But his eyes were still dead.

When Giancarlo saw that the high priest's lifeless eyes were now looking at him, he knew his turn had come. He felt a powerful tingling in his hands—the warning that, within seconds, his mind too would be lost in a deep void. But he felt a sense of rejection rather than acceptance. It was as if something—

something or someone—was projecting a helping hand over him: a savior. At that moment, a memory washed over him: *In the end, Gian, he will come and go from your mind whenever he sees fit—and when he is within you, you are less than nothing. Until one day he comes to collect on every one of the feats he performed for you. While they pile the earth over your dead body, he will carry your soul off to a second death. That is the true price of the pact between you.*

"Disciple Giancarlo," the high priest's quavering voice echoed again. "Step forward for your oath of loyalty."

◆ ◆ ◆

SUDDENLY, SOMETHING akin to a centrifugal force sucked the high priest up off the ground and sent him flying ten feet in the air.

Everyone's trance was abruptly broken.

The three hooded men lowered their hoods but didn't appear to know what was happening.

Amaro Maggio's mouth was gaping, his eyes bulging.

McDowell was prostrate on the floor where he had been thrown.

Michel, who had also fallen over, was gasping for breath and looked stunned.

Over in the corner, Menendez was as astonished as all the others and stood immobile, holding the dogs by their leashes.

Caesar and Nero growled menacingly and bared their teeth.

"What madness just happened?!" the high priest yelled from the ground, but his voice was now lacking the vibrato of possession. His enraged and indignant eyes searched for Maggio. Amaro was still gasping, adhered to the ground, trembling.

The dogs' growls increased in volume. Maggio managed to get up and take two steps. He looked wildly in all directions.

"Who are you?!" he shouted to the darkness.

Turning around quickly, Giancarlo saw a man in dark clothing standing next to the first torch. He was tall, full-bodied, with a wispy beard and whitish hair.

"Get him!" Maggio shouted again.

Quickly, the man raised a hand, grabbed the torch off the wall and fled. The chase was on. Three of the costumed men discarded their cloaks and ran after him.

Giancarlo was still frozen in the middle of the circle. McDowell was already on his feet and Maggio at his side.

"Who is that man?" McDowell asked.

"I don't know! I don't know!" Maggio responded, annoyed. "A crazy person! This was not supposed to happen."

"No one is crazy enough to intrude on a place such as this—not for anything!"

Maggio ran both of his hands through his hair. He was bewildered, his eyes still bulging. Neither of them wanted to admit the truth: that a power greater than their guides had, as if by magic, driven away all the spirits gathered there. They both felt empty, weak, impotent—and fearful.

Maggio stroked his cleanshaven chin. He was still tense. He saw a piece of black tubing on the ground and, with trepidation, knelt down to pick it up. But it wasn't plastic: it was the tip of a stick someone had set alight and turned into charcoal. He threw it far away.

"The dogs!" he shouted. "Sancho! I want the dogs at my side! Now!"

Still standing in the center of the circle, Giancarlo saw Maggio's desperation when he could not see Menendez or the dogs. Giancarlo looked back at the perplexed severity of McDowell's features. Then he glanced at Michel. Visibly exhausted and sweating, Michel was raising and lowering his heels to stretch the ache from his legs. He had just emerged from a grueling possession and, because of this, was the most shocked of all. Michel seemed totally confused by what was happening in the chamber.

A growing panic began to overtake Giancarlo. He looked back at the irate Maggio. And again at the exhausted Michel. And then he ran out the door.

"Giaaancaaaaaarlooooooo!" Maggio's shout echoed through the castle. "Get back here, you FOOL!"

◆ ◆ ◆

From inside her parked car, Jill first saw the light of a torch. Then she saw a man holding it. He was running toward her. He threw the torch away and vanished into the woods to the left.

Seconds later, the barking grew louder and soon two dogs appeared with four men. Jill recognized one of them as Menendez. The dogs also banked left and disappeared into the night. The men did the same.

Jill was scared. She thought about Giancarlo. She started the car, put it into gear and slowly drove forward, toward the bridge. Behind Maggio's vehicles stood McDowell.

As she got out of the car, she could see Giancarlo running toward the bridge.

"Gian! What happened?" she shouted.

Seeing Jill in front of the castle somehow seemed natural to him.

"Jill, where did that man go?"

She pointed. And he started running again.

"Gian! Wait! What's going on?"

But there was no response.

After twenty minutes, Jill went from being scared to terrified in the gloom of the night. Now back in her car, she sunk down in her seat when she saw Menendez coming back with the dogs. They crossed the bridge and went back into the castle. Five minutes later, the other three men appeared too and went back in.

She got out of the car, walked a few yards away from the looming castle and shouted, "Gian!"

Nothing. The waxing moon broke out from behind the sparse clouds. Jill came upon a small ravine, which she descended, and walked up to the bank of a stream. Around sixty yards in front of her, she finally caught sight of Giancarlo. He was walking back in her direction.

"Finally!" she said when they met. "What happened?"

The question didn't seem to have reached Giancarlo's ears. He started slowly rubbing the points and angles of a small gold crucifix on a chain around his neck. Stopping, he turned back and looked into the darkness, as if trying to hear something. Or see someone.

"Gian! What is going on? Please! Say something!"

Twenty-Five

I t had all been a complete mess.

"I was with him, Jill... with the old man. Yes, he was old but, from the distance, he didn't give me that impression. Those men searched everywhere, but they never found him. Neither did Menendez with the dogs. By going through water, he managed to throw them all off. And eventually they gave up and went back to the castle."

"I was about to go back too. But suddenly, next to the stream, someone grabbed me hard by the arm and pulled me. It was dark... the moon had gone behind a cloud. And then, lying on the ground, I felt the tense breath of a face very close to mine. His grip was strong and he was still holding onto my arm. His clothing was wet. Then I saw those eyes... and that closely groomed whitish beard. It was him, the man from the castle. 'They are blind and dying to catch someone,' he said to me in Italian. Then he said, 'let's make sure it isn't you, *figliolo*.' He held his strong arm across my chest, then I saw him staring at my neck. And his eyes looked like... like my eyes. Do you understand? I don't know how to explain it better. This feeling, Jill, it was something... something

I can't explain. His eyes felt familiar."

Giancarlo stopped talking. His gaze was still lost in the night as if searching for the slightest movement—or more memories. His left hand just kept rubbing the edges of the gold crucifix on his chain.

"And what happened next, Gian?"

"We stayed silent and waited for the three men to walk back to the castle. When that happened, he took his arm off my chest and said, 'Now you may go, *figliolo*.' 'But who are you?' I asked. 'What just happened in that castle?' He said nothing. We just stayed standing there until he started to leave. Then suddenly he stopped. He turned to me and said, 'I'm just an old man.' He took a brief pause, looked again at my neck and said, 'An old man... an old man who discovered more than twenty years ago that the Lamb is gloriously alive—and not nailed to a cross.' After he said that, he vanished into the darkness. That was when I heard you shouting my name, Jill. And I started to walk back."

Stopping, Giancarlo looked at Jill. He let the silence linger for a moment. Then he said, "You know what idea crossed my mind after he left, Jill?"

"What?"

"That I... that I had met him before... that I had seen him somewhere."

Twenty-Six

They were back in front of the castle. All the vehicles were still there.

"They're still inside," said Giancarlo.

"What now? What are you going to do?"

"I'm going back in. You coming with me?"

They started across the bridge.

"You hear that, Gian?" Jill asked. They both stopped to listen more carefully.

"Yes. It's Maggio's dogs."

They ran through the large gateway and saw Menendez crossing the atrium with a small torch in his left hand. His other hand was holding the leashes of the two dogs. They waited for Menendez to disappear into a gap in the ruins and went after him. It was a long corridor.

• • •

IN ONE OF THE DEEPEST CHAMBERS, Maggio was on the verge of hysteria. Hair completely disheveled, scratches around his mouth and eyes bloodshot, he took his twitchy hands off the stone wall and then turned around to face the representative of the Order.

"Enough, McDowell! Enough! You've said enough! I know it was my mistake.

And I know where and when I messed up. I don't need any more accusations."

"I'm not accusing you, Maggio. I just recited a few of our rules."

"Rules? I know the rules very well. All of them, McDowell. You know that. What have I done for the last fifteen years if not uphold them? And it is by those rules that I am here in Vallencantado. I am following my orders to the letter. I came to be instructed—and only I know how much I need that. Despite everything that's happened, I don't regret coming."

"And someday, will someone explain to me what happened tonight?"

Maggio returned to his pleading, "I am just asking you to have a bit more patience. And to give me some advice. I have a rendezvous tonight in this castle."

"Well, I do not!"

McDowell walked a few steps and came right up to Maggio. He was still perturbed. The two torches on the wall distorted their features.

Maggio half-begged, "Please, McDowell! I need help, I haven't been able to establish contact with my mentor for days."

"Sometimes I don't feel the proper ambiance either, Maggio. I already told you. If this turbulence continues in any way, I don't see how we can proceed. This is my final decision. Who knows about tomorrow..." After declaring this, the representative of the order picked up one of the torches and started to leave.

"McDowell! Please! Wait!"

The appeal was of no use. McDowell kept going. Maggio stayed there, his hand trembling as he lowered his arm that had been begging for help.

He wiped his face with a handkerchief. It came away soaked with sweat. The flickering light of the last torch bestowed a phantasmagoric quality on his appearance.

Suddenly he heard an echo of footsteps from the corridor. He turned quickly, thinking it was McDowell.

"How nice that you returned...! I..."

It was not the representative of the Order.

"Sancho! Where have you been?"

"I had to go round up the dogs, Boss."

Maggio was still using the handkerchief. He was puffing like he was short of breath.

"It's actually a good thing you brought Caesar and Nero," he said.

More footsteps. Another figure emerged and thankfully they were on the side of the torch Menendez was holding in his left hand.

"Michel...! How nice that you came, Michel. I need help... I... I..."

The ensuing silence served to multiply Maggio's panic. Michel's eyes were again frozen, cold. Then a familiar voice spoke to Maggio through Michel's mouth,

"And why do you think I'm here? Weren't we supposed to meet now?"

It was *him*. Maggio was sure it was his mentor. He didn't even notice that his guide was in Michel. A nervous tick twitched and stretched his lips and, in a poor imitation of laughter, Maggio said, "Oh! It... *is it you...?*"

"Yes, it is I. Why are you trembling?"

Eyes fixed on Michel, Maggio swallowed a lump in his throat. Then he followed Michel's gaze, looking for Menendez. Menendez's eyes were filled with hate and scorn.

"Sancho...!"

Menendez asked Michel,

"Has the time come, *Sete Flechas?*"

Whipping around, eyes full of fear, Maggio turned toward Michel.

"*Se-sete Flechas*... it's *you?*! But how? It isn't possible! All these years, have you been my guide... my advisor, and...!"

The voice said, "*Fool! I have always been whatever you wanted me to be. I have claim over you. Your mind has belonged to me since your old days searching for the 'inferior forms of spiritism'!*"

Maggio's panic rearranged his features into an expression of pure terror. He saw Michel's dead eyes signaling to Menendez. And he saw Menendez open his right hand to loose the dogs.

"Nero... Caesar... what...!"

Maggio backed up against the wall.

"No! No! Go away! Leave me alone! Sancho! Michel! It's me, Maggio! Get these dogs off me!"

Panting, Maggio climbed the spiral staircase up the tower.

♦ ♦ ♦

"HEAVENS!" EXCLAIMED a frightened Jill. "Who is that screaming? What's going on, Gian?"

Giancarlo was the first to see Menendez and Michel leaving the chamber. The screams continued, now mixed with the dogs snarling louder and louder.

"It's Maggio," he was sure.

Suddenly the dogs fell silent. And the screams died as well. Next, Giancarlo saw the Dobermans leaving the chamber. They quickly caught up to Menendez and Michel. Jill was tense.

"They're coming our way, Gian."

Grabbing Jill's arm, he pulled her aside and shoved her into a crack in the dilapidated wall. Not long after, the two men and dogs walked right past them. They kept walking until they disappeared off to the right at the end of the corridor.

"How strange," said Jill. "I thought the dogs would smell us. They were so close."

"It really is strange."

They started walking again toward the bright light of the torch spilling out of the chamber Menendez, Michel and the two dogs had come from. They stopped under the arch of the entrance.

"Oh my…!" Jill exclaimed when she saw the body on the ground.

Maggio, his face purplish and pale, frozen in an expression of agony and terror, was no longer breathing.

"No, no!" said Giancarlo in growing amazement. "What could have done that to him?"

Jill looked from side to side and shook in fear.

"Gian, I want to get out of here," she said quietly.

◆ ◆ ◆

NOT LONG AFTER, from the safety of the car, they both watched as six men entered the castle, leaving again shortly after. Three of them were carrying Maggio's body shrouded in a body bag. Minutes later, two vehicles drove away and just one police car remained parked outside the castle.

Jill noticed that Giancarlo was withdrawn.

"What is it?" she asked.

"I wish I had the courage to run after them… and tell them to stop, to drop all this. Poor Michel… Menendez…"

"Maybe one day you will."

"Yeah. Maybe one day I will."

They waited fifteen more minutes. Giancarlo wanted to give the vehicles enough time to leave the village too. Neither of them mentioned Maggio's death—they were still too shocked.

On the way back, they didn't say much. The dramatic scenes of that night were all replaying in Giancarlo's head, especially those of the man—of the old man who had suddenly appeared at the exact moment of his consecration.

Next to him, Jill was thinking about how she was going to meet Giovanni di Stefano tomorrow. And that caused her a certain degree of anxiety. She was also thinking about Mike. In other circumstances, marrying Mike would have solved everything. But now it didn't make any sense.

"What are you thinking about, Jill?" said Giancarlo, emerging from his private world.

She wasn't going to lie,

"At this exact second, I was thinking about a letter I got from Mike. He asked me to marry him."

"Ah," replied Giancarlo, dejected. "Congratulations. I hope Mr. Five-Foot-Eleven will be good to you."

She cracked a smile. "How tall are you, Gian?"

"Six feet. Why?"

"No reason."

They looked at one another. But this time they didn't laugh. They were still in shock.

After a brief silence, she said, "I was also thinking about the man I'm depending on—Giovanni di Stefano. I'm afraid of being disappointed again."

He reflected for an instant before saying, "I think *noi due* are still wandering the desert, Jill."

"And you think... you think we'll end up finding the Well of the Morning Star?"

"Who can say? According to Nicodemus, it all depends on our thirst."

"And how thirsty are you, Gian?"

He didn't respond because they were reaching the village. They arrived exactly as Maggio's truck pulled onto the highway access road. McDowell's car was further ahead.

"They left," said Giancarlo. "I knew they would get out of here as quickly as possible. They've definitely cut ties with me."

"Well then, what should I do now?"

"Go to the next corner. Then turn left."

Shortly after that, Jill stopped the car in front of Don Miguel's guesthouse. Everything was silent, the lights turned off. She thought Giancarlo was only going to get his bags, but he surprised her. He said he was going to stay.

"Stay here? In this village? To do what?"

"I'm going to find that man, Jill, and I'm going to do it bright and early tomorrow morning. Maybe somebody from the village will know where he lives."

"Gian... you aren't thinking that man might be your grandfather, are you?"

The question came unexpectedly. Giancarlo looked at Jill.

"Well, is there something wrong with that? Because my *nonno* couldn't possibly be alive? He seemed familiar." Giancarlo touched the chain around his neck. "And this thing used to belong to him. I saw the way he looked at this chain."

Jill's face wore an expression of pity.

"Gian... this is like something out of a movie. Stuff like that never happens in real life. Traveling over twelve hundred miles, going into the ruins of a castle... and then finding your grandfather right there, a man who disappeared twenty-five years ago? That's just too much of a coincidence. It sounds more like a tall tale."

"It just so happens I am not thinking of coincidence. According to Nicodemus, everything that happens to us in life is actually the result of providence."

"Ah, Nicodemus...!"

"And why couldn't it be my *nonno*? You didn't see him up close like I did. And you didn't feel what I felt."

His words were sharp.

"Calm down, I don't want to argue. I just think... that what you saw and felt could be nothing but the fruit of a strong desire for your *nonno* to be alive. Tomorrow you'll see how ridiculous all this is."

Giancarlo's response was to leave the car. Jill's reaction was to start the engine. A small gale of rage had begun blowing across her face as she watched Giancarlo circling around the front of the car.

216

And he heard, "I thought your master's death would have finally freed you of your obsessive ways. But it looks like I was wrong."

She revved the car in neutral and then threw it into reverse.

"But it's fine," she said, her lips narrowed. "Have it your way. I think it's actually good for everything to stay the way it is. I'll never understand your mind—or your dreams. Suit yourself. Nor will you understand mine."

"Jill..." Giancarlo tried to say something.

"See you around, Gian."

She didn't want to hear anything else. She took off with a certain violence. A minute later, her headlights disappeared around the side of the mountain.

Twenty-Seven

Dawn was breaking.

Giancarlo heard a faint knock at the door. He got off the bed and went to open the door. It was little Pedrito. He turned shy when Giancarlo opened the door. Giancarlo smiled at him.

"*Hay un hombre...*" the boy told him.

"*Gracias*, Pedrito."

Giancarlo quickly pulled a shirt on and left the room. Pedrito was still outside waiting. There didn't seem to be anyone else in the building—it looked like everyone was out. As Giancarlo headed for the front door, the kid ran out ahead of him.

"Nicodemus!"

Nicodemus was leaning with his back against a car—a white Spanish sedan. Nicodemus was no longer dressed like a drifter. He was wearing light-colored linen pants and a white cotton shirt with two pockets. He was also no longer wearing a hat, and his beard had been expertly trimmed. His old sneakers, too, had been swapped for black suede leather boots. He took a step forward.

"Hello, Gian. Did I wake you from a dream?"

Giancarlo gave a sad sigh.

"I think you woke me from a nightmare, Nicodemus. I was dreaming about those dogs."

"Then it was a nightmare. Some things imprint themselves on our souls. Can we take a little walk? I like to think while I walk... and talk, too."

They started off on a little stroll. Unhurried. It was still a cool morning. Giancarlo had a lot of questions.

"How could a man have so much power... such a simple man disrupting such a high-level meeting?"

"It wasn't the man who did it: it was He to whom was given all power in heaven, on Earth and below the Earth. It's a question of faith."

"And those dogs... the dogs must have cornered Maggio, and..."

"Gian, I am very sorry for your loss. Maggio was your master and also your friend. But no. That wasn't what happened. It wasn't the dogs at all. All these years, Maggio's Dobermans were never there just to guard his property. His tormentors had been policing him up until that very day, hour, and place. The demons did what they wanted to. They led Maggio to his end. Then they left."

Nicodemus said something that caught Giancarlo off guard, "I tried to make Maggio see reason."

"Did you speak with him?"

"For a few minutes. It was back at *El Rincón*. He mocked me, didn't want to listen. But let's leave that in the past, Gian. I'm here for another reason." Nicodemus gave a slight smile. "Of course, you are no longer talking to a drifter..."

"Nor an angel. Did you know that Jill thinks you're an angel?"

"Jill! She is very precious to God—and to you as well, I think. Right?"

Giancarlo didn't have to respond. Nicodemus understood. But he didn't understand the sudden look of defeat on Giancarlo's face.

"A rival?" he asked Giancarlo.

"His name is Mike. A rich guy from America. You think God could win me a battle like that?"

Giancarlo wanted to laugh, but Nicodemus was serious,

"Gian, you're the only one who can win this battle. God already did his part: he put her in your path."

They had looped back and were returning to the guesthouse. Pedrito was walking back and forth nearby rolling an iron hoop with a stick.

"Gian... I came here to say goodbye. I have to get back to my business. You know, at a certain point in my life I knew in my heart that I was going to guide you all the way here. And now I've done just that. Are you surprised?"

"I think so. And I don't get it."

"You will soon. You remember the legend of Three Magi... their thirst and the well?"

"Yes, of course. And the Star shining up from the bottom."

"We all reach our own well in the end—even if it takes us until the last second of our life. And the earlier it happens the better, because then we find the Holy Grotto sooner. In my case, Gian, it took fifty-one years. And it's been a year and a half since I saw the Morning Star reflected in my well of rubble. I believe that you already suspected I used to be a warlock."

"I swear I didn't."

"I used to spend hours in a hypnotic trance having discussions with those *particular geniuses*... without knowing that I was conversing with deceitful demons—false guides masquerading as spirits of light. Then one night, a year and a half ago, I found out I was going to be a priest at the initiation of a disciple, but surprisingly, something similar to what you saw last night in the castle happened. Except that it happened somewhere else not far from here."

Giancarlo stopped. Nicodemus did the same. Pedrito halted his hoop's momentum with his hand and stood staring at the two from the distance.

"And it was the exact same man, Gian."

"The old man?"

"Mm-hm. I went after him that same night—and I was thirsty. I went as Nicodemus did in the Bible: in the dark so no one would see me. He made me see that I was at the bottom of a dark well, and he lifted me out so I could gaze upon the Morning Star. Those were marvelous days. That meeting changed the course of my life, Gian."

They walked up to the car. Pedrito had stopped playing with the hoop and now was sitting on the car's rear bumper.

"I have one more thing to tell you after our walk, Gian. I know you have a lot of questions—and you want answers. People with questions have thirst. But you don't need anything else. You are close to being found by the Morning Star."

Opening the car door, Nicodemus picked something up off the seat.

"I brought you a present," he said, handing Giancarlo a book-shaped package. Giancarlo was going to unwrap it, but Nicodemus reached out and stayed his hand.

"Later."

Giancarlo stopped. Nicodemus extended his hand to shake goodbye.

"See you around, Giancarlo."

"See you around, Nicodemus."

Two minutes later, Pedrito was already back to rolling the hoop with the stick in a vain attempt to outrun the car as it drove off.

Then Giancarlo unwrapped the package.

The Death Of A Mystic

"And many of those who practiced magic brought their books together and began burning them in the sight of everyone; and they added up the prices of the books and found it to be fifty thousand pieces of silver."

— Acts 19:19, Holy Bible

Dear Gian,

I hope reading this book can undo the catastrophe my earlier works produced in your mind. Soon we will meet again for another great bonfire.

Your friend,
Fernando "Nicodemus" Sierra

Twenty-Eight

Giancarlo spent the whole morning scouring the area around Vallencantado castle. He didn't go as far as to enter the castle, but he returned to where he had been with the man the night before. He stood there next to the stream for some time.

It was a sunny day and the images of the previous night would not come back to him clearly or easily. But the words did—*I'm a simple old man... an old man who discovered more than twenty years ago that the Lamb is gloriously alive—and not nailed to a cross.*

Then, slowly but decisively, he grabbed the chain around his neck and tugged at it. He removed the cross with the small body crucified on it and put the chain in his bag.

In front of him, the stream slipped and babbled its own kind of hymn as it strummed the slick stones, and it was there, in the sonorous tow of the waters, that he made the golden object disappear. He felt better. He didn't know how to explain it, but he felt like he had just been freed from shackles. Ancient shackles.

Then he carried on.

He combed the nearby part of the valley and saw no signs of habitation.

He only gave up when he caught sight of Don Miguel. He was coming back from the vegetable gardens he tended in the valley. With a wave, Giancarlo went out to meet him.

"Apart from the people in the village," Don Miguel responded, "I don't know anyone else who lives around here. This place is very dangerous. Every year at least one tourist falls off those ruins. I heard about what happened last night. I'm sorry for your loss."

And with a distant gaze, Don Miguel continued, "People used to think this place was cursed. Many centuries ago, some important men were beheaded in this castle. They were Knights Templar. They were accused of many crimes. A great deal of blood was spilled here—and that's not counting the fight against the Moors."

They ambled back to the village together. When they were twenty yards from the guesthouse, Don Miguel's grandson came running out to meet them.

"What's all the fuss about, Pedrito?" he asked his agitated grandson.

The boy looked at Giancarlo.

"*Hay una mujer…*" said Pedrito, but didn't finish, as he started running off in front of them, leading the way.

Giancarlo didn't have to turn the corner to know it was Jill. Already having been notified of their impending arrival by Pedrito, she had come out to meet Giancarlo.

"Hi, Gian."

There was a special glint in her eyes. And her expression was unusually tranquil.

"Hi, Jill. What a nice surprise. What... what happened?"

Jill gave a slight smile. And even that was different—totally disarmed. She kept looking into Giancarlo's eyes.

"I came... I came looking for you, Gian."

"Looking for me?"

Now her eyes were shining over-bright.

"I met someone... a man who found the Morning Star," she said.

"What?"

"It was the guy from the castle," Jill extended a hand.

"Let's go. I'll tell you everything on the way."

224

Twenty-Nine

The wasteland, strewn with rocks, extended for miles. And far off in the north, high up, you could see the western edge of Los Ancares Leoneses Biosphere Reserve with its remaining population of wolves and brown bears. But down below, the soil was poor except for some stretches where age-old vineyards had been restored.

"It is not the best land, *Señorita*," said Jorge Valverde from the back seat of the car, "but it is where I was born and raised."

"*Señor* Jorge," said Jill when he had stopped talking, "what is Giovanni di Stefano like? How long have you known each other?"

"I only know him by sight."

"Oh. But aren't your properties next to each other?"

"*Sí*, they do touch. But my house is a good ways further up, *Señorita*. And what I know about Giovanni is that he is a... a peculiar old Italian man."

"I don't think so, *Tío*," said the girl on the front seat. "He came over to talk to me and *Tía* Carmen once. He's a nice guy."

"Hush, girl."

They passed in front of a fence to the left with a wire gate.

"Here it is, *Señorita*. I'll open the gate and you can drive through. You shouldn't leave the car blocking the road."

Jill stopped the car and the other two got out. Valverde unlatched and opened the gate, and she drove the car through. Then, as he was closing the gate, he said, "Giovanni's house is at the back, *Señorita*, next to the forest. Just follow the path around the orchard." He slung his backpack onto his back. "*Buenos dias*, and *gracias* for the ride."

"I'm the one that should be thanking you, *Señor* Jorge. Thanks for the help."

She stopped to watch the man walk away with his niece. Then, putting her car into gear, she said to herself,

"Good job, Jill. You made it. Now ask God to bring your long voyage to an end. And pray for it to end well."

She set the car in motion and followed Valverde's directions. She drove around the orchard and proceeded down the road. In the distance, she spotted a house right on the edge of a forest.

◆ ◆ ◆

RECENTLY WHITEWASHED, the house was a good deal smaller than it seemed from a hundred yards away. The door was open, but Jill didn't go in. She rapped at the door with her knuckles. Seconds later, a man appeared.

Tall and still strong-looking, he had sun-kissed skin and abundant hair, which was as whiteish as his carefully cultivated beard—no one would have taken him for older than sixty-eight. His green-brown eyes carried an air of indescribable peace.

"*Signor* Giovanni... Giovanni di Stefano?" she asked.

"*Sì.*"

"My name is Jill."

In the living room, there were three artisanal armchairs made of cedar and spotted goat hides. Giovanni extended his arm.

"*Prego*, come in and make yourself at home," he invited in perfect Italian.

They sat in the two closest armchairs.

"How can I help you, *Signorina*?"

"*Signor* Giovanni, what I'm about to tell you may seem strange, but I traveled almost one thousand miles to find you."

"Hmm!" the old man teased. "Then I must know a secret that's very important to you."

"You can't even imagine."

He crossed his right leg over his left and got settled more comfortably.

"I hope you're comfortable in my rustic armchair, *Signorina* Jill. I made it myself... with the help of two little goats, of course." The old man smiled. "And now, why don't you tell me what brought you here?"

"My full name is Jill Lane Piomondo Heston. Does that mean anything to you?"

She saw his ears perk up.

"I am the granddaughter of *Barone* Vittorino Tedesco Piomondo."

He leaned back in search of better support from the back of the armchair.

"Go on, *Signorina*," he encouraged.

She began telling him of her *Nonno* Vittorino's grave health. She told him how her grandfather was ruined and that Villa Piomondo now belonged to the bank. And she told him about her search for her grandfather's old friends.

"They say there were four of them, and all very rich. Isn't that right? Every one of them, in one way or another, received many favors from my *nonno*. That's what my mother told me. Well, today it's *Nonno* Vittorino who needs favors, *Signor* Giovanni. And that's why I'm here."

"Are you talking about... about money, *Signorina*?"

"*Sì.*"

"How much?"

"Three hundred thousand, at least."

The man stood up. He walked over to the wall and stood there thinking for a few moments. Then, quite slowly, he sat back down. Jill noticed that his face seemed to be carrying an invisible burden.

"It's very... it's very hard to explain," he said.

"Explain what?"

"And very... very shameful."

"Shameful?" That struck Jill as odd. "I don't get it. Why is it shameful to ask a friend to repay favors? What are you trying to tell me?"

"So, you... you left to look for the four men to help you and you were... thinking of their money?"

"Yes."

His small eyes stared at Jill.

"Well, there is no money to be had."

"Of course there is!" Jill balked. "There were four men. One of them, *Signor* Decchi, might have lost everything, but there are three more. I have to know who and where they are. Can't you see that I... oh, *Signor* Giovanni, I'm so very tired."

Jill's eyes brimmed with tears and her cheeks were pale. She was struggling with the idea that she may have come all this way for nothing.

"Try to calm down, *Signorina*."

"Calm down? How? You are not in my position, *Signor* Giovanni."

"Of course not, *figliola*. Of course not."

The old man remained silent. Jill took a handkerchief from her bag to dry her eyes. They were tears of rage, and of fatigue.

"*Signorina...*" Giovanni di Stefano resumed, "it wouldn't be fair to let you leave here without knowing the truth."

"What truth?" she asked, curious now that her emotions were once again in check.

Bit by bit, dredging up the words from the deepest depths of his soul, with great remorse in his voice, the old man began to tell her of the shameful origins of the four men's fortunes.

"It all happened after the Germans were driven out of Italy. They were four ex-combatants, all young and irresponsible, who had allowed many fellow soldiers to die in combat. Some of those who died were rural landowners. Once the war was over, the four friends ravaged the already depleted south of Italy by coercing the widows and orphans of the fallen soldiers to sign their vast tracts of land over to them for virtually nothing—exchanging them for a basket of food or a box of medicine."

"It was honest-to-God robbery, *figliola*. They pillaged the families of their dead war buddies. And that was when it all started. The four men had to forge documents... papers. To enjoy their newfound riches, they had to obtain new identities. *Capisci?*"

"Times change, but men remain the same. Those times also had their influential men... conniving... and corrupt."

The old man continued, "The four managed to get two such influential men to legalize their paperwork. And because of that, the four ex-combatants were able to multiply their fortunes in the 1960s."

After a brief pause, feeling a mixture of frustration and disgust at what she had just learned, Jill told him that one of the four men, Luigi Decchi, had died.

"*Oh Signore!*" Giovanni exclaimed in grief.

"But there are three more left..." Jill continued, thinking out loud. Looking at the old man, she said, "I need help... I need to liquidate the villa's debt before my grandfather... do you understand my predicament, *Signor* Giovanni? I have nowhere else to turn. And I can't come back empty-handed. On top of everything else, I'm racing against time."

Getting up again, the old man paced a few slow steps and came back.

"I always have to stay in shape, *figliola*... it's my age. Walking is nice, and sometimes I have to run after a rebellious goat."

Then he added,

"I'm sorry to hear about Romeo Bellomo."

"Romeo Bellomo? Who is he, one of the four?"

"Romeo Bellomo is Luigi Decchi's real name. It was the name he had when the war ended."

The old man sat back down.

"You asked about the other three..."

"Yes," said Jill, recovering her hopefulness slightly.

"Pietro Accetta is a patient at a retirement home in Genoa. A public one for... indigents."

"Indigents?" Jill started digesting this new surprise. She was already starting to feel like her head was in a fog. "And... and the other two?"

"The third man—Enzo Bonetti—is doing time in a penitentiary near Venice. He killed his business partner. And his children took care of dismantling what was left of his estate. Like the others, he also changed his name in 1946. And it wouldn't help you one bit, *figliola*, if I told you the name he's registered under in prison."

"That leaves one more," Jill said. Again, she was thinking out loud. A skeptical thought. Nothing—nothing and no one—could convince her now that this fourth and last man was somehow anything other than impoverished too. Or dead.

Jill needed to leave this place. She crossed her arms and went over to the window Giovanni had been standing at shortly before. She saw nothing outside but trees, trees, and more trees. And a few sheep fenced into a pasture next to the woods.

What a joke! What a nice little hole I have dug myself into! She thought hard, already stepping away from the window. *So much running around, so much wasted time... for nothing! They are all dead... or ruined.*

The thoughts washed over her almost like a convulsion. She stopped in front of Giovanni di Stefano, continuing to mentally berate herself.

Why are you afraid to accept that the fourth man might be this guy here, this sad old man with no money? He's so pitiful he thinks it a grand feat to have made armchairs from the hides of goats he killed for food. Say this to him, Jill P. Heston. Say that you hate him—because he killed all of your dreams. And lay blame on him. In the end, those four men robbed and destroyed defenseless families—the widows and orphans of men killed in war. Throw that in his face, Jill P. Heston. He might be the fourth one of those repugnant men.

Still standing, Jill looked at Giovanni di Stefano. He stared up at her from the armchair.

She said, "*Signor* Giovanni... I am ready. Tell me one thing, please."

"*Sì, figliola*" said the man, getting to his feet.

"*Signor* Giovanni... the fourth man… is it... is it you? Are you one of the four who... who robbed the widows of friends who died in the war?"

Without taking his eyes off her, the old man slowly shook his head.

"No, *figliola*. I am not one of them."

"Don't call me *figliola*!" she half-yelled in a hoarse shout. "I am no daughter of yours."

The old man shot a gaze of compassion at Jill.

"Of course, *Signorina*. But try to calm down."

Pensively, the old man took two slow steps to the side.

He turned back to face her with his fingers half-interlaced to confirm,

"Just like your *Nonno* Vittorino, *Signorina* Jill, I did not fight in the war. I... I already had my properties... my prestige... and I stayed out of it. I stayed and defended what was mine. Your *nonno* did the same."

This old man is lying, to you, Jill P. Heston.

"Are you telling the truth, *Signor* Giovanni?"

"*Sì, cara.*"

"Then... Tell me, please!" Jill was exasperated, "Who is the fourth man?"

The old man walked slowly around the armchair. He locked eyes with Jill.

"Would you be... even be able to accept that kind of money, *Signorina*?"

"Well, what difference does it make? Could you help me by any chance? Is there maybe some... some treasure buried around here? How many goats do you have in your flock... five? Well, there would have been seven, but two of them are stretched over these armchairs. *Nevvero?* My cause is just, *Signor* Giovanni. I am not asking for money for myself. It's nothing like that. I have to finish what my father started. Any money will do, I have no choice. I have thirty-three children depending on me."

Jill finished her fusillade of harsh words. But the old man was meek when he asked,

"*Bambini?* Did you say thirty-three children, *Signorina*?"

Jill stayed mute. Giovanni tried to break the ailing rhythm the conversation had taken on.

"I know you are *Barone* Vittorino Tedesco Piomondo's granddaughter... and I know your *nonno*'s villa belongs to a bank now. But you just mentioned children... more than thirty of them. And something about your father. I don't think you took this trip only because of your *nonno*'s situation. There must be more. So, why don't you tell me the truth...? All of it."

"And what good would that do? How would you be able to help me?"

Jill was close to weeping. She knew she had been hard on the old man, but she didn't have it in her to act any other way. A profound sense of frustration had come over her.

"Only the Lord knows if I can help you or not, *Signorina*."

She heaved a deep sigh. Suddenly she felt exhausted. She went back to the armchair and began to tell him the whole story. She talked about her father, Benny Marshall, and Vietnam—and most of all about the *Pellegrino*, which had thirty-three Kurmanian orphan refugees in its hold.

And finally, she got to the money from America that seemed to have been sent but never arrived.

"I don't know what else to say, *Signor* Giovanni!"

"Trust in the God of providence. He knows how to move people and he will move the right people at the right time."

"I can't even do my job. Is there any way God doesn't see that? Is there any way he doesn't see these dozens of children with no chance at life?"

"Trust in the Lord," the old man repeated. "Love always triumphs."

"Love?" she balked. "Look, I'm giving all the love I have. So then why do I have to go through all this trouble? To love is to do, *Signor* Giovanni. And don't go spouting off any more fancy words."

"*Signorina*... I cannot love only the cause itself of the thirty-three children who fell victim to thoughtless men. I must first love the children."

Jill stopped.

"Tell me about the orphaned children *Signorina* Jill Lane Piomondo Heston loves so deeply."

Suddenly, she was unable to open her mouth. She was falling apart. In the blink of an eye, she realized that she had never been aboard the *Pellegrino*. Never seen a single one of the children's faces. Never met any of them. Never touched their scars or their prominent bones. How many cried at night, waking up afraid of the terror of war? She knew none of that. She had only dealt with them as numbers, figures, and plans. Like some inconsequential distraction, she got carried away running here and there and making waves and even lying— yearning to show leadership but instead showing only sterile and metallic love. And a spirit and force that were nothing more than the rotten fruit of her ego.

Or rather, it was all a simple and bombastic way of escaping her own self. Escaping the problems she'd left behind in Atlanta.

The old man before her didn't have to tell her any of this. But, just by looking at her with those eyes, firm and meek at the same time... it was as if he were doing just that. And because of it, she felt a lump swelling up to block her throat.

"It's very unfortunate, *figlia mia*". The old man flashed a smile. "Excuse me for calling you *figlia*. But if you depend on any of those men's money to do your work... you won't be doing any work at all. They lost everything they had. All of them."

She already knew that—she thought it, but didn't say it. She was still caught up in the previous topic. The old man's words were pounding in her head like a hammer. She thought about the children. For the first time, she thought about them like... like they were the only thing worth thinking about. Maybe she was losing it, but she could swear she could see those little faces she had never met holding hands in a circle around her—a living circle that smiled and sang and jumped.

That was when she heard new words—words that gave her the power to change everything:

"What is more important to you, *figliola*: a fistful of money or... the children?"

She looked at his little eyes, which seemed to be smiling. And opened her arms for the old man to hug her. It was a clear way of saying: the children.

Then, slowly backing out of the tender embrace, Giovanni di Stefano touched Jill's chin lightly with his fingers.

"*Figliola*... if I... if I were one of those men... would you be able to forgive me?"

Jill flashed a smile. It was an innocent question. The man looking her in the face was like... like a child. He wore a gentle expression of peace and love.

"You, *Signore*?" she asked, half smiling as if gearing up to tell a joke. "What about everything you just told me, that you never went to war because you had property... were influential... and stayed behind to protect your interests?"

"Would you be able to forgive me, *Signorina* Jill?" the old man insisted, not turning away. "If I were one of those men..., would you be able to forgive me?"

"But...! But of course! How could I not?"

"*Grazie, figliola.* Then forgive your *Nonno* Vittorino as well. We were not four foolhardy men: we were six. The fourth soldier, however, died when he was still young."

"As I told you, your *nonno* and I did not fight in the war. Back then, we were two of the most influential men in southern Italy. There was nothing... nothing our influence couldn't get from the authorities. Nothing. Papers... titles... identity documents... *Capisce, figliola?* Those times also had their influential men... conniving... and corrupt."

"Many years ago, more than twenty, when I was a pilgrim in the desert of my life, I reaped the fruit of my own evil sowing: I was buried alive by my own son, who forged a document attesting to my death. All of a sudden, I saw myself leaning over and looking into the bottom of my well. That was when I caught sight of the Morning Star reflected down in the bottom. I looked next to me, and there was the Holy Grotto of the Savior. Now, where did you leave Giancarlo, *figliola?*"

• • •

JILL STOPPED TALKING. They had already parked the car beneath a tree fifty feet from the little white house. Giancarlo's eyes were lost in a nearby part of the forest. Nevertheless, he was not able to hide the tears streaming down his cheeks.

He got out of the car and approached the house.

The door of the small house was ajar. He entered without knocking. There was nobody in the living room. No signs of life at all inside the house. He left. Standing in front of the house, he examined his surroundings. Then he looked for Jill. She was still in the car. He went over to her.

"There's no one in the house," he said.

"Then he must be with his flock near the forest. Go look there."

"Do you really not want to come with me?"

"No, I want you to go alone. This moment is all yours. And he's expecting you, Gian."

"Okay then. I'll take a look."

He went. He walked through the small pasture and saw the little flock. He followed a path down through the forest. Tall, ancient trees filtered the rays of the sun pleasantly as it carried on its slow conquest of the second half of the day.

After walking a small stretch of the path that curved ever downward, he began to feel a fresh breeze on his face. The cool wind was coming from straight ahead of him. A few more yards and he reached the last turn.

The surprise made him stop.

Thirty

At first he thought it was a huge mirror lying flat on the ground in front of him. In it, he could see the reflections of trees and clouds. Suddenly, a gust of wind rippled across the glossy surface, breaking the illusion, and he realized it was a lake. A breathtaking lake at the far edge of the forest.

He approached the water's edge. Crouching down, he cupped his hands to scoop up a bit of water and drank a sip. Then, after sitting down on the grass, he realized he had done it naturally, without thinking. *The lake is there to serve you, you needn't bow before it*—the words washed over him. And he flashed a smile. He liked knowing he had learned that first lesson.

He stayed seated on the ground. It was a magical moment. He looked at the lake and tried to conjure up the memories of the other lessons he had learned in his dream about the lake in the Apennine mountains. Then, getting up off the ground, he went back to the shore. He stood staring at the water at his feet. Some kind of uncontrollable internal desire made him raise his right foot, about to place it on the water.

"You won't be able to do it."

He turned around quickly. And saw his grandfather. He was sitting on a rock in front of a hut. How had he not seen him before? Overcome by profound emotion, Giancarlo started walking over. His grandfather's small green-brown eyes stared at him over the eternal seconds of his slow approach.

Once he was standing in front of him, Giancarlo muttered,

"*N-nonno...*"

There was no response. Giovanni di Stefano kept his eyes fixed on Giancarlo's face. There wasn't a second stone in front of the hut, so Giancarlo sat on the ground. They stared at one another in silence for some time.

"One day, *figliolo...*" said his grandfather, "twenty-five years ago, I went up into the Apennine mountains in search of the knowledge of how to perform miracles. And way up there, I had a dream. I dreamed of a lake... and there was an angel there with copper-colored hair... and an old man who called himself a prisoner of that lake. But the angel had taught me how to walk on the water to escape, so I laughed at the old man. And I didn't concern myself with him. I ran back to the lake and placed my foot on it... and it sunk."

"That's unbelievable, *Nonno!* I had the same dream and... and my foot sank too."

"*Figliolo...* at all times, God gives us the power to perform miracles. At all times. But we almost always want to see them shouted about from mountaintops… or plastered on the sides of tall buildings—when they could simply be in someone's lost eyes... or in two empty hands reaching out for our help."

Giancarlo was slightly amazed.

"I... I think I heard something like that from the angel... I'm starting to remember."

"Today you know that memory does not bring ability. But now you are not remembering: you're starting to nourish yourself with what has entered your heart."

"What I learned in the dream on the mountain... what you learned, *figliolo*— and what our memory transformed into garbled words—is that he spoke of extraordinary miracles, yes. But walking on water is the final one... perhaps the least useful of them all. Listen to your heart. That is the wellspring of life. And it knows that the path of miracles is something different."

"Different?"

"In that dream we had, we were thinking only of ourselves, and that was why the miracle passed us by."

"The way the angel treated us, Giancarlo, extending an arm to help us get up off the ground—we did not treat the old man from the hut the same way. We wanted to go on alone. That was why we sank."

As he said that, he got to his feet, and extended his lithe arm openhanded toward his grandson.

♦ ♦ ♦

THEY MEANDERED ALONG the path to the edge of the lake. Giancarlo still had many questions. At a certain point he said, "Tullio fought to save the vines, but every day they got worse, *Nonno*."

"If the branches aren't grafted, the vines won't bear fruit. We'll have to help your brother with that. Harvest time has already come."

"I have been blind, *Nonno*. And so selfish. My father wanted the best for me, and I let him and my family down. I hope *Mamma* and Tullio will be able to forgive me," Giancarlo said repentantly.

"But I will start over…by keeping my promise to bring you back and by finishing my training in agriculture and helping with the land. I just wish my father could be here to see all these changes."

Giancarlo told him about his father's death and his last words. *Nonno* Giovanni observed a moment of silence, perhaps in pain. Then he replied,

"What your father said was not a delusion brought on by the fever. The spirit of man is above the effects of an illness. One day, alone with your father in a barn, I told him everything I'm telling you now. He sneered at me—his own father. But it wasn't truly your father who was sneering and calling me crazy… it was the one who ruled over him. And that hate was not directed toward me—it was hate of the name of the Holy Lamb. Hate of the *Stella Mattutina*. I left, but the kernel remained. And it remained because it never belonged to me. And I believe, *figliolo*, I believe that in the final moment of his life, your father reached the Holy Grotto."

A minute later, Giancarlo continued, "*Nonno*…I met Fernando Sierra."

"He is a good friend. He wanted to repay me somehow. That's why he got close to you."

"But how did he know that I would be in Aquila Colorada?"

"From your mother, Albertina. He came to the farm looking for you, but you had already left that morning. Then, yesterday afternoon, he came to my farm to get me so we could go to the castle. He said you were ready to make peace with God... or make a pact with the Devil."

Shortly after, Giancarlo asked,

"*Nonno*... Giovanni or Enrico?"

"Saul of Tarsus... or Paul, *figliolo*?"

Just then, Jill appeared at the edge of the woods. *Nonno* Giovanni waved at her. She walked over.

"I see everything turned out well."

Nonno Giovanni shook his head.

"Everything is just getting started, *figliola*."

◆ ◆ ◆

AN HOUR LATER, they had just finished a lunch cooked by Jill. Now she was washing the dishes. While she worked, she was watching the two men outside through the small kitchen window. They were enjoying the pleasant shade of a large tree.

They chatted a bit longer. Then they came back into the kitchen. *Nonno* Giovanni announced that he was going to put two straw sleeping mats out in the sun to dry.

"There's no need, *Nonno*," said Jill. "We're leaving today. I have a lot to do in Italy."

"I do too, *figliola*. My mission here is over."

"*Nonno* is coming home, Jill. He's decided to come with us."

"Is that right?"

"*Sì*. And I want the two of you to rest today and tomorrow. We have a long trip ahead of us."

So they stayed.

A day and a half was long enough for *Nonno* Giovanni to rid himself of his belongings. The man who bought his small property off him was Jorge Valverde.

After closing the deal, once Valverde had gone, Jill asked *Nonno* Giovanni,

"That man was quite kind to me when he showed me the way here. But the thing is, he didn't want to set foot on your farm. It stood out to me. He seemed to be mad at you. And now... now I saw that he was frowning the whole time. So why did you want to negotiate with him, *Nonno*?"

"That scowl was definitely for me, *figliola*. That was why I thought it best to hand my property over to him."

"But why?"

"Because it was the dream of his lifetime. He always wanted the lake I made eighteen years ago."

"But...? I don't understand. If he got a good deal... if he ended up getting what he wanted, why the sour face?"

"*Figliola*... he is not to blame. The blame lies with the dream he sowed. His dream definitely did not involve making friends with me. Whatever his motives, he never truly accepted me as his neighbor. *Capisci?* The mouth only conveys what's inside the heart, even when it is closed."

That day, the three of them spent a series of unforgettable, joyous hours together. Every minute, Jill discovered more polished facets of a possible new life filled with kindness and forgiveness. Giancarlo absorbed the way the light shone through the trees of the forest and the beauty of the lake. He used his observations to do a couple of quick sketches for future paintings.

When Jill mentioned that Giancarlo attributed his landscapes on canvas to memories of past lives, *Nonno* Giovanni responded,

"Giancarlo took his first steps when he was just a year and a half old. Back then, I used to go on horseback rides with him sitting in front of me. His mother Albertina didn't like that. She thought it was dangerous. But what was so dangerous about taking him with me through those valleys... down those mountain paths?"

Looking at his grandson, he concluded,

"No, *figliolo*, you have never painted anything from past lives. That's just a tall tale. If you let me see a few of your paintings, maybe... maybe I could tell you where the place you painted is—and that you saw it when you were not yet two."

On the afternoon of the second day, Giancarlo made a comment about the wise voice Jill always heard. Then *Nonno* Giovanni stood in front of her.

"From *where* or *whom* do you think this voice originates?"

"Obviously not some spiritual guide. My subconscious takes it from the wisdom of the world. Have you ever read about the collective unconscious, *Nonno?*"

"No, no I haven't. But if you think your subconscious is giving you all that wisdom and that it can... it can help people, *figliola*, then why not return to the well your unconscious mind drank from when you were just a girl at the side of her Christian father?"

"The thing is she hears two voices," Giancarlo added.

"We all *always* hear two voices. We have to learn to tell them apart. The Spirit of God speaks in our hearts, and the trickster spirit speaks in our minds."

Little by little, Jill withdrew. She let the two men continue their conversation and walked away. She looked out at the sun already turning red in the west.

"Have faith in God, *figliola*," she heard *Nonno* say next to her. "He is God the Provider. That which does not exist, he calls into being."

The look Jill gave Giovanni didn't inspire much faith. It still bore the weight of pessimism—of frustration. In the end, the greatest objective of that grueling trip had not been attained. But she didn't argue.

On his last night on the farm, *Nonno* Giovanni said, "I'm happy to go. My heart is not here, on this little patch of land, even though I lived here for almost twenty years."

"*Il mio cuore* is with the people God placed in my path. There have been many of them. And I showed them He who is the Only Way. Many of them, I'm sure, will never go on a pilgrimage again. They accepted that the Long Walk... the pilgrimage that truly matters, had already been made almost two thousand years ago."

♦ ♦ ♦

MORNING BROKE ON THE DAY OF THEIR DEPARTURE.

Bright and early, Jorge Valverde and his scowl were there to take the keys. They got into Jill's car and drove off. At no point did *Nonno* Giovanni look back.

Less than an hour later, already in Villavieja del Campo, Jill decided to call Villa Piomondo. She wanted to know how her *Nonno* Vittorino was doing and tell them she was coming home.

"*Signorina* Jill!" said Genoveffa, sounding more startled than usual.

"Can I speak to my mother, Genoveffa?"

"*Sua mamma... sua mamma* went to take flowers to the chapel, *Signorina*."

Jill's legs went weak.

"The chapel?"

The villa's chapel was the tomb of the Tedesco Piomondo family. They only brought flowers there for All Souls' Day. Or when somebody died.

Thirty-One

The drive took them two days.

Now they were less than twenty miles from Villa Piomondo. *Nonno* Giovanni was snoring in the back seat. Giancarlo, who had shared the burden of driving with Jill, was now sitting tightlipped behind the wheel. Jill reclined her seat a bit and tried to relax.

To Giancarlo's surprise, without moving her head, she said, "You know Gian, I've been thinking back on when I left Villa Piomondo for the whole drive. Some things are falling into place now."

"For example?"

"The couple who were following me. I knew I'd seen them before. You know where I saw them? At a bar in Monte Carlo. I'm sure it was them. They must have been following me all along."

"And they disappeared. Do you think one day you might find out what they were looking for?"

"Well, it wasn't just to try exciting new dishes."

It was a brief moment of casualness. Moments later, Giancarlo said, "I don't know why, but I can only see Nicodemus as a drifter."

"To me he's still an angel. An angel-poet."

They both flashed brief smiles.

"How much longer, Jill?"

"We're basically there. Take the first right and go straight. But be careful, the road up is narrow and very windy."

Giancarlo took a right. He slowed down. The higher they went, the more magnificent the view became. From some of the bends in the road, he could glimpse the waters of the Mediterranean far in the distance.

"It's very beautiful here," he said.

But there was no response from Jill. Giancarlo noticed she had withdrawn again.

"I think you're disappointed deep down. Am I right?"

"Yes. And it isn't just my grandfather's death. I failed at everything, Gian."

"Something is weighing on you more heavily."

"Of course. It's the villa's debts. It was only going to be possible to pay them while my *nonno* was alive. We'll all have to leave now. My mother must be devastated, poor thing."

And then it all spilled out of her,

"Gian... try to understand me. I can't—I can't keep fooling myself and I don't want to. I have to face reality. It was all nice, what..." she looked back to check that *Nonno* Giovanni was snoring, "what *Nonno* said. But how can I leave it up to God to fix something... something that is only mine to fix? Or does God not wait for us to act?"

"I'm starting to get freaked out again, Gian. It's okay that my *Nonno* Vittorino died... that is, I was preparing for that ever since I brought him home from the hospital a few days ago. As for my mother... well, she has relatives here in Italy: my uncles. And she has my father's pension. But as for me, sooner or later, I'm going to have to face the problem I left behind in Atlanta. And I'll have to fight for my career. But... what about those kids?"

"It isn't proving easy. The more I try to run away from my worries... the more they come jumping back, those little kids... jumping and growing before my eyes... their empty hands... their eyes full of tears and terror. It hurts, Gian. It hurts that I did all that running around for nothing—only to come back with nothing."

After a brief pause, Giancarlo asked, "And what about Mike?"

"We're here, Gian!"

Thirty-Two

Peppino smiled jubilantly in the midst of his small flock. Ever since *Signorina* Jill's car came around the last bend before the villa's front gate, Peppino's joy had been bursting forth from him in short monosyllabic phrases. He figured that would be enough for the nearest sheep to understand why he was so delighted. He ran over to the bars of the gate. Dante Migliano was already there.

On the back seat, only then did *Nonno* Giovanni wake up to find the trip was over.

"We're there, *Nonno*," Jill announced. "We're finally home." And she added, "At least for now."

As soon as they pulled in and stopped, she stuck her head halfway out.

"*Grazie*, Peppino. *Grazie*, Dante."

"Did you have a good trip, *Signorina*?" Dante asked with restrained joy. He was wearing a black stripe on his shirt sleeve.

"We did, *Signor* Dante."

"*Sua mamma* thought you would be arriving yesterday afternoon, *Signorina*."

Jill didn't respond. She couldn't say anything because Peppino's gaping smile was right there. And his eyes were gleaming. Jill felt so sorry to disappoint him.

"Poor Peppino..." she whispered to Giancarlo. "He's expecting me to have brought a lot of money."

"Why?" Giancarlo wanted to know.

"Before I left, I told him I would buy back all the sheep *Signor* Dante had sold... to feed the people that live at the villa."

"I'll talk to you later, Peppino," she said.

"*Sì, sì, Signorina!*" he responded with enthusiasm. Just then, Jill saw her mother waving from an upper balcony above where a white convertible was parked. Someone next to her was also waving—someone in an impeccable dark-brown suit. She nibbled her lower lip. She put the car in gear and slowly drove forward.

"Who is that?" Giancarlo asked. But he was just asking for asking's sake. He was already sure it was Mike.

◆ ◆ ◆

ALWAYS RESPECTFUL OF TRADITION, Maddalena Heston was wearing black. Jill got out of the car and went to hug her mother. Maddalena cried a bit into her daughter's shoulder. *Nonno* Vittorino's death seemed to have taken a piece of the villa with it.

Next came Mike's turn. With a confident grin plastered on his face, he embraced Jill and planted a kiss on her cheek.

"I feel like I haven't seen you in years, darling," he said, still holding Jill's hands.

"What happened, Mike? Are you investing in Italy now?"

Mike laughed loudly.

To escape his clutches, she went to introduce *Nonno* Giovanni and Giancarlo to her mother. She started with Giancarlo.

"Hello, Giancarlo," said Maddalena Heston, greeting him with her hand.

"*Piacere, Signora.* My condolences about your father's death."

"Thank you."

"Now I'd like you to meet Giancarlo's *nonno*," said Jill.

"How have you been, *Signor* Giovanni?" Maddalena Heston asked, surprising her daughter.

"Have you met before?"

"So, he didn't tell you he was here visiting your *Nonno* Vittorino almost two years ago?"

"Two years and three months, *Signora*. No, I didn't tell her. I was saving that for now."

As a mere spectator to the conversation, Mike just stood there with the same sophisticated smile on his face. Jill introduced him to the others.

Maddalena Heston then said, "*Signor* Giovanni... I want to thank you for that day. After your visit, *mio padre* changed a lot. At first, I didn't understand. But later... I don't know what you said to my father. But he... how can I explain? I started noticing that he was kinder, so concerned about everyone... sometimes he would shy away from people and... he would cry like a child."

"But he always found a way to hide it," Jill added. "He was constantly blaming that cataract."

She smiled thinly at her mother. Mike guffawed.

"Yes, it's true," said Maddalena Heston. "That's a nice memory of your *nonno, figliola*. And before he died, he said that... that he died at peace... that he felt like he had been forgiven by God."

"Repentance is the first step a child of God makes on the path of return, *Signora*."

Jill froze. She craned her head to listen to something.

"Mother... where is that coming from...?"

"That's the children singing. They got here this morning."

"Chil-dren?"

"Why the surprise?"

"Well," Mike cut in, "unfortunately, I have to go now. I have to get to Rome for a meeting tonight."

"Ah, what a pity," said Maddalena Heston.

Mike grabbed Jill's hands again.

"But of course I'll be back. Probably the day after tomorrow."

Jill didn't say a single word. She let Mike kiss her on the cheek.

"See you when I'm back, darling. Rest up. We have lots to talk about."

He kissed Maddalena's cheek too, said goodbye to Giancarlo and his grandfather, then planted himself in the white convertible. Two minutes later, he left the villa.

The four walked in the direction of the restored mansion. Jill was in front with her mother, with *Nonno* Giovanni and Giancarlo behind.

"How did they get here, mother? Where did the help come from?"

"What are you talking about, Jill? So, it wasn't you who provided for everything?"

"Me?!"

"I got a call from the bank saying some money had been deposited in your *nonno*'s account. They asked me if it was to pay off the debt and I said yes. Didn't you go traveling to find your grandfather's friends?"

"Mother! I didn't get any money! Those men are all either dead or ruined! Every last one!"

"What? I don't understand."

"I'm the one who doesn't understand. Tell me everything."

"After the bank called me, I called a taxi from Salerno and took your *nonno* to the bank to sign some papers. That was in the morning. That afternoon he started to feel unwell. It really must have been God's plan. One more day and all would have been lost. But now you... Jill, I don't know what to think."

They entered the house. For a moment, the topic was forgotten.

◆ ◆ ◆

IN A LARGE ROOM that had been painted straw yellow, Jill stopped, astonished by everything she was seeing and hearing. She couldn't make out what the words being sung with such stunning ability were—but music isn't made of words only. So, she wept. She saw no sadness there—only joy in the small multitude of eyes, all amazingly large and bright. She could feel the warmth radiating from their dignified faces, all of them singing with voices that were unique, human, content, and loved.

They sang the song Mary Marshall had taught them in sweet, finely honed voices. But more than that: they were all striving to prove that they had not just remembered how to smile but now they also felt like doing so.

Jill gazed into their little faces and saw that they were tearing up as well.

Then she looked at the couple of American missionaries. She was touched by Mary's meekness. She smiled at Benny Marshall, whose serene joy and glistening eyes were perhaps now seeing in her, Jill, something of her father.

One four-year-old boy, the youngest of them all, was not singing: his big eyes were fixed on Jill. She signaled to him with a smile and he stepped forward. Crouching down, she picked him up, set him on her hip, and went to join Giancarlo. She was surprised at how natural it felt for her to have that little boy in tow while standing next to Giancarlo.

Looking around, she asked, "Where is your *nonno*, Gian?"

"He walked away with the Missionary. Why?"

"I have to talk to him. He must know who made this happen."

She traded smiles with the boy and chatted to him for a few moments. Then, returning him to his friends, she left the mansion with Giancarlo.

♦ ♦ ♦

Not long after, Jill had managed to track down *Nonno* Giovanni. The feeling of sharing Mary and Benny Marshall's love for those children had already been processed. Now her rational mind craved explanations.

"*Nonno*... you must know something. Tell me. I want you to tell me what's going on. You were one of those men, weren't you?"

"No, of course not... it's impossible. What I told you about them is true, *figliola*."

It was a frank answer. Jill looked at Giancarlo.

"Do you know something, Gian? Money doesn't just fall from the sky."

"Are you sure?"

"Listen, I'm being serious!"

Missionary Marshall walked up. He placed his hand kindly on *Nonno* Giovanni's shoulder and said, "I heard you're planning to go home today."

"Yes, in two, maybe two and a half, hours."

"Then we still have a bit of time to talk."

Just then they both heard a car horn at the front gate. Dante Migliano hurried over to open it. A vehicle came in with two men sitting in the front seats. The man in the driver's seat exchanged a few words with Dante. Then the car drove up to the house.

Kurmanian War Orphans Finally Have Somewhere to Call Home

The Hero of Atlanta

Judge John Molden has ruled in favor of the clinical psychologist Dr. Jill Heston, PhD, in her counterclaim of defamation and charged businessman Alfred G. Dickson with perjury.

Dr. Jill Heston

Who is Dr. Jill Heston, PhD, the unjustly accused Atlanta psychologist?

She was working to help her father, the late Consul Wesley T. Heston, on a mission to rescue 33 little victims of turf wars in Kurmania.

The arrival of a one-million-dollar check donated by US Senator Frank Borsato to the plight of the Kurmanian orphans, now refugees in southern Italy, is scheduled for next Friday.

◆ ◆ ◆

WHEN JILL had finished reading the newspaper article, she looked, stunned, at Giancarlo.

"Gian!" she proclaimed euphorically. "God is so great!"

Then, in English, she said to the grinning journalist,

"Mr. Benson... I... I don't know what to say. One million dollars...! I don't need that much money... my father was expecting three hundred thousand. It was enough to buy a small farm and make a few arrangements."

"I understand your surprise, Miss Heston," said Bill Benson. "But great that it's a million, isn't it?"

Jill looked at her mother. Maddalena Heston was smiling and weeping.

"Now it's all explained, daughter. Now we know who paid the debt and the boat fees."

"Did Senator Frank Borsato also get the authorization for the children to disembark, Mr. Benson?"

"Well... Not that I'm aware of," he answered, somewhat surprised by Jill's lack of awareness of what had happened." He probably had someone else do it. But, Ms. Heston, now I'd like to finish my report. America is waiting... and I think the rest of the world as well. Everyone's attention is focused on this incredible little corner of Italy. And they all want to meet the hero of Atlanta."

William Benson signaled to the man accompanying him. He was a cameraman from a Naples TV station. Getting his camera out of the car, he walked over.

Jill realized what was about to happen.

"Oh, no. Please, not now," she said running a hand through her hair. "I'm... I'm tired, I've been traveling for two days."

"Maybe tomorrow morning, then"

"That would be better, Mr. Benson."

Turning to the cameraman, Bill Benson asked him, in Italian,

"What do you say?"

"*D'accordo*. But the earlier the better."

"Is nine in the morning okay?" Jill proposed.

They agreed.

"Can I keep these newspapers, Mr. Benson?"

"Of course."

Feeling somewhat unwelcome, Bill Benson said his goodbyes and started heading for his car.

Giovanni followed him to the car, as he had noticed that the journalist appeared tense, as if he still had news to share. Genoveffa joined them. As Bill Benson quietly explained the initial mix up with the donated money, their faces lit up.

Unaware of this development, while still inside the house, Jill turned to celebrate with her mother. They hugged and cried. Then Jill extended a hand to Giancarlo. He was somewhat taken aback. It was the first time she had done that.

"Gian! I'm so happy!"

"And I'm happy for you, Jill."

However, six feet behind them, Benny Marshall's forehead was creased.

He motioned for them to sit down and talk to Jill and *Signora* Maddalena. Excusing himself, Giancarlo left to meet *Signor* Dante to ask him a long list of questions about the farming operations in the villa.

Maddalena and Jill listened attentively to Benny Marshall with their joyous expressions gradually fading away.

"On the day the Consul died, I had called him to explain why I had not accepted that suitcase full of cash. I thought it was dirty money. And it came with no information about the sender apart from an acronym. I called the bank, but they could not confirm the origin of the money. You see, a few days prior to that, I had heard about certain suspicious acts of money laundering in connection with cash donations from Washington, DC. Later that day, the Consul called me back to report that he had heard the same stories of money laundering and that he would investigate the matter further. He asked me to keep this confidential. Unfortunately, he died before we had the opportunity to clarify the matter."

At the end of their meeting, Benny Marshall left them in stunned silence. Now with grief in their hearts, Jill and Maddalena sat quietly trying to process this new information. Benny Marshall excused himself and walked outside for some fresh air but was intercepted by Giovanni.

"*Signor* Giovanni…" he said, staring at a fixed spot on the ground, "I must confess I don't understand something."

They started walking away from everyone else. *Nonno* Giovanni didn't ask any questions. He just wanted to ease the missionary's burden.

Marshall turned to the other man,

"Join me in prayer, *Signor* Giovanni. I need God to take certain thoughts off my mind—or to enlighten me."

They started praying in low voices while their feet carried them toward the orchard.

Five minutes later, far on the other side of the property, they had no way of knowing another car had arrived at Villa Piomondo.

♦ ♦ ♦

THE CAR CAME THROUGH the gates and stopped, blocking Bill Benson's exit. It was clearly an intentional maneuver.

Jill traded a perplexed look with Giancarlo.

"But…? What are those two doing here at the villa?"

Maddalena Heston came over to stand next to her daughter.

"The missionaries and children are here now thanks to them, Jill."

"What?"

"If not for those two, the *Pellegrino* would have set sail the day before the authorization to disembark arrived."

Jill was perplexed. With a slight smile, Tonelli gave her a quick finger wave.

But the person Tonelli wanted to see was Bill Benson—that was why he had parked behind him. Isabella went to join Jill, Giancarlo, and Maddalena Heston. Tonelli walked up to the American journalist. Bill was still standing by his vehicle.

"Hey there, *bello*! I went to all our favorite bars in Naples looking for you. You really are unbelievable! You don't waste any time!"

Without the slightest bit of ceremony, Tonelli opened the back door and climbed into Bill Benson's car, motioning for him to join him. He said to the cameraman,

"Buddy, would you mind stepping out for a cigarette?"

◆ ◆ ◆

MEANWHILE, NEAR THE ORCHARD, Giovanni and Missionary Marshall were deep in conversation underneath an olive tree. Totally oblivious to the confrontation between Tonelli and Bill Benson nearby, they were watching three boats slowly sailing the blue of the Mediterranean. Closer to the horizon, a speedboat sliced through the waters, leaving a trail of white behind it. This stirred up Marshall's memories of the two and a half months he had spent aboard the *Pellegrino*—including the voyage from Kurmania to the Bay of Naples.

"But you still haven't told me what's bothering you, Missionary."

Marshall let out a half sigh.

"It's true, I haven't. All I said was that I didn't understand the news that American journalist brought about that US senator donating the money—and that's why I asked you to pray with me. *Signor* Giovanni, did I make a mistake in not accepting that suitcase with the cash? We certainly felt God's provision with the many things that happened while we were on board the *Pellegrino*. But did I bring unnecessary suffering upon us all?

"The morning after I met the Italian journalist, the harbormaster of the Cagliari port got in touch with Captain Sbroggio and said there was money waiting for him at some bank. Mary and I fell to our knees on the deck, *Signor* Giovanni. And we raised our hands to the sky. 'Yes, Missionary,' said Captain Sbroggio, 'if that is true, I think I'll have to believe that miracles do happen sometimes.'"

Marshall then stressed, "The way it all happened seemed like a miracle—a miracle involving many people, *Signor* Giovanni. I remember how flabbergasted Tonelli looked when he wasn't able to get a single photo of the children. Then he left. And he left without saying anything. That was when Mary and I began to pray. We didn't know what was going to happen—but God did. And he knew that everything was going to be resolved in less than fifteen hours."

Thirty-Three

"*Ma cosa…*? She… she left?" Tonelli asked, half afraid.

"Yes," responded the captain of the *Navigatore*. "I told her my dinghy was basically a bathtub, but she didn't care one bit. So, I ordered a sailor to take her bag and lower the dinghy. It's already on the way back now."

Tonelli looked toward the port of Cagliari. Night had fallen, but nevertheless he was able to spot the *Navigatore*'s dinghy. And he saw only the sailor inside it.

"I'll go ashore too then, Captain."

"And how long are you two going to keep smooth talking me with this back and forth? I have a schedule to stick to and commitments to uphold."

"Then the best thing for you to do now is get rid of me as quickly as possible."

Twenty-five minutes later, suitcase in hand, Tonelli set foot on dry land. He went right to the departures area of the port. The sailor told him that Isabella was planning to go to Naples that very night.

They ran into each another near the ticket office. Isabella was doubly disenchanted: both with her fiancé and the ferries. The last one had just left. Setting his suitcase down next to hers, Tonelli sat down by her side.

Isabella was in no mood to talk, but ended up saying,

"When I was coming here in that old dinghy... me and that fishy-smelling sailor... looking at all those anchored fishing boats... I thought about our trip around the world. What a fool I was to believe you...! I felt like I'd fallen from a transatlantic cruise into a bathtub with two holes in it. In the past fourteen years, I think this is the first time I've actually had my feet on the ground."

Tonelli said nothing. He didn't open his arms, or say he was hungry... he didn't even curse. And that made Isabella feel strange.

"What scheme are you cooking up this time, can you tell me?" she asked.

"I'm thinking about the pictures I screwed up... and about those kids."

Another surprise to Isabella. Her voice came out almost sickly.

"What do you mean screwed up? There were three or four shots left on that film."

"Dunno. All I know is that I wasn't able to get a single decent shot."

Isabella let out a sigh of relief.

"Thank goodness. At least my camera won't have a headache because of your scheming."

Tonelli was in no mood to argue. Not now. He felt empty. What he wanted now was to eat something. And fall into bed.

"It's been more than thirty hours since the last time I slept."

"Are you sure nothing else happened on the *Pellegrino*?"

Tonelli wasn't going to mention the children's hymn, his jaw locking up... or his tongue getting tied. He didn't know how to finish.

"And now, what are *noi due* going to do?"

Isabella's question relit a ten-year fire. Or fourteen. She had said *we two*.

"Bella... Bella *mia*...! Are you trying to say that... that *noi due* are still...?"

"What else am I supposed to do? Try to run away from you? I already have and that didn't work."

Revitalized, he got up off the bench.

"First let's get ourselves a hotel nearby, Bella. *E poi*... after that, let's get something to eat."

Tonelli picked up both of their suitcases. And they left. As they walked, he started fanning the flames again,

"Tomorrow morning we'll go back to Naples, Bella. And I'll put the whole truth to paper. Despite the exhaustion and everything else, I did it."

"I'm sure you did something. You got the missionaries mixed up in your lies. Poor things. They'll be waiting around until noon tomorrow for something that will never happen."

Changing the subject, Tonelli started talking about food.

◆ ◆ ◆

A NEW DAY DAWNED in Cagliari.

Tonelli heard a knock at the door and went to see who it was.

"Missionary!"

"Good thing you stayed at this hotel close to the docks. This is the third place I checked, Tonelli. I had to thank you."

"Thank me? What do you mean, Missionary? Please, come in."

Drawn by the conversation, Isabella stuck her head out of the bathroom door.

"Hi, Missionary Marshall."

"Hi, Isabella," he said walking in. "I can't stay long. I came just to say that you two are amazing. Mary, the kids, and I are all grateful. May God shower you with blessings."

Tonelli felt a nervous tick and started rubbing his jawline.

"A bit less than an hour ago, the Cagliari port harbormaster contacted the *Pellegrino*. They wanted to know the total of our bill, since someone decided to settle up for us. Captain Sbroggio is already at the bank picking up the money. And I just picked up a fax giving the children authorization to disembark from the harbormaster."

Tonelli's jaw froze, his tongue was rendered useless. But he held firm in collecting someone else's laurels.

"Only God can repay what you have done," came the missionary. "It doesn't matter if it was your paper putting pressure on certain people or what... what does matter is that God put you two in our path. We were just about to set sail for the Suez Canal. May God bless you."

Marshall was already leaving. Then he remembered,

"Oh yeah, we just have one problem. We don't know where Villa Piomondo is."

"We can take you there."

The person who said that was Isabella. Very gratefully, Benny Marshall agreed on the details. Then he left.

◆ ◆ ◆

THERE WAS ABSOLUTE SILENCE.

Sitting on their beds across from each other, Tonelli and Isabella were staring into one another's eyes. They were still slightly afraid.

"Did you hear what I heard, Bella?"

"*Sì.*"

"Then have we made up?"

"*Sì.*"

"Then explain to me what happened."

Isabella shrugged her shoulders.

"What's going on with your jaw?" she asked.

"I don't know... it's been kind of stiff. It started when I took those bad pictures of the kids. But I think my TMJ is acting up... I should go see a dentist."

After a bit of thought, Tonelli asked,

"Bella... do you believe that... that someone is capable of doing something good by accident?"

Isabella shrugged her shoulders again. Then she added,

"I guess so. Don't people often do something bad and then say they didn't mean to do it?"

"What does that mean, Bella?"

She reflected.

"Maybe... maybe it means that there are many things we do not mean to do, *Amore*. Both good... and bad."

He raised his head.

"But you don't think it was us, Bella? Then... then who was it?"

◆ ◆ ◆

"As I SAID, *Signor* Giovanni," Benny Marshall continued, "neither Mary nor I know what really happened. All we know is that this journalist, Tonelli, came into our lives and suddenly everything just happened. But now... after what we just saw..."

Marshall took a deep breath. He was visibly worried.

"That's why I'm feeling so down right now, *Signor* Giovanni. I need God to give me an answer. I wonder if I refused to receive God's providence because I judged someone too quickly, and too harshly. Until very recently, I only knew to thank divine providence for... for putting people like Tonelli and his fiancée in our path, and... and mainly for having moved you, *Signore.*"

"*Io?*" *Nonno* Giovanni asked, putting his hand on his chest. Now he was the one who didn't understand.

Marshall explained everything. He said what Tonelli told him about an old friend of Jill's grandfather—a friend called Giovanni di Stefano—who had offered the money to solve all the problems concerning the children.

Benny Marshall flashed a smile and looked for *Nonno* Giovanni's small eyes.

"I was happy, *Signor* Giovanni... happy and anxious to meet and embrace the benefactor God had provided for us."

"Well, I am not that benefactor, Missionary."

As if to confirm, Marshall kept slightly shaking his head.

"Unfortunately not, *Signor* Giovanni. That was why I asked you to come pray with me. I need to understand. I'm starting to find it hard to accept that all this... that all these providences might have come from the same dirty source as before... or not. I'm not sure. And I am conflicted."

Nonno Giovanni blinked in surprise.

"What do you mean? Dirty source? *Non capisco.*"

"Let me tell you. And I know you'll feel the same way."

Thirty-Four

"What extraordinary talent you have!" said Tonelli in a voice laden with sarcasm. "I must confess that I underestimated your abilities, Bill. How quickly you arranged for some dirty plates to be cleaned over in America! What a nice concert!"

Tonelli was sprawled out on the back seat. Keeping his calm, Bill Benson was gazing forward without really looking at anything in particular. The TV man was smoking a cigarette not far away. On the other side, around fifty feet from the car, Jill's group was completely surrounding Isabella. This meant the two of them were totally isolated inside William Benjamin Benson's car.

"I don't know what you're talking about, *Pingue*," Bill Benson changed the subject. He took out a cigarette, lit it and blew some smoke out the window.

Tonelli was verging on blasphemy. He leaned forward until his nose was almost touching the back of the American man's head.

"Don't play stupid, Bill. You know perfectly well what I'm talking about."

Taking a few pages from his internal jacket pocket, Tonelli chose his next words carefully,

"I don't know *when, where* or *how* you got the information to run out here before me and put this whole circus on in Jill's name, Bill. But nobody is going to stop me from publishing the truth. It's all right here."

Tonelli tapped four fingers on the pages. Blowing another wisp of smoke out the window, Bill Benson turned his head to look at the paper.

"Well, *Pingue*... why write an opera with so little to go on? I was drinking from the same well as you were. You know very well how much Miro Vaccaro appreciates a good whiskey—and the way he talks your ear off after his second glass."

"Ah, so it was that jerk Vaccaro! I should have known. And you didn't waste any time. Isn't that right, Bill? You made one call, spooked your fellow countryman Senator Frank Borsato and, in two or three calls, he took care of everything before the castle crumbled."

Bill Benson kept his cool. He knew it was impossible to debate with *Pingue*—especially when he was convinced of what he was saying.

And Tonelli continued,

"But I will fight to the end, Bill. You'd better believe I will. And everyone will learn the truth. Here and in America."

"And what truth might that be?"

Massimo Tonelli drank in the American journalist's slight tone of mockery. He restrained himself from puffing up like an angry toad. He spewed out that American society had been fooled. And that since the beginning, Frank Borsato's so-called *donation* had stayed right where it was as a slush fund for his re-election campaign. Meanwhile, using his connections to certain shady characters in the USA, he had had someone order a Sicilian friend of Nico Sacchi to leave a suitcase full of dirty money with Missionary Marshall on the *Pellegrino*.

"Bill, do you really think this one-million-dollar check and emotional manipulation using Jill's name will distract the American public? And that this will keep everyone from learning about that windbag politician pretending to help a handful of desperate children just to pick up some votes? Do you think a garbage lid today will cover up the stench of yesterday's rotten food? Didn't that jerk Vaccaro ask you these questions, Bill?"

"And there's more," Tonelli emphasized, his face now almost pure white. "This con... all this nastiness made Missionary Benny Marshall indignant. Of course he had to refuse the dirty money. And even so, Marshall didn't lose much—practically just some time. It was worse for the late Consul Heston, who died when he found out about the machinations using his name and the impoverished war victims."

Tonelli touched Bill Benson's right ear with his pointer finger.

"Now answer me, Bill: what is it worth? The death of an honorable man, whose biggest mistake was trusting the corrupt temperament of a politician from his own homeland—what is that worth? Huh?"

Wanting to laugh, William Benjamin Benson was shaking his head.

"You know, *Pingue...*" he said quite calmly, "you could have been a Hollywood screenwriter... you have an extremely fertile imagination. Why don't you try your hand at writing spy novels?"

"The Berlin Wall fell a long time ago, Bill. And the Soviet empire, too."

"So what? There will always be someone who wants a piece of their neighbor's backyard."

Tonelli put an end to it. Pulling the cassette tape from his pocket, he shook it next to Bill Benson's face. He turned to look at it, but Tonelli pulled his hand away.

"I have a recording, Bill. And you're gonna listen to it."

Tonelli put the tape in his mini-recorder and pressed play, starting the conversation between Senator Frank Borsato and Consul Heston. Bill Benson listened in silence.

"With everything else I've discovered," Tonelli said, "it's as good as an admission of guilt."

"Enough," they both heard. It was Jill. Her face was pale and her hand was outstretched next to Tonelli. "I've heard enough. Give me the tape, *per favore.* I think I have rightful claim to it. After all, it did belong to my father. Give it to me, please."

The person who opened the car door and pulled the mini recorder from Tonelli's hand was Isabella. She took out the tape and placed it in Jill's hand.

"I also think you've done enough, *Amore,*" said Isabella with a firm tone. She gave the recorder back to her fiancé.

Speechless and somewhat afraid, Tonelli got out of the car. His cheeks pale, Bill Benson stayed in the driver's seat.

"Do you smoke, *Signor* Tonelli?" Jill asked him.

"No, *Signorina*. I don't."

"Well, I do," said Bill Benson, already opening the door with his lighter lit.

Then, pulling the tape out of the cassette, Jill let flames consume it to the end.

"*Mi perdoni*," she said to Tonelli's gaping face. "I know it's hard to understand. But if my father were alive, he'd have done the same thing."

Turning back to William Benjamin Benson, she said in English,

"I think our interview is off for tomorrow morning, Mr. Benson. And everything else is off, too. I promise to pay Senator Frank Borsato back what he already spent to get those children off that ship. Same goes for the bank debt. I'll settle this, you can tell him. I don't have anything else to say about this—not to you and not to anyone else. Good afternoon, Mr. Benson."

Bill Benson's forehead was now glistening. He ran three fingers over it. He thought about getting out of the car and explaining everything to Jill, but he also understood that he was no longer welcome there. He hoped *Signor* Giovanni could clarify things later and he prepared to leave.

Without saying anything else, Jill walked a few steps over to Giancarlo. They said nothing, and this time they didn't hold hands. He could see that Jill was heartbroken. She hunched her shoulders, shrinking into herself. It had all been just a fleeting dream.

Maddalena Heston walked over.

"*Figlia mia*, don't be like that... don't let it get to you."

In response she bit her lower lip, her shimmering eyes darting away from her mother's glance. Maddalena tried to hold her daughter's arm.

"Jill!"

With no response at all, Jill started walking quickly toward the main house. Maddalena Heston turned to face Giancarlo.

"*Dio mio*! Did this have to happen?"

"Try and talk to her, *Signora*. She needs our help."

♦ ♦ ♦

STILL IN THE SAME SPOT, his hands stuffed hopelessly into his pockets, the look in Tonelli's eyes was now somehow pathetic as he allowed Bill Benson to order him to get out of his car and out of the way so he could quickly drive off.

The cameraman, seeing it was time to leave, threw his cigarette on the ground and went to take a seat next to Benson.

Benson threw it into reverse to get around Tonelli's car. That was all the time Tonelli needed. With a quick sprint, he was in front of the car and he made Bill Benson stop again. Leaning into the car window, he said quite close to the American's ear,

"Bill... we lead a hard life. You know that better than anyone."

"Spit it out, *Pingue*. What are you suggesting?" Bill Benson said straightforwardly.

"Well... it just so happens I have a copy of that cassette tape..."

"Of course. I knew it. I might be able to use it for a follow-up story. How much?"

That was all Tonelli wanted to hear. Giving the American a pat on the shoulder, he put on a triumphant half-smile all the while he was being judged.

"I'll see you soon, later tonight in that restaurant by the market."

"Sure, *Pingue*. I'll see you there."

◆ ◆ ◆

JILL'S WORLD had come crashing down all over again. She forced herself not to cry, but her head was throbbing. It was her ingrained nature. But the tears she was choking back weren't just for the million dollars she just turned down—they were also for the pain of knowing how much her father had suffered in the last moments of his life over all this mess.

Maddalena Heston walked away from the window from which she'd been staring at the Mediterranean and reflecting. Then she said, "That afternoon... the afternoon your father called me saying that everything was fine. I guess he didn't want me to worry about him. Your father was a discreet man and never brought problems from work home to his family. He only said that he would be coming home late since he had to make some arrangements. He died moments later, *figlia mia*."

Jill got up from the rattan armchair.

"But I told that journalist that I'll pay Senator Frank Borsato back every last cent. It might be good money now, but it's still stained with father's blood."

"We'll pay him back, *figliola*. I don't know how, but we will. Thank goodness you are free to work as a psychologist again."

"Yeah, thank God," said Jill, walking over to the door. "Now I have to go.

Giancarlo and his *nonno* have to catch the train to Cosenza."

"Do they have to leave today? You've all been traveling for so long."

"It's Giancarlo's *nonno*'s idea. He is in a hurry to get home."

"Jill."

She stopped. She stared at her mother.

"What about Mike?"

Jill took the question a different way than it was intended.

"*Mamma*... are you sure you didn't ask Mike for help? When did he get here? Why did he come?"

"Well... he started calling again the night your *nonno* died, and the next day he was here for the burial. I let him stay at the villa, and that was how he learned you were going to be arriving from Spain. So, he waited until now."

"I see. And I guess he already knows why I went to Spain."

Her mother's eyes were incapable of lying.

"Well, *figliola*, I... last time I called, I already told him something about your trip... and about the situation at the villa with your *nonno*'s health."

"Mom...! Why did you do that? I know you're on his side—and I can even understand that. But haven't you noticed that Mike only became interested in me again after I won the lawsuit in Atlanta? I actually thought he might be feeling bad about that... but no. If I have another problem like that, Mike will no doubt invent some urgent business trip to the North Pole."

And Jill added,

"Maybe we don't owe that senator anything. Mike could easily be behind all of this. I know him. He puts a price on people. And if that's the case, *Mamma*, what a nice little pickle I'm in! I don't know what would be worse: owing the senator or owing Mike."

"Jill," Maddalena walked over to her daughter and stroked her hair, "don't look at me like that. I want the best for you, and this has nothing to do with the problems we're going through. I didn't ask Mike for help, but I also can't say for sure that he didn't do anything. I just think you need to forget about Atlanta."

Jill's lips flashed the outline of a wry smile.

"Then our life would be a bed of roses, isn't that right, *Mamma*?"

After a brief silence she said, "Mom... an idea just occurred to me. Call the bank and ask where the deposit into *Nonno*'s account came from."

"But I know where it came from: Spain. That was why I thought you sent it."

"You know it wasn't me. And I want to know exactly who it was. It coming from Spain would eliminate Mike, anyway."

Maddalena Heston made a call to the bank in Naples.

"I'd like to speak to *Signor* Vilacqua, *per favore.*"

"May I ask who's calling?"

"Tell him it's Maddalena Piomondo Heston."

"One moment, *Signora.*"

Moments later, the manager picked up.

"Good afternoon, *Signora* Maddalena. How can I be of service?"

"Good afternoon, *Signor* Vilacqua. I'm looking for some information. That money... the deposit made into my late father's account came from Spain, according to what they told me at the bank. But I need to know who actually sent it."

"Just a moment. I'll have someone check that for you."

Maddalena waited for six minutes. The whole time Jill stood on the balcony staring out at the sea. She heard her mother thank the man for the information then hang up the phone.

Maddalena Heston walked over to her daughter.

"There is no way to know who made the deposit. It wasn't an electronic transfer: it was made in cash at a bank branch in Málaga."

"Málaga?" Jill repeated.

"That's what they told me. Well, Jill, I guess you can cross out Mike at least. And Senator Frank Borsato, too."

After a brief reflection, Jill said, "I'm not so sure about that, *Mamma.* There are many ways of getting dirty money into circulation. And as for Mike... what a deadend! My head is pounding. I never thought the solution to the problem with the children would be such a hassle. Mike... Senator Frank Borsato... what's worse, *Mamma?*"

Jill was already in the doorway again.

"You like him, don't you?"

Jill said nothing in response. She just held her mother's gaze.

"I'm talking about that guy... Giancarlo."

"I know, *Mamma.*"

"That was what I wanted to hear. You like him. If you like him, then why are you being so hard on yourself? Listen to what your heart is telling you. It's your life, not mine. You can make your own decisions."

"I have to go. The train to Cosenza will be leaving in a little over an hour."

"But won't they have a bite to eat? Or a cup of coffee? I forgot to offer them anything with all this running around."

"They don't have time and we had lunch before we arrived."

On the ground floor, Jill ran into Genoveffa.

"Find *Signor* Dante for me, Genoveffa. I need him."

"*Sì, Signorina*," answered Genoveffa, who was rather anxious to have a word with Jill but seemed to have no luck in finding the right moment.

Jill rushed to find Giancarlo and *Nonno* Giovanni.

◆ ◆ ◆

TIGHT-LIPPED AND ARMS CROSSED, Giovanni took a few steps forward and stood watching a speedboat carving arabesques on the surface of the sea.

Then he walked back to Benny Marshall, who still had a despondent look on his face. The mark of a smile that seemed eternal had gone from his lips. The missionary exclaimed,

"Goodness! This is all so uncomfortable. I never thought we could still be mixed up in all this nastiness. Now Captain Sbroggio's words ring clear to me, *Signor* Giovanni. The ways of God are unfathomable, I know. But I cannot forget the look on the Captain's face... such an ironic look. When he came back from the bank with the money in his bag, he said, 'It's no big deal to me, Missionary, but I don't know why you didn't want to keep that suitcase full of dollars right at the very beginning. Where do you think this new money from Málaga came from? Sicily is not all that far from southern Spain, Missionary...'"

Marshall stopped talking. He didn't even notice that Giovanni had raised his eyebrows.

"Málaga?" he asked. "You said the transfer came from Málaga, Missionary?"

"Yes, Captain Sbroggio told me."

Giovanni kept running his fingers through his trimmed beard.

"And the name... the name of the man who sent it—did he tell you that?"

"Yes, of course."

Giovanni's small green-brown eyes rediscovered their habitual sparkle when he heard the name.

"Don't worry, Missionary. The money is not dirty."

That eternal smile reclaimed its place on Benny Marshall's lips. He listened to everything Giovanni had to say in silence. He asked for Giovanni to pray for him for his wrongdoings, even though they had been well-intended. After their prayer, Benny Marshall's countenance reflected the freedom he felt from having the heavy burden lifted from his soul.

In the end, Marshall said, "Ms. Heston will be happy to hear that."

"But I am not supposed to say anything yet, Missionary."

"Yes, I know. I was just thinking of her emotional state."

"Peace comes from God. And the wind blows when He sees fit."

"And where He sees fit."

"Perfect, Missionary. She will know when the time is right."

◆ ◆ ◆

JILL MET GIANCARLO halfway between the mansion and orchard.

"Isn't it time for you to be going?" she asked.

"I think so. But what about you—how are you? You seem so tense."

"I'm fine now. I'm not mad anymore. But my head is splitting."

"In pain or from thinking too much?"

Dante came over. She said, "*Signor* Dante, please go take my suitcase out of the car. It's the brown one." Jill handed him the keys. "Then please drive Gian and his grandfather to the station in Salerno. I have a lot to sort out here at the villa."

"*Sì, Signorina.*"

Dante walked away.

Giancarlo said, "Jill... I thought the children arriving would be a relief. In the end, that's what you were fighting for."

"Of course it was. But now I have to manage things, don't I? You know what's bothering me. Money doesn't just fall from the sky, as I already said. And now someone might come out of the blue and present me with a big fat bill. Did you think of that? I have to be ready. It's the way I am."

And she continued, "Try to understand: before, when my grandfather was alive, everything was going well. The mansion was restored, and all I had to do was get the children off that boat. But now... now it's hard to accept that maybe we owe everything to the man who caused my father's death. Or even worse: that I might be indebted to Mike."

"Ah," replied Giancarlo, "I see. He's roping you in with those numbers of his."

Silence. Arms crossed, looking at the landscape but not seeing it, she continued,

"I didn't say he was for certain, but he *might* be."

And turning toward him, she said, "But we have one way out: we can sell the villa. It has historical value and it could fetch a good price. Then we would be able to buy a much cheaper farm down south. The leftover money would be enough to reimburse... Mike—or whoever it is."

"Of course. And after you pay all that, what's the next thing for you to worry about? And after that? And after that?"

"Hey! What's the matter? I thought you were only worried about Mike. Now you've decided to tackle my personal problems as well?"

She turned away so he wouldn't see the severe line of her lips. She added while still turned, "You know? You aren't helping me with anything like this, Gian. I'm the one who owes somebody money—not you."

"I am sorry," Giancarlo replied.

Jill tried to regain control over her emotions. She stared at the grass on the ground. She raised her head just to say, "I think it's time for you to get going."

Thirty-Five

Massimo Tonelli had been waiting, bored, for an hour and a half. Cooped up in his car, he had watched his life play out two or three times already in his mind. He did not like the way it ended in any scenario. Each time he saw Isabella near the mansion, he thought his fiancée might come down to the car. But she never did. And time just passed like that. He felt like an outsider at the villa.

Then he saw Giancarlo coming over to say goodbye. They shook hands, exchanged a few words and Giancarlo walked back to Jill.

◆ ◆ ◆

He stepped in close to her. They looked at one another. They looked at each other's hair, their necks, the tips of their noses—everywhere but into each other's eyes. The looks in both sets of eyes were both firmly entrenched behind the walls of their own motives.

As they were saying goodbye, they could hear that the children were still singing in the mansion. The missionaries Mary and Benny Marshall—the latter now pleased once again with how quickly God had answered his prayers—were with the children. And they had a thousand plans.

Genoveffa and Isabella were chatting in front of the mansion. Maddalena Heston had already gone back into the main house to get a few things done.

Finally, Dante Migliano and *Nonno* Giovanni got in the car. They were only waiting for Giancarlo.

Then Giancarlo smiled at Jill.

"You know what just crossed my mind?"

"What?"

"That piece of plaster crashing to the floor. That was crazy, wasn't it?"

She gave a half smile and just said,

"Yeah, it was pretty crazy."

"Jill, you have a lot on your hands and… I know I don't have much to offer, but if there is anything, anything at all, that you need me to do to help, please let me know. With my *nonno*'s help, and…" Giancarlo paused and smiled, "perhaps even with my *mamma*'s help, I am sure we could be of some use to you and the children."

"That is generous, Gian. Thank you."

Then she toyed with a lock of her curly hair. Giancarlo extended a hand, and she let go of her hair.

"*Ciao*," he said.

"*Ciao*."

Then she asked, "You gonna drop by to visit some day?"

"Who knows? But what could happen then that couldn't have happened today? I think I heard you say something like that."

She didn't break the ice.

"My offer stands. We have to go now, but you know where to find us."

She willed her lips to smile but the command failed. She wanted to look deep into his eyes, but she couldn't find the courage.

Then he got into the Alfa Romeo. Moments later, they drove out of the villa.

◆ ◆ ◆

Tonelli got out of the car. He slammed the door and leaned against it. Then he crammed his hands into his pockets.

"Bella!" he let slip when he finally saw his fiancée coming out to meet him.

Isabella walked up to him. Her eyes widened.

"*Ma cosa…?!*"

Tonelli pulled back his arm and closed his hand in refusal because Isabella was trying to put her engagement ring into it.

"I'm tired of waiting around, *Amore*. I know you're going to come up with some other excuse soon. And I know you're going to go running off like a madman. I can't do this anymore. I've had enough. I'm staying here."

"Staying... here?!"

"I'm going to work with Jill. She needs my help. And you know how I adore children."

Tonelli's face drained of its color. Bella couldn't be serious.

"I'm being serious, *Amore*," she confirmed, as if reading his mind.

"But... what about your job?"

"I'm done with that too. Here, take it."

She tried again to give him the ring but he moved his hands away. Then he started swaggering around his soon-to-be ex-fiancée, talking, and talking, bringing up the little flowers on their hope chest, searching for the promises from ten, eleven years ago.

"Twelve, *Amore*," Isabella corrected.

To avoid accepting the ring, Tonelli started repairing the foundation of his age-old arguments. Isabella pretended not to hear.

"You always have your newspapers... your life. You won't be alone."

"I-I-I am ne-ver going back to any pa-per! *Mai!*" Tonelli spluttered out.

Finally, Isabella managed to slightly open one of his hands. She roughly stuffed the ring in. Then she crossed her arms.

"You aren't going back to the newspaper? Then what are you going to do?"

"I don't know. I really don't know!"

Then, Massimo Tonelli started bawling like a hungry baby.

"I'm bad luck, Bella! In my hands, everything turns out to be a spectacular failure..."

"That isn't true. You have done a lot of important things. If not for you, those children wouldn't be here. You kept Missionary Marshall in Italy... kept the *Pellegrino* from leaving until... until everything happened. You kept the *Pellegrino* with a... with a lie—but you still did it. *Nevvero?*"

Tonelli swallowed a lump. He had no way of refuting Isabella.

"But even still, you were used by God, *Amore. Capisci?*"

"*Dio*, Bella?"

"*Sì*. And you know why? Mary explained to me how God can make springs dry up in an instant and bring forth springs on dry land. She told the whole world what we did... what you did to keep the boat from leaving."

Tonelli raised his head a bit. Isabella saw a slight glimmer in his eyes.

"Those two hundred thousand dollars, *Amore*... that money you were planning to get from Nezzo Bologna... it wasn't going to be clean money. Was it?"

Tonelli shook his head. But said nothing. His eyes were still teary. He pulled out a handkerchief and resoundingly blew his nose into it.

Meanwhile, Isabella had more high-caliber ammunition,

"And same for that money you were just thinking of extorting from that American senator. That is what you wanted the pictures of the children for, *nevvero?*"

"Bella!" Tonelli laid his hand reverently on his chest. "That's ridiculous!"

"How much were you going to ask him for, *Amore*? Five hundred thousand dollars?"

Taken by surprise behind the handkerchief he had raised to his nose, slowly Tonelli found his voice again.

"*I-iio*, Bella? An extortionist? How could you think I would do something like that?"

Isabella shrugged.

"Well, if you say I'm wrong... then I believe you. But what about your little last-minute whisper with Bill Benson?"

"*Ma cosa...?*"

"Think I didn't see you sticking your head into his car? When did you agree to bring him a copy of the cassette tape?"

Now Tonelli let out a huge sigh. He gave up.

"Come clean."

"Hmmm... well, I was thinking of fifty thousand dollars."

"How much?"

"Hmmm... a hundred thousand dollars. Or two."

"Is that all? And is that pittance supposed to be enough for a round-the-world cruise for two, *Amore?*"

"For two, Bella?" Tonelli took that as encouragement. His eyes took on an expectant glint.

"I was just joking, *Amore*. I wanted to see if you could be salvaged. But forget that two hundred thousand dollars, *caro mio*. The copy of the tape is not at your apartment. Here's what's left of it."

Isabella threw the burned remnants of the tape at Tonelli's feet.

"You are wrong, Tonelli, as you so often are. The money from Frank Borsato was clean. Missionary Marshall suspected the money was dirty because of the way it was delivered—as a suitcase full of cash. This caused a lot of suspicion and confusion. Benny Marshall is a man of character who likes to do things right and he could not accept a donation from a questionable source. But there is no dirt to be found in the money. It was all a big misunderstanding. The money has been returned to the bank and it is waiting for Jill. Bill Benson explained all of this to *Signor* Giovanni and *Signora* Genoveffa, who then shared it with me. Bill Benson came here to tell Jill but then he never got the chance. Then you came and made things even worse for her!"

He stopped himself from falling over, then put the handkerchief back in his bag and mumbled something unintelligible. Then, with the tip of his shoe, he started brutalizing a lone tuft of grass. The scene broke Isabella's heart.

"*Amore*, if you don't want anything to do with the paper... then why don't you write a book?"

"*Cosa hai detto*, Bella? A book?"

"Yeah, a novel... a work of fiction. You change some things... names... situations—but keep the most important parts. And no one has to believe it was true. *Nevvero?*"

Isabella had already stepped aside. She was uncomfortable making the decision, but she had to do it. If he had taken away the strategy of giving back the engagement ring, then now she had to try something else. She had to be tough. She had to make a dramatic retreat. It would be a kind of blackmail— but all's fair in love.

"Then... goodbye, *Amore*," she mewed while taking a step and a half back. "*Addio, mio caro!* You write your book and I... I will follow my path."

Next, turning her back to Tonelli, Isabella started walking away.

◆ ◆ ◆

SILENT, STILL AND ALONE at the edge of the garden, Jill was watching a long stretch of narrow road down below. Before too long, the car would be coming around the bend.

Then she heard her mother shouting from the balcony,

"Jill! Phone call! It's Mike!"

Without taking her eyes off the distant bend, she said quite loudly,

"You talk to him, *Mamma*."

She didn't even notice that Isabella was back after leaving Tonelli. Isabella furrowed her brow. She followed Jill's gaze. Then she looked into her eyes. And said,

"I can't believe it. I can't believe you two didn't patch things up before he left!"

Still without taking her eyes off the bend, Jill asked how she knew.

"Because your eyes aren't even damp, come on. You have everything locked up inside you—even your tears. Why did you let him leave?"

"He had to go."

"That wasn't what I meant. I meant why did you let him leave your heart?"

Then they both saw the car in the distance. It was pretty small, almost nothing. The size of a stifled goodbye.

◆ ◆ ◆

THE LIGHT FROM THE SETTING SUN was still blazing on the road. Nevertheless, the dismal shadows of the mountains running westward seemed to have brought profound melancholy to Giancarlo's heart. And it wasn't only *Nonno* Giovanni who made this observation: Dante Migliano, in partnership with the interior rearview mirror, was driving the car and at the same time contemplating the devastation on the *ragazzo*'s face. "Ah! Splendid, foolish youth...!" he almost let slip.

But *Nonno* Giovanni had to say,

"Are you sure... sure that this is what you really want, *figliolo*!?"

Hiding alone in the back seat, Giancarlo looked at his grandfather's face in silence. *Nonno* Giovanni, seated in front, hadn't said anything until then. But now he had addressed his grandson.

And he was expecting a response.

"Once..." Giancarlo said in a moan, "once I asked Nicodemus if God could help me fight this war. And he told me that God had already done his part—he had put Jill in my path. It was up to me to fight for her. I don't know exactly where in our journey it happened—but I lost the fight, *Nonno*."

♦ ♦ ♦

"YOU KNOW, JILL," Isabella continued, "while we were at *El Rincón*, I noticed something being born between you two... forgive me, but I... I started to feel envious. Don't let something that amazing slip away from you."

Isabella stopped talking. She looked back. She sighed. Seeing her fiancé, she said, "I just spent ages doing the impossible not to lose mine."

Slowly, Jill turned her gaze back to the empty road—a void that was now the color of the sunset. She didn't notice her mother coming over.

"Giancarlo," Jill mumbled to herself. "I've never met someone so… sincere and so… thirsty."

"I told Mike everything that had to be said, *figliola*," Maddalena Heston replied.

Without taking her eyes off the void, Jill asked,

"What do you mean everything, *Mamma*?"

"I said you had met someone amazing. God forgive me if I lied."

"You didn't lie, *Signora* Maddalena," said Isabella.

♦ ♦ ♦

"BACK AT THE FARM in Villavieja, *figliolo*, I was certain that you two would live together in a shared dream. Why did you give up the fight?"

Giancarlo let out a sigh. Discreetly, Dante winked in expectation at the rearview mirror. *Nonno* Giovanni remained half turned toward the back. He was awaiting a response.

"*Nonno*... a man has to know where and when he is not needed, right?"

"A man has to know that pride cannot come before love."

Giancarlo stayed quiet for a moment. Then he said,

"Then do you think she is only torn because of the money Mike might have sent? Did you really not see the way she changed when we got to the villa?"

"I know what I saw in her eyes. And I've seen it a lot in the past few days. The eyes are windows into the soul—but they're also the way out. What matters most is what is spoken with the eyes, not the mouth, for the mouth doesn't always speak the fleeting phrases that pass through our eyes—even when our eyes are closed."

And *Nonno* Giovanni added, "Leave Mike out of this. He has nothing to do with the children—nor the woman you love."

♦ ♦ ♦

"MIKE LAUGHED when I brought up the money, can you imagine that! But that's just how he is, right? And he took the chance to say that he has to go from Rome to a conference in Paris. He doesn't know where he's going after Paris, but it involves a consortium of multinationals. Poor thing. Consider yourself free of him forever, Jill."

Her mother went on to finish,

"But I didn't come here just to say that."

Jill was still staring into the distance. She didn't seem interested in what her mother had to say. But nevertheless, she asked in a dull voice,

"And what else is there, *Mamma*? Has that Senator already hired a lawyer to get his money back?"

"I guess not—unless he has a front man called Fernando Sierra."

Jill quickly turned to face her mother.

"The drifter?!"

♦ ♦ ♦

"NICODEMUS, *Nonno*?! But how?"

♦ ♦ ♦

"THE DRIFTER? What are you talking about, Jill? I'm trying to say that I got a call from the bank saying the man in Málaga who made the deposit into your *nonno*'s account is called Fernando Sierra. Just like the Spanish writer."

"But he's the drifter, mom!"

"What drifter? *Figliola*, are you sure you're feeling all right?"

And Isabella, overhearing the exchange, had finally found the opportune moment to share the much-needed clarification that had been delivered by the American journalist.

♦ ♦ ♦

GIANCARLO COULD SUDDENLY FEEL a cool breeze—a breeze blowing from within him. His lips stretched to form a smile and he started to laugh until he broke down. He laughed then felt a tug at his heartstrings as he digested the message—the silent and selfless message from a former mystic who had pretended to be a drifter as an act of service.

"But how can that be, *Nonno*?!" he asked again.

"It is not love from mankind, *figliolo*—it is the love of God acting in the heart of a God-fearing man. Do not try to understand it. It is a love that exceeds all human understanding."

"But...? But he was with me... we talked so much... and then... Then why did he never mention it?"

"Why does the right hand have to know what the left hand is doing? Still, *figliolo*, it was through you that he heard about Jill—and her children."

"But can't I even say thank you, *Nonno*?"

"What for? To rob him of his gains?"

"Rob him?"

"What is the greater blessing? To give or to receive? In truth, God controls all payment."

Giancarlo felt moved. He had started to feel a desire inside himself—a supreme desire bearing no external influence. It wasn't coming from his soul; it wasn't coming from his emotions: it was coming from somewhere deeper within. It was coming from his spirit. He could feel that there—in the heart of his being—the Spirit of God was at work.

He could now see the work that needed to be done. His mother needed his support, and his family's farm needed his attention. And he knew he could help them. He thought of Jill and of all the work she had ahead of her.

He thought about how he could help Jill and his own family if he finished his degree in agriculture. Giovanni listened quietly to the planning session. Giancarlo hadn't even realized he was speaking out loud until he concluded it with a quiet and reflective smile, and just one more word, "Jill."

◆ ◆ ◆

SHE WAS STILL CRYING. But she also wanted to laugh. She could sense that it was the same power that flowed through her father's veins... just like the power in Benny and Mary's rough hands... and perhaps also in Isabella and Tonelli's reckless journey. She could sense something, she could see it—not in the arid landscape of her goodbye, but within her very self—deep down she glimpsed something shining. It was the Morning Star.

Then she raised her head. And when she did, she saw the most beautiful day of her life.

"Oh, how wrong I was! How could I have thought so badly of Senator

Borsato, who was always such a good friend to my dad! Chasing a wild idea for thousands of miles when the help I needed was right here. What a waste of time! How could I have made such a mistake!"

"It wasn't a waste of time. You two would have never met! Now don't make another mistake! Go on, then, Jill!" she heard Isabella's excited voice, "You still have time to catch up to him!"

◆ ◆ ◆

FOR THE FIRST TIME, Dante dared to interfere in the conversation—he had obviously heard everything. Through the rearview mirror, he could see Giancarlo looking jubilant in the back seat. And, adding more fuel to the fire, he asked the man in the mirror,

"So, are we turning around then, *Signor* Giancarlo?"

"*Sì, sì, per favore, Signor* Dante! *Alla svelta!*"

In two minutes, Dante had turned the car around.

◆ ◆ ◆

JILL PRACTICALLY FLEW to the door of Tonelli's car from where she'd been standing with her mother and Isabella.

"Can I borrow this?" she said while getting into the vehicle. Not waiting for a response, she started it, put it into gear, turned it around and tore off honking the horn. Peppino ran to open the gate and the car disappeared.

Isabella smiled at Maddalena Heston. Then she dried her eyes with a handkerchief and stared off the balcony in front of her, at her *Amore*. Saddened, hands still crammed into his pockets, he didn't react at all to the sudden theft of his car—just went back to kicking that poor tuft of grass with the tip of his shoe.

Isabella made use of the handkerchief again. She sighed deeply. Then she followed Maddalena Heston into the mansion.

◆ ◆ ◆

IN THAT MOMENT, the Earth felt too big for Massimo Tonelli. He was scared by his solitude.

And then, looking down at the dirt, he realized the only reason he could pick on that stupid tuft of grass because it was by itself.

In a decisive motion, he turned and ran after the only thing that truly mattered.

"Bella! Bella *mia!*" he shouted. "Wait!"

Bella came over to him, worried.

"I know," continued an excited Tonelli, "I can keep writing as a journalist. I'm gonna write about the children's rescue and write their stories as they grow! Who knows, maybe more children will be rescued because of their stories. It will be an international success!"

Bella smiled and hugged him.

"Brilliant! I always knew you had a kind heart, *Amore*." And she sealed their plans with a kiss.

◆ ◆ ◆

THE TEARS WERE STINGING HER CHEEKS. But she soldiered on, foot on the accelerator, making daring turns, pulling onto the highway, merging left, accelerating faster—until she saw the black Alfa Romeo… on its way back to the villa.

"Hey!" she shouted, waving her arm euphorically out the window.

One minute later, once the vehicles had both stopped on their respective sides of the road, Giancarlo jumped out. He started crossing the highway, paused, waited for a car to pass. Then another. Then he ran to catch her. She jumped into his arms and he lifted her into a midair twirl that ended in an embrace. Both were totally unaware of the smiles on Dante and *Nonno*'s faces on the other side of the highway, oblivious to the motorcyclist giving them a funny look, and ignorant of the fact that all the people on the passing bus were cheering for them.

"Should we make our two dreams into one?" he asked before setting her down.

"Yes!" she answered.